MAGIC'S MOST WANTED

Also by Tyler Whitesides

The Wishmakers

The Wishbreaker

MAGIC'S MOST WANTED

TYLER WHITESIDES

HARPER

An Imprint of HarperCollinsPublishers

Library of Congress Control Number: 2020942414
ISBN 978-0-06-256837-3

Typography by Jessie Gang
20 21 22 23 24   PC/LSCH   10 9 8 7 6 5 4 3 2 1

First Edition

To Mrs. Foster

PROLOGUE

NOVEMBER 28
6:56 P.M.
INSIDE THE MORRISON MAILBOX

The man watched the house from his hiding spot inside the mailbox. The little door was dangling open, flapping slightly as a winter storm blew in with the sunset. The mailbox was sheltering him for now, but he wouldn't be able to stay much longer.

The man wasn't always this small, of course. The pair of magical glasses he was wearing shrank him to just under an inch tall. These glasses weren't his, but the Mastermind had let him use them for surveillance today.

The garage door trundled upward, catching his attention. The man checked his watch: 6:56 p.m. The Morrisons were trying to make it to a movie at 7:05, but at this rate, they were going to be a few minutes late.

He watched the car back down the driveway. Mr. Morrison was driving, his wife in the passenger seat. Through the tinted window, the man couldn't see Mason, but he knew the boy would be seated on the passenger side where he always was—easier to climb in with his bad leg.

The car rolled onto the street, neither parent seeming to notice that the mailbox door was hanging open. The family sped away through the cold night, unaware that anyone was watching them. Unaware that the man had been watching them for weeks now.

He reached into his pocket and pulled out his cell phone.

"This message is for the Mastermind," he began. He didn't expect a reply. This was just a recording to be given to his boss at a later time.

"This will be my final report on Mason Mortimer Morrison," the man said. "Tomorrow I'll be heading back to Magix Headquarters to resume my work there. I think my time here has been very worthwhile. I've placed several surveillance boons in and around the house to continue monitoring the boy until we are ready to make our move."

The man paused, stepping up to the edge of the mailbox. The cold wind howled, and he ducked back inside to finish his report.

"You were right about Mason," the man said. "The boy is

exactly who we need, although it might take some time for us to set him up. His limp will probably fade with time, but it has only been six months since the accident. Mason has no brothers or sisters, but he has a good relationship with his parents. We will probably have to do something about that. He is a good student. Does well on tests. Gets his homework done. That will probably need to change, too."

The man looked at the house, wondering if he should add anything else.

"I believe your plan will work, Mastermind," he finally said. "It won't be easy, but it's the right thing. By the time we're done with him, Magix will be eager to arrest him. And we'll make sure all the evidence is in place so they have to find him guilty. Then he'll be ours, and we can use him to do what needs to be done." He drew in a deep breath. "To destroy all magic forever."

It felt good to say that. And the man was excited to finally see the pieces of Mastermind's plan coming together.

"I've rented a place in New York City so I can keep an eye on Lawden," said the man. "In the meantime, I've got Talbot and Vanderbeek taking shifts outside the Morrison house. This is a once-in-a-lifetime opportunity. It could take years, but we won't let it get away from us."

The man ended the recording and slipped the phone into his pocket. Then he ran forward and jumped out of the mailbox.

As he fell, he reached up and pulled off the glasses. Instantly, he returned to his regular size, feet striking the sidewalk. The man glanced once more at the house, tugged at the collar of his coat, and strode off down the dark street.

TWO AND A HALF YEARS LATER

CHAPTER 1

WEDNESDAY, MAY 13
2:05 P.M.
EAGLE FIELDS CHARTER SCHOOL, INDIANA

I was definitely not ready for this book report. But that wasn't a surprise. Reading and homework were for kids who didn't have better things to do. Things like . . . video games.

But I found myself rethinking my choices as I stood in front of my whole class, filled with dread as Mrs. Dunlow circled closer like a vulture in the desert, just waiting for the helpless critter—*me*—to finally die.

"I'm just . . . ," I stammered. "I'm not sure where to begin." Speaking to my classmates was always terrifying. Especially when I was supposed to be talking about a book I hadn't even read . . .

"You could start by telling us the title," my teacher said.

That seemed like a good idea. Why hadn't I thought of that on my own?

"Right," I said, holding up the book in my right hand. "It's called *The Music in the Box*."

Honestly, I was feeling a little embarrassed about it. The librarian had actually made it sound pretty cool, but once I got home, the book had looked totally boring. I had tossed it on my dresser and forgotten all about it (and the report) until last night.

"And what was the book about?" my teacher asked.

"Umm . . . music," I said. "In a box."

A few kids snickered, and that made me feel pretty good. But I didn't want Mrs. Dunlow to call my mom again. Then I'd get another lecture about being a smart aleck, and by the end, my mom would somehow find a way to blame my behavior on my dad. Because, if he were still around . . .

"Okay, Mason," Mrs. Dunlow said. "I think you're done."

I felt my A+ quickly turning into a daydream.

"Wait!" I pleaded. I had one chance to recover my grade. My mom had found me a good visual aid, just like the librarian had suggested. I whipped it out from behind my back, holding it aloft for all my classmates to see.

"This is a music box," I explained. "I know it's a little different from the one on the cover of the book." I glanced at the novel for reference. "The one on the book is made of metal. This one is made of wood. The book one has a little robot that spins around doing a techno-dance. This one . . . doesn't."

I actually had no idea what was inside this music box. My mom had found it for me after I'd gone to bed last night. We'd argued about the book report. I'd told her that it didn't matter if I'd read the book as long as I had a good visual aid to show off. She'd opened the box at breakfast, but I'd been disappointed by its dainty appearance and hadn't paid it much attention. The happy little song it played was so annoying that I didn't think there was any chance it would win me an A+.

In fact, I hadn't even planned to bring it to school, but Mom had stuffed it into my backpack, saying that she hadn't gone through so much effort to get it for nothing.

"Does it open?" asked Mrs. Dunlow, unimpressed with the item in my hands.

"Yeah," I said, not wanting to do it for fear of the cheesy song that would play for my classmates.

"Mason," the teacher said in her serious voice, "did you even read the book?"

"What?" I said. "I couldn't hear you over the song that's playing in my music box . . ."

Slowly, in the most dramatic fashion, I lifted the little wooden lid.

That was when my life changed forever.

In the blink of an eye, Mrs. Dunlow, all of my classmates, and I disappeared. I had just a moment to wonder what the classroom must have looked like as we left it behind—suddenly vacant, a few papers fluttering off desks and drifting to the floor like leaves on an autumn breeze.

Fortunately, every single one of us reappeared. *Un*fortunately, we were no longer in Indiana. In fact, I was pretty sure we were no longer in North America.

The air around us was freezing cold, my breath catching in my throat and escaping my lips like a white cloud. As I spun my head around in surprise, I realized that there was nothing but snow and ice in every direction.

"Whaaaaa . . . ?" Mrs. Dunlow couldn't get the whole word out. She was either too astonished or partially frozen. I was feeling a bit of both myself.

"Where are we?" asked Kyle Henderson, standing up and dusting snow off his backside.

I realized that we'd all been transported in the exact same positions we'd been in in the classroom. Mrs. Dunlow was closing in from the side to give my book report an F, and everyone else was seated. Only, here, in this snowy wonderland, there were no desks or chairs, so everyone had instantly collapsed, taking an unwanted seat on the frozen white ground.

I was standing in front of my classmates, holding the open

music box. I saw now what was inside. Two little wooden figurines—a fox chasing a goose. The annoyingly cheerful song was playing in my hand, the tune almost lost in the howling wind.

"I'm not getting any service," said Thomas Grand. His hand was shaking from the cold as he held up his cell phone.

"Phone!" Mrs. Dunlow said, changing directions and going after Thomas. "Give me that phone!"

"Are you serious?" he cried as she snatched it out of his hands. Like me, Thomas must have thought that Mrs. Dunlow was enforcing her strict no-phone-during-class policy. I had been wise, leaving mine safely in my desk. But we were soon proven wrong about Mrs. Dunlow's motives.

"Hello?" our teacher cried, pressing the phone to her ear, voice desperate. "This is an emergency! Hello? Can anyone hear me?"

"I said I don't have service—" Thomas tried.

Mrs. Dunlow yowled in rage and threw the phone down into the snow. "Why don't you get better service?" she yelled at Thomas.

He took a step back. "It's not my fault. We're in the middle of nowhere—"

"Antarctica," Sandra Park cut him off. "I'd say we're in the middle of Antarctica."

"How could you possibly know that?" shouted Ingrid Selbaker.

Sandra pointed across the frozen wasteland. "Penguins," she said. I spotted them a short distance away, black blobs that I had first mistaken for rocks.

"Just because you see some penguins doesn't mean we're in Antarctica," continued Ingrid.

Sandra shrugged. "It's just a guess. The orange color around their necks means they're emperor penguins, and that species is found exclusively in Antarctica, so—"

"Stop being such a know-it-all, Sandra!" yelled Damian Fawks. "I don't care *where* we are. I just want to know how we got here!"

"Yeah!"

"What happened?"

"How do we get out of here?"

"I'm cold!"

Everyone started yelling and talking at once. I stood in silence, watching the sun dip toward the horizon. It would be dark soon. I had a feeling that without the little warmth the sun was providing, we'd all be icicles in a matter of moments.

The music box was still going in my hands. The tune wasn't really helping the mood, so I snapped the lid shut, giving the fox and the goose a rest.

"Class, class!" Mrs. Dunlow's voice cut through the chaos, her hands clapping with her words. It did the trick, just like in the classroom, quieting the nervous bunch in a second.

"There has to be a logical explanation for what happened," our teacher said, voice warbling from the chill. She seemed to have gotten control of herself again. "We have to think back to what was happening in the classroom."

"The last thing I remember was Mason failing his book report," called one of my classmates.

"Yeah! This is Mason's fault!" shouted another.

"What?" I cried in defense. "That doesn't make any sense! You think failing my book report somehow transported us all to another continent?"

"Wait . . . maybe this *is* the book report," said someone else in a mysterious voice.

"Did the book take place in Antarctica?" asked Kyle.

"I don't know," I admitted. "I didn't actually read it."

"I knew it!" howled Mrs. Dunlow, pointing a failing finger at me.

"Waaaahhh!" cried Ingrid. "This *is* your fault!"

"You guys!" I shouted. "I swear I don't know how we got here. One second I was standing at the front of the classroom, trying to sound smart. Then"—I lifted the item in my cold hands—"I opened the music box and . . . *poof.*"

I flipped open the wooden lid of the music box, and everything changed again.

This time, we were instantly transported to a tropical beach. In a heartbeat, the ice beneath my shoes was replaced with soft sand. Instead of the cruel Antarctic wind, there was a gentle, warm breeze carrying a salty scent as it rolled in over the turquoise water in front of us.

"Whoa . . . ," muttered Kyle. "This is way better than—"

In curious wonderment, I clicked the music box shut again and then lifted the lid once more.

Zoom!

My classmates and I were immediately whisked away to a different kind of sandy landscape.

A desert.

Dry orange sand surrounded us in an endless field. The sun was beating down so fiercely that I immediately felt uncomfortable. No trees, no shrubs, no shade. And worse . . . no water.

I found it completely understandable that several of my classmates were now having full-blown panic attacks. Mrs. Dunlow was taking attendance, which was actually a pretty good idea, to make sure that no one had been left behind.

"Really, Mason?" Kyle yelled over the tinkling music of the little box. "We could have been happy on that beach!"

I wanted to say that it wasn't my fault, but I was starting to think that, somehow, it really might be. I turned my eyes to the music box in my hands. The fox chased the goose like nothing was out of the ordinary.

What was this thing? Some high-tech transporter? Magic? It definitely hadn't done anything but annoy me during breakfast. What was going on?

"Mason Morrison!" Mrs. Dunlow shouted once she was satisfied that there were no absences. "Explain yourself at once!"

I couldn't. I really had no idea what was going on. I clicked the music box shut again.

"No!" screamed Noah Miles, suddenly tackling me from behind. The box went flying out of my hands, skidding through the sand as the two of us went down. I didn't want to fight Noah. He was usually pretty nice. Luckily, he didn't seem interested in pounding me into the sand, either. He rolled away, letting me rise to my knees.

"I was just going to open the music box again," I explained. "It seems to be connected to whatever is happening."

"Obviously," said one of the girls behind me.

I didn't dare move toward the fallen music box for fear that Noah would pounce again. In fact, nobody seemed interested in picking it up. We all just stared at it like it was a musical bomb about to go off.

"Maybe if I open it again," I said, "it'll transport us back to Indiana."

"Or maybe back to Antarctica," said Noah. "Or drop us in the middle of the ocean. We can't risk it."

"Then what're we supposed to do?" asked Thomas. "We

don't have any water, and the sun's going to fry us before we can walk a mile."

"Maybe someone at the school will notice we're missing," suggested Natalie Burgon. "They'll send someone to look for us."

"In the desert?" cried Kyle. "They might check the cafeteria or the gym, but we've got to be halfway around the world!"

"Everyone remain calm," Mrs. Dunlow said. "We're all together, and we're all safe. For the moment."

"Yeah," said Natalie. "Someone's going to rescue us."

"How?" argued Kyle. "No one knows where we are. *We* don't even know where we are. Do you really expect someone to show up out of nowhere and save us?"

There was a loud sound to our left, and everyone turned in surprise. An archway of bricks had appeared out of thin air, looking very strange and out of place in the landscape of never-ending sand. As we stared speechlessly, a man and a woman suddenly showed up out of nowhere, stepping through the arch. Both were wearing light gray suits and tall black top hats.

"Is everyone okay here?" asked the woman, who had a braid of black hair falling over one shoulder. "Anyone injured?"

"Agent Nguyen," the man muttered, his eyes falling to the music box in the sand. "There it is." He took a step toward it, but the woman grabbed his arm.

"Could be another decoy," she said. "You don't want to end up like Jacobsen. I say we get these people to safety and then return with a verification team to retrieve the boon."

"What is . . ." Mrs. Dunlow took a deep breath as if trying to steady herself. Then she lost all control and started shouting. "SOMEBODY BETTER TELL ME WHAT'S GOING ON!"

"We've tracked the signal of an unauthorized boon," said the man.

"Boon?" said Mrs. Dunlow.

"It's what we call magical items," answered the woman named Nguyen.

"Hold on." My teacher raised a hand. "*Magic?* As in . . . magic?"

"But magic's not real!" called one of my classmates.

"I'm gonna need everyone to keep their doubts and concerns to themselves," the man said firmly. "None of you are even going to remember this, so don't slow us down with your tedious and meaningless questions."

"That music box has been linked to one of the biggest magical crimes in recent years," Nguyen continued. "We believe it was being used by a dangerous young criminal."

Criminal? Were they talking about *me*? No. That was a

word my mom and I had heard a lot, but never about me.

"Did any of you see the person who used this boon?" asked the man, pointing to the music box.

"It was Mason Morrison!" shouted three of my classmates in unison, all fingers suddenly pointing in my direction.

For the first time since their arrival, the adults in the gray suits got a good look at me.

"That's him, all right," the man whispered under his breath. Then he stepped forward, pulling a pair of handcuffs from his jacket.

"Mason Morrison," he said, his voice gravelly. "We're here to apprehend you for a major crime against magic."

Then he said those words. The words I hated.

"You are under arrest."

CHAPTER 2

WEDNESDAY, MAY 13
2:21 P.M.
MIDDLE OF NOWHERE, SAHARA DESERT, MAYBE

Under arrest? But I hadn't done anything wrong! Okay, so transporting my teacher and entire class to some of Earth's most extreme climates might have been considered *wrong*, but it wasn't my fault!

I watched the big guy in the gray suit move closer, his feet churning through the loose desert sand, his top hat casting a shadow over his face.

In that moment, staring at those silvery handcuffs, I had a crazy idea. I wondered if my dad had had a similar thought when the cops had surrounded him. He hadn't been able to get away. But I had something magical lying right in front of me. . . .

The man was almost to me when I leaped forward, snatched the music box out of the sand, and flipped open the wooden lid.

At once, the orange desert disappeared as I was transported to a new environment. This time I found myself in a dense jungle, my wind-up song met with a chorus of chirping birds. Low-hanging vines drooped from towering moss-covered trees.

As before, Mrs. Dunlow and my entire class were transported with me. And much to my disappointment, so were the two strangers in the gray suits and top hats.

Basically, I was still in danger of being arrested. Only now it would happen in the jungle instead of the desert.

But the teleportation had given me the element of surprise, and I took advantage of the man's momentary confusion to take off running. I didn't really have a plan as I leaped over a decomposing log, snapping the music box shut. All I could really think was, *Don't get arrested. Don't end up like Dad.*

Maybe if I got far enough away from the others, the music box would transport me alone. I could keep opening it and shutting it until I landed somewhere I recognized. Preferably somewhere closer to Indiana.

Damp ferns slapped my legs as I sprinted through the dim jungle. But I could hear the man in the gray suit running right behind me.

"Mason Morrison!" he shouted. "Running will only make this worse. Surrender the boon and turn yourself in!"

Yeah, right! I was obviously faster than this guy, and I could run longer than—

I came to a screeching halt as I burst through the jungle trees and found myself at the top of a massive cliff. Far below, I saw a wide river tumbling along. In the movies, people always jumped, somehow landing safely in the water. In real life, that didn't seem like such a good idea.

I turned as the gray-suited man arrived at the edge of the trees, stopping just a few feet away from me. He raised his hands in a peaceful gesture, his top hat tilted slightly from his run.

"My name is Special Agent John Clarkston," he began. "I'm with Magix, Investigation Division. But you already know that."

"Nope. Never heard of it," I answered.

"Come on," he said. "We both know that's not possible. I want you to toss the music box toward me—slowly."

I clutched the small box with both hands. "And what if I don't?"

"You're Magix's most wanted criminal, Mason."

Most wanted criminal? This was nonsense!

"Agent Nguyen and I are authorized to bring you in by any

19

means necessary," he said. "Obviously, I don't want it to come to that. You're just a . . . a kid."

"I don't know what you're talking about," I said. "I didn't even know magic was real until I started failing my book report."

"This is the end of the road, Mason." Clarkston started reaching up for his top hat. "You're coming back to Magix to face the consequences of your crimes."

"What if I come?" I asked. "What would you do with me?"

"Honestly, there's not much hope for you after what you did," he said, slowly taking off his black hat. "I'd expect a life sentence."

Locked up forever? All because of my terrible book report? No way!

I didn't want to know how Special Agent John Clarkston planned to bring me in with force. I had a plan of my own. Risky? Yes. But any risk was better than getting taken in by the crazy magic police.

"Sorry," I said. "But you've got the wrong guy."

Then I jumped off the cliff.

My plan was to get some distance between Clarkston and me, and then flip open the music box midfall. The music would start playing, the fox would chase the goose, and if all went as expected, I'd be safely transported to a new location before I hit the river.

Unfortunately, things did not go as expected.

The moment I dropped off the edge of that cliff, the wind whipped the music box right out of my hands.

Plunging to my certain death, I let out a terrified howl. Just then, I saw Agent Clarkston leap over the edge and plummet rapidly toward me, his arms lowered to his sides. He gripped his top hat in one hand, and it flapped in the wind.

He caught up to me in a flash, his left arm reaching around my middle. In total panic, I clung to him like he might be able to save my life, his top hat pressed against my chest.

With his free hand, Agent Clarkston reached into the flapping hat and pulled something out.

"Seriously?" I cried. "A pillowcase?"

The fabric was pink, with little red hearts all over it. What good was that going to do us? There wasn't even a pillow inside to pad our landing!

Suddenly, the pillowcase filled with wind, billowing like a huge parachute. Our breakneck fall slowed and we were soon drifting peacefully downward, Clarkston somehow steering us gently toward the far bank of the river.

We touched down ungracefully, tumbling onto the muddy ground. Clarkston recovered much quicker than I did. Before I could move, he pulled both of my arms behind my back, and I felt the cold steel handcuffs clipping into place around my wrists.

"I told you running would only make it worse," he said, stepping aside and tucking the pillowcase, which had returned to its regular size, back into his top hat. When his hand reappeared, he was holding a pair of tweezers. How much stuff did he store in that old-fashioned hat?

"You didn't happen to see where your boon landed?" he asked with a threatening tone.

"If by *boon* you mean *music box*, then no," I answered. "I'm guessing it landed in the river."

"I was afraid of that." Clarkston sighed wearily. Then he held up the tweezers and spoke into the pointy end like it was a microphone. "Special Agent Nguyen, I have the suspect in custody. What's your status?"

To my surprise, the tweezers spoke back. The voice was crystal clear and obviously belonged to the woman who had arrived with Clarkston.

"I made contact with Magix Headquarters," she answered through the tweezers. "I let them know that our brick archway was left behind in the Sahara. They're working out a new rendezvous point with the Doorman. Stand by."

"I'm going after the music-box boon," said Clarkston.

"Negative," answered Nguyen. "You can't pursue the boon with a criminal in tow. Bring the boy up to me. We can send a recovery team back to the jungle once he's properly locked up."

Clarkston fumbled in his top hat for a moment before retrieving a blue marker. "I can put him out."

"Negative, Clarkston!" Nguyen's voice sounded more forceful this time. "If we're right about him, this kid isn't an ordinary criminal. He could be carrying immunity boons. Just bring him back to my location. Magix can deal with the music box later."

Clarkston looked downriver and grunted. "Understood." He pulled off the marker's cap. "But I'm still putting him out so he doesn't try to escape."

"Do what you've got to do," answered Nguyen.

Clarkston lowered the tweezers and turned to me.

"Put me out?" I asked. That didn't sound too friendly.

"Don't worry," he said. "This shouldn't hurt a bit." He reached out with the marker and drew a blue line on my forehead.

I tried to shout, "Hey! What was that for?" But the words came out all jumbled. I suddenly felt very sleepy, the sound of the rushing river soothing me.

Then everything went black.

CHAPTER 3

WEDNESDAY, MAY 13
4:53 P.M.
INTERROGATION ROOM 6, MAGIX HEADQUARTERS

I woke up slowly, my vision blurry as I blinked against the bright lights shining in my face. I tried to stand up, but apparently I was strapped into a chair.

"Mason Mortimer Morrison," spoke a bold, deep voice.

"Who said that?" I mumbled, my tongue feeling as if it were wrapped in toilet paper. And how did they know my middle name? I guarded that secret with my life!

"You are in a high-security holding room in Magix Headquarters," said the voice. "My name is Director Frank Lawden."

My eyes had finally adjusted enough to see my surroundings a little better. The windowless room wasn't very big, with cinder block walls and a low ceiling. There was a wide desk in front of me and a man sitting on the other side.

He was thin, with dark skin and short black hair. His gray suit was even fancier than the ones Clarkston and Nguyen had been wearing in the jungle, but he didn't have on one of those ridiculous top hats.

"Do you know why you are here?" he asked.

"Because I failed my book report?" I guessed.

Lawden leaned forward. "How old are you, Mason?"

"Twelve," I responded. "No, thirteen."

"What, you're not sure?" he asked.

"Thirteen," I stated. "I just had a birthday last week." A boring one, with no friends and only two presents. But it was waaaay better than last year's. "I'm still not used to saying it. But I'm thirteen."

He drew in a deep breath and shook his head. "That's awfully young to find yourself at the top of Magix's Most Wanted list."

"Sir," I began, deciding to be polite and make my mother proud. "I think there's been a terrible mix-up. I am not a criminal, and I don't know anything about magic."

"Knowledge is power. Power is magic, Mr. Morrison," said Lawden. "Did you, or did you *not*, use that music-box boon to transport your teacher and classmates to multiple locations across the globe?"

"Well, yes," I replied. "Apparently, I did. But I had no idea the music box would do anything . . . *magical.*"

"You and I both know that's impossible," Lawden said, repeating almost the exact same words that Clarkston had said.

"Why?" I begged. "Why is it impossible?"

"It's the most fundamental rule of magic," he said. "Knowledge is power. Power is magic. You had to know that the music box was a boon in order to activate its magic."

"But I didn't know!" I shouted. "I swear!"

He rubbed his forehead as if to push back a headache that was coming on. "That's not something we have to decide right now. Save it for the trial."

"Trial?" I squeaked. I had a lot of bad memories from my dad's.

"I'll let you know what additional charges you're facing for today's little stunt," he said. "You won't have a lawyer, but you'll be able to prepare a defense on your own, if you wish."

"What?" I cried. "No lawyer? That's against the law!"

"Forget what you think you know about the law," he answered. "You're with Magix now, and we do things our own way." Mr. Lawden cleared his throat. "Four counts of unauthorized use of a magical boon."

"For opening a music box?" I yelped.

"Four times," Lawden answered. "Twenty-nine counts of Ignorant magical exposure."

"What does that even mean?" I asked.

"One teacher and twenty-eight students witnessed the use of a magical boon today," he said. "All of them were commoners with no knowledge of magic—Ignorants, as we call them. Which leads me to your next charge—endangering civilians."

"Where are they?" I asked, suddenly feeling a gut-wrenching nervousness that they'd been left in the jungle to be devoured by pythons.

"Everyone is safe, no thanks to you. They've been returned to the school. I believe they're preparing for a math test about now."

"What?" I shouted. "You expect them to just dive back into their studies like nothing ever happened?"

"Luckily, what you did today was isolated and contained," said Lawden. "We were successfully able to wipe all memories of the magical incident."

"You can do that?" I asked in amazement.

"We're an organization specializing in magical items," he replied. "There is very little we can't do." He drummed his fingers on the desk. "And finally, the last charge—fleeing the scene of a crime."

"Huh?"

"When you ran away from my agents," Lawden clarified. "Which also led to defying arrest and endangering and injuring Magix agents."

"Who got hurt?" I asked, my stomach sinking in fear again.

"Agent Clarkston stubbed his toe while landing the parachute pillowcase."

"A stubbed toe? He didn't seem hurt to me."

"Clarkston filed the paperwork," said Lawden with a half shrug. "He was pretty upset that you ditched the music-box boon in the river."

"Have they found it yet?" I asked.

"Our people are on it." Lawden remained expressionless.

"What now?"

"We'll hold you here until the committee has a chance to review your case."

"How long will that be?"

"We're planning for seven o'clock this evening," he said. "If you're found guilty, we'll deal with the consequences tomorrow morning."

"You're keeping me overnight?" I gasped. "I haven't spent a night away from my house in, like, three years. My mom is way too paranoid for that. She's going to call the real police, and you guys are going to be in serious trouble."

"She thinks you're at piano lessons," answered Lawden.

"She *what?*" I yelled. "Nothing you say makes sense. I don't take piano lessons. Why would she—"

"My agents located her shortly after you were brought in," he cut me off.

I narrowed my eyes at him. "What did you people do to her?"

"We simply gave her a gift," he said. "It's a magical boon bracelet activated by Agent Nguyen. As long as your mother is wearing it, she wholeheartedly believes the last thing Agent Nguyen told her—that you are at piano lessons. The magic also establishes your mother as a reputable source to other Ignorants, who will believe the same thing without question."

I shook my head. "It won't work. My mom hardly ever wears jewelry. She'll take it off."

"Agent Nguyen also told her that the bracelet was lucky," said Mr. Lawden.

"My mom doesn't believe in luck anymore."

"But you forget that the magic of the bracelet will force her to believe it," said Mr. Lawden. "Besides, it's quite true. As an Ignorant, your mother will benefit from the boon on her wrist. She'll have a great time until you get home."

"So, you *are* planning to send me home?" I said hopefully.

Mr. Lawden nodded. "Best-case scenario, you're looking at

ten years of limited Magix correction for today's little esca-pade."

"Wait. You're going to lock me up and let my mom think that I'm at piano lessons until I'm twenty-three?"

"Oh no. That's not how the system works." Lawden shook his head. "We're not talking about ten years of your future. We're talking about ten years of your past."

My eyes bulged. "Hang on. . . . You're going to turn me into a three-year-old?"

Lawden wrinkled his forehead as if I'd just said something ridiculous. "A limited correction means we enter your memo-ries from the last ten years and erase anything that could have led you to your first magic exposure. It's not a very precise procedure, but we usually do our best not to interfere with fun-damental memories."

"Umm . . . I don't like this."

"Well, you should have thought of that before you began your life of crime," said Lawden. "Because I'm telling you—it doesn't look good."

"I'd say! Ten years of patchy memories?"

"Remember, that was the best case. I expect it to be much worse when the committee considers your previous crime."

"*Previous* crime?" I squeaked.

"The committee has evidence linking you to one of the

most significant crimes in Magix history."

"What? No!" I cried. "I didn't—"

"Save it for the committee," he answered, rising abruptly from his chair. "Look, Mason. The entire Magix organization exists to uphold goodness in the world. We'll treat you fairly and kindly, even if you are our enemy."

"I'm not your—" But Frank Lawden didn't care what I had to say. In a heartbeat, he had crossed the room and exited through the door, leaving me alone and terrified.

CHAPTER 4

WEDNESDAY, MAY 13
5:12 P.M.
INTERROGATION ROOM 6, MAGIX HEADQUARTERS

I had been sitting there for only a few minutes, wondering when they would dim the lights that were shining in my eyes—or at least untie me from the chair—when the door opened.

I turned, expecting to see Frank Lawden again. But this time it was a girl who looked to be about my age. So far, she was the first person in Magix Headquarters that I'd seen *not* wearing a gray suit. Instead, she wore a denim jacket over a green shirt. She had deep brown skin, and her black hair was done in lots of small braids all pulled back into a ponytail.

Strangely, she was plugging her nose as she quietly shut the door behind her.

"Mason Mortimer Morrison?" she asked in a nasal voice.

"That's me." Why did all these people know my middle name?

The girl let go of her nose and sniffed.

"Did something smell funny out there?" I asked.

"No," she said defensively. "Why?"

"You were plugging your nose."

"That's irrelevant," she said. "I'm here to prepare you for your trial with the committee."

I raised an eyebrow at her. "And they chose you because . . . ?"

"Magix thought you might be more comfortable with someone closer to your age."

"What's your name?" I asked.

"Avery," she said. "Avery Laaa . . . Lobster."

"Your last name is La Lobster?"

"Just Lobster," she said. "It's a family name."

I nodded. "That's what last names are."

"Anyway, I'm here to answer any of your questions." She crossed the small room and seated herself across the table.

"I didn't think I was allowed to have a lawyer," I said.

"Oh, I'm not a lawyer," said Avery. "I'm an apprentice detective with Magix. So, of course I've been trained to deal with criminals."

"Then I'm afraid you'll be disappointed, because I'm not a criminal."

She exhaled slowly, shaking her head. "That's what they all say."

"You're here to answer my questions?" I checked. "Let's just pretend like I don't know anything. You can start at the beginning. Treat me like a regular person who doesn't know anything about magic. What do you call those people? *Ignorants?*"

"They said you were stubborn. I guess I'm wasting my time," she said, standing up.

"No, wait!" I lurched forward against the straps on my chair. I took a deep breath. "Please?"

Avery didn't even try to hide her curiosity as she looked at me. She seemed to relax a little, sitting once more. "What do you want to know?"

"How did that music box get magical powers?" That seemed like a good place to start, since it was the beginning of my confusion.

"The magic core," she said, like it should be obvious.

I raised my eyebrows, silently begging her to explain.

"The center of the Earth is filled with magic," Avery expounded. "There's no way for it to get to the surface on its own, so it has used people as a conduit for thousands of years."

"How?" I asked.

"Well, magic is attracted to goodness," she said. "Whenever someone does something good in the world, the magic level rises. Eventually, someone does something that causes it to boil over."

"And then what?" I asked. "The person turns magical?" I gasped. "Is that what happened to me?"

"No, no," she said. "*People* can't turn magical. That's not how it works. Good people are just the *reason* the magic surfaces."

"Then what?" I asked. "Magic just comes shooting out of the ground? I'd think people would have noticed that before."

"The magic isn't visible," said Avery. "And when it boils up, it doesn't just go anywhere at random. The magic trickles into specific objects that mean something to the person who caused the boil-over."

I scratched my head. "I don't think I understand."

She drummed her fingers on the table in thought. "How do I explain this . . . ?" Avery muttered. "Let's say you're just a regular person."

"I am," I said.

"No," she replied. "You're Magix's most wanted."

I sighed. "Fine. *Pretend* I'm a regular person."

"Okay. So, you're going about your life, and then one day you do something really amazing."

"Get an A on my book report?" I suggested.

She shook her head. "Probably has to be more amazing than

that. Maybe you save a dog from getting hit by a car, or you give all your money to the poor. . . . It has to be an act of true goodness. That can include bravery, kindness, creativity . . . stuff like that."

"Okay. So, I do something amazing."

"Well, if the magic in the earth's core has been building up, bubbling higher, looking for a way out," continued Avery, "then your act of goodness tops it off and opens the way. The magic comes up, and it soaks into any item you may have touched up to that point in your life. Specifically, items that were significant to you for some reason."

"Whoa," I said. "So, who created that magic music box?"

"That's a good question," she said. "And we'll probably never know. It had to be someone who had once touched the music box and then done something worthy of making the magic boil over. Magix has given up on trying to learn the origins of the magical items. There are just too many possibilities, and it's impossible to track."

"Okay," I said. "So, what exactly is *Magix*?"

"We're the worldwide organization responsible for managing all of these magical boons."

"So, Magix's goal is to capture all the magical boons in the world to make sure no one can use them?"

Again, Avery looked confused. "Not even close," she said.

"Do you know what the word *boon* means?"

I shook my head. I'd figured it was a special word that Magix had made up.

"A *boon* is like a blessing," Avery said. "It's something that benefits you, or gives you a boost. Magix wants as many boons as possible out in the world. They're meant to help people. When an Ignorant person comes into contact with one, a little bit of the magic rubs off on them. It makes their day go a little smoother, makes everything around them better for a time."

"That's definitely not what happened with me and the music box," I muttered.

"That's why we know you're not an Ig," said Avery. "Knowledge is power. Power is magic."

"That's the same thing Mr. Lawden said to me," I said. "What does it mean?"

"Most people don't know anything about real magic," said Avery. "That's what keeps them safe."

"And you call them Ignorants?" I said. "Seems kind of rude."

"Not rude, just the truth," said Avery. "We call them Igs for short."

"And what do you call people who *do* know about magic?"

"Eds," said Avery.

"Why?"

"If someone is able to use the magic items, it's because

they're *Educated*," she clarified, "which is the opposite of being Ignorant. See, if an Ig had opened that music box today, it would have improved their day, times ten."

"But it didn't!" I cried. "It ruined everything!"

"And that's why we know you're an Ed," she said. "Those of us with knowledge of magical boons don't simply get a little bit of good luck rubbed off. The knowledge makes us able to use the full power of the magic in the item."

"Knowledge is power. Power is magic," I said, finally understanding. But my story still didn't make sense. "Why did I activate the music box's true magic if I didn't have any knowledge that it was a boon?"

Avery shook her head. "You *did* have knowledge."

"That's not true!" I yelled loud enough to make Avery flinch.

"I'm sorry, but it has to be," she said. "There's no other explanation for how you could have used the music box's magic. You're an Ed. You had to have knowledge."

I slumped in my chair. "This doesn't make any sense. If Magix *wants* boons out in the world, then why was I arrested for using one?"

"Magix wants as many boons as possible for *Ignorant* people to use," explained Avery. "That's the way magic is supposed to go. When Igs brush up against the boons and a little bit of the magic rubs off, that action helps to raise the core magic level. When people are having a good day, they're more likely to do acts of goodness, which will eventually cause the magic to boil over again. But when Eds use their knowledge to access a magical item's full power, it doesn't do anything to make the level rise."

It sounded ridiculous, but I actually believed everything she was saying. How could I not? Earlier today, my class and I had experienced the impossible. It was just nice to be finally getting some answers. I only wished that I wasn't the bad guy in this story.

"All right," I said. "Tell me more about this committee that's reviewing my case."

"Fifteen of Magix's most powerful administrators," she said. "Basically, three members from each division are elected to serve on the committee for a term of five years."

"What are the divisions?" I asked.

"Investigation Division," she said. "That's everybody you've met so far. They're in charge of tracking unauthorized uses of magical boons and generally keeping the peace."

"Is Frank Lawden their boss?" I asked.

My question made Avery fidget a little bit. She nodded. "Yeah. He's definitely the boss of Investigation. He also oversees the Memory Correction Division—"

"Are they the ones who zapped Mrs. Dunlow and the rest of my class before sending them back?"

She nodded. "And the Boon Recovery Division."

"And I'm guessing they're the ones searching the jungle for the music box," I said, remembering what Nguyen had said about sending in a team. "What are the last two groups?"

"Boon Identification Division," answered Avery. "They're in charge of finding out what new boons can do if their full magic is used. And the Manipulation Division. They experiment with boons to refine or alter their magical effects."

"So, how do I convince a committee full of magical experts that I'm innocent?" I asked.

Avery stared at me for a long minute. Long enough that it got a little uncomfortable for me.

"*Are* you innocent?" she asked.

"YES!" I hollered. Hoping for the first time since I'd opened that music box that someone might believe me.

"Hmm . . . ," she mused, narrowing her eyes as if to inspect me closer. "Well, the committee's definitely going to find you guilty. They have overwhelming proof against you for that big crime last month."

"What crime?" I asked. "What proof?"

Suddenly, an alarm on Avery's wristwatch started chirping. She sucked in a breath. "I have to go." She turned sharply toward the door.

"Wait!" I called. "That's it? You're not even going to tell me what my major crime was? No tips for the committee?"

She glanced back at me and shrugged. "Just tell them the truth."

"Will you be there?" I asked hopefully. It might have been nice to see a familiar face.

Avery grimaced. "They won't let an apprentice detective anywhere near the Hall of Justice."

"Thanks for finally giving me some answers," I said as she gripped the doorknob.

"Mason?" she said without looking back. "Do me a favor and don't tell anyone that I was here."

Then Avery Lobster pinched her nose shut and slipped through the doorway.

CHAPTER 5

WEDNESDAY, MAY 13
7:00 P.M.
HALL OF JUSTICE, MAGIX HEADQUARTERS

O h boy. And I thought it was terrifying to stand up in front of my class to give a book report. . . . The Magix Committee was a million times more intimidating.

I felt puny, sitting in my little chair in the vast Hall of Justice while fifteen adults filed in to take their seats on elevated platforms so they could all scowl down in my direction.

Frank Lawden was the only face I recognized, but he wasn't one of the fifteen. Instead, he stood off to one side at a podium with a large screen hanging behind him.

The focal point in the room—besides myself—was a huge thermometer. It stood on a pedestal, several feet tall, with the numbers representing Fahrenheit on one side and Celsius on the other. The red liquid bar had risen from the bottom, indicating that the temperature in the room was about 35 degrees Fahrenheit.

No wonder I was trembling! Although it didn't feel cold in here, the thermometer showed that this room was nearly freezing!

"For the record," Mr. Lawden said to me, "please state your name."

"Mason Morrison," I said.

"Your *full* name."

I grimaced. "Mason Mortimer Morrison."

Mr. Lawden cleared his throat. "The Magix Committee assembles at seven o'clock on the evening of Wednesday, May thirteenth, to review the charges against Mason Mortimer Morrison."

I wanted to shout, "I'm innocent!" but I decided to wait. He told me I'd have a chance to defend myself.

"Will the defendant allow the use of a truth boon?" Lawden asked, looking at me. I knew enough from following my dad's court case to know that *I* was the defendant.

"What's a truth boon?" I asked. From the platforms, I heard some of the committee members scoff in annoyance. They probably thought I was being a smart aleck, but I really didn't know.

"It is a magical boon that will force you to speak the truth."

My eyes grew wide. This was it! This could save me and prove my innocence! "Yes!" I cried. "That's an option? I'll take it!"

"His eagerness is suspicious," said one of the committee members with a noticeable French accent. "Perhaps he has come prepared for this moment, protecting himself with boons to counter the truth."

"That's crazy!" I shouted. "I didn't even know magic was real until this afternoon."

Mr. Lawden came toward me, holding something small covered by a cloth bag.

"You have to understand that the use of a truth boon does not guarantee anything," he explained quietly. "It shows the committee that you're willing to cooperate, but as it was mentioned, there are known ways to combat its effects." He pulled off the cloth bag to reveal the item beneath.

It was a shoe. An old dirty black sneaker with frayed laces.

"Once your foot is inside the shoe, you will only be able to answer questions truthfully. Also, any information you voluntarily share must be the truth, and nothing but the truth. You may also choose not to answer our questions, although your silence will likely be as incriminating as an answer." He handed me the shoe. "You are now educated and have the knowledge of this boon, which means you can activate its full magical power. Go ahead and put it on."

I stooped over, slipping out of my regular shoe and into the dirty sneaker that Mr. Lawden had given me. I didn't feel any different once it was on. It was a little big for me, but I didn't need to run a mile in it. I just needed to answer some questions, and they'd see that I was innocent.

"Let us begin." Back at the podium, Mr. Lawden lifted a remote and clicked a button. At once, the screen behind him lit up with the picture of a redbrick church. "Do you recognize this building?"

"I can tell it's a church," I said. The steeple was a giveaway.

"Have you ever been to this church?"

"No." I heard a few of the committee members scoff again, so I added, "At least, I don't think so."

"This is the Church of the Faith at an undisclosed site in the eastern United States," explained Lawden. "In truth, Magix uses this building as a top secret storage facility for over a hundred magical boons. Just over a month ago, on April third, at eight o'clock p.m., this facility was robbed of every single magical boon in storage. This represents the greatest theft of magic in the last two decades, making you Magix's number one most wanted criminal."

"Me?" I cried. "Why do you think *I* did this?"

"There were two guards on duty in the facility," said Lawden. "They report that a person matching your description took them by surprise and quickly overpowered them. You then loaded the boons into a large hiking backpack—itself an illegal boon capable of reducing items in size and weight to fit—and exited the church. The guards gave pursuit, but you reportedly opened a music box and transported to an unknown location."

"That's crazy!" I yelled. "It wasn't me. The guards are lying. I'm being framed!"

"Fortunately, we have more than the word of the guards," said Lawden, pressing another button to change the slide behind him.

A video started playing on the screen, the time in the bottom right of the screen showing 8:02 p.m. It wasn't great quality and looked like footage from a security camera. In view was an empty street approaching twilight, but in the background, I could clearly see the Church of the Faith. As I watched, a kid wearing a sweatshirt exactly like one of mine came running into view, a large black-and-blue hiking backpack flapping empty on his back. He skipped up the front steps and blasted forcefully through the front door.

"That wasn't me!" I said. "Just because I have the same sweatshirt. . . . You couldn't even see his face!"

46

"Please hold your comments until the end of the video," said Mr. Lawden. He sped through the next several minutes and slowed the video again at 8:13 p.m. The church's front door opened and the kid reappeared, his large backpack bulging. He glanced around nervously and then moved down the steps. At this point, I could see his face. But it was far away. I guess he sort of looked like me, but it wasn't enough to accuse me like this!

The kid in the video moved around the right side of the church, disappearing from view.

"That could have been anybody," I said. "Lots of kids look like me. There's a fifth grader in Mr. Marchant's class. People get us mixed up all the time . . ."

I faded away as Mr. Lawden pointed back to the screen. For some reason, the thief had reentered the frame. And this time, he was moving right toward the camera!

As strange as it was, I began to be convinced. With every step, the person looked more like me. Then he paused in the middle of the street. I could see the music box carefully cradled in his hands. Then the boy looked directly up at the camera. At this close distance, there was no mistaking it.

"That's me," I whispered. At least, it looked *exactly* like me, down to the big freckle on my forehead. The church door opened behind me, and the two guards ran down the steps.

The boy that looked like me ducked under the camera and out of sight.

"I don't understand," I muttered as the video ended. "That was me."

"Then he admits to the theft," said one of the committee members.

"No!" I shouted. "I didn't steal anything from that church! You know I can't lie!" I wiggled my right foot to remind them of the sneaker.

"He's clearly found a way to immunize himself against the truth shoe," said another committee member with an accent I didn't recognize. "We cannot trust his word."

"How can you be sure that was me?" I asked. "Maybe somebody used a magical item to create an evil twin. Or disguise themselves like me . . ."

"That is not possible," said Mr. Lawden. "Magical effects cannot be recorded by common cameras. And this footage was from an ordinary security camera belonging to a company of storage units across the street from the church."

"You can't record magic?" I said.

Mr. Lawden shook his head. "In the event that a common camera attempts to record magic in action, something will always interfere to prevent it—something will obstruct the view, or the lens will break, or the camera's battery will suddenly die. Magic *cannot* be recorded. Which is why we know the person in the video must be you."

"No, I—it's not—" I stammered. "What about . . . what about the backpack? You said it was magic, but I could see it on the video."

"The backpack *is* a boon, but it was not doing anything magical in the video," explained Lawden.

"Then maybe someone was wearing a mask," I said. "Not a normal mask, it looked too realistic for that. But what about a magical mask that—"

"I oversee the Boon Identification Division," a voice from the committee said, cutting me off. "We had detectors analyze the video. I can personally assure you that the only two boons in play were the backpack and the music box."

I swallowed hard and folded my arms. This was looking bad for me.

"Do you recognize any of these items?" Mr. Lawden clicked his remote. The screen showed a mash-up of several ordinary-looking things.

"Of course," I answered. "That's a hockey stick, a coffee mug, a blanket, a flowerpot, and a motorcycle helmet." I hoped this wasn't a trick question. Even if it was, I wasn't supposed to be able to lie with that shoe on my foot.

"Shortly after your arrest this afternoon, a Magix Artifact

Recovery team located these five magical items in your bed-room."

"*My* bedroom?" I repeated. "Like, at my house? That's not possible! I've never seen any of these things before."

"These five items were all registered boons being stored in the church," said Lawden. "They were reported stolen on April third and were found in your bedroom on May thirteenth."

"Well, I don't know how they got there!" I cried. "I'm innocent. I didn't steal anything."

"We found stolen items in your room," called a committee member. "We have a video of you fleeing the crime scene! What more do you want?"

"Like father, like son," another person mumbled from the stands.

"What did you say?" I spat, rising from my chair. My hands were in fists at my sides, and I could feel my face turn hot.

"I'm only saying that your determination to deny obvious evidence is unsurprisingly like your father," the committee member continued.

"What do you know about my father?" I pressed. "Leave him out of this!"

Mr. Lawden stepped away from his podium, motioning for me to take a seat. "Mason, please. The committee has been reviewing every aspect of your case. Your father's bank robbery and trial was a relevant bit of backstory."

"How is it relevant?" I asked, refusing to sit.

"It is a sad truth that children with criminal parents are more than twice as likely to commit crimes themselves," said the committee member. "It's a pattern of behavior that passes from father to son—"

"Crime isn't genetic!" I cut him off. "And my dad didn't actually rob that bank!" It had been months since I'd said that out loud. It felt good to shout it again.

"Five hundred thousand dollars," said another. "The bank recovered most of it in the trunk of your father's car, but he managed to squirrel away a hundred thousand dollars that is still unaccounted for."

"He didn't—" I tried.

"Go ahead and roll the footage, Lawden," continued the man.

"Footage?" I said. "Of the bank robbery? They said the bank's cameras were cut."

"Yes," the committee member said. "But much like your situation, an outdoor camera captured it all."

Mr. Lawden pressed a button and another video started. I sat forward in plain curiosity. I'd heard there was footage, but it was supposed to be confidential. Magix seemed to get anything it wanted.

On the screen, I saw someone who looked exactly like my dad run into view, holding four huge bags of cash. He exited the frame quickly, and a moment later I saw his car veering away. I could still see my dad behind the wheel, swerving out of control. He was almost out of view when he crashed into the back of a delivery truck carrying custom windows and mirrors. Broken glass sprayed everywhere, and it looked like the truck slammed against the pole where the security camera was mounted, causing the picture to shake as my dad's car sped out of sight.

Then the video stopped and everyone stared down at me. But seeing the footage hadn't convinced me of anything. In fact, it had done the opposite. I knew *I* wasn't guilty. There had to be some kind of magical explanation. And maybe that same explanation meant my dad was as innocent as I was.

"I think that shows what kind of household young Mason was raised in," said the committee member.

"Not at all!" I shouted. "My dad is a good person! He never broke the law!"

Mr. Lawden held up his hand. "Mason is the one on trial tonight. Not his father. Let us return to the case." He moved back to his podium. I finally sat down again, still breathing heavily from seeing that footage of my dad.

"After stealing the church boons, the defendant kept a low

profile," said Mr. Lawden, "until today when—"

"Hold on," I cut in. "You've known who I was for over a month?"

"It wasn't difficult to get a positive ID off that video," Lawden said.

"Why didn't you just surround my house and arrest me right away?" I asked. "Or grab me on the way home from school? Why'd you have to wait and do it in front of my whole class?"

"We needed to recover the music box," Mr. Lawden explained. "We had identified it from the security video, but there was no way of knowing where you had stashed it. So we placed an alert on its magical signal. The alert went off the moment you opened the music box in your classroom. We dispatched Agents Clarkston and Nguyen immediately."

"But I had already transported Mrs. Dunlow and my class to Antarctica," I said.

"So, you admit to doing that?" asked one of the committee members.

"Sure," I replied. "But how was I supposed to know it was a crime? How was I supposed to know that music box did anything other than play a little song?"

"That was the nature of the boon," answered Lawden. "When you opened the box, you were transported to an uninhabited region of the world. Anyone looking at you, or anyone looking at them, was transported with you."

It was nice to finally understand how that had worked.

"Nguyen and Clarkston traced your music box to Antarctica, then to the Caribbean, and then to the Sahara Desert, where they quickly caught up. You resisted arrest, endangered civilian Ignorants, and put Magix agents in harm's way. Do you deny that this happened?"

"No," I said. "But I didn't understand what was going on. I still don't. I had no idea what that music box would do when I opened it."

This comment really sent the committee into a tizzy. Many of them started talking at once. Several rose from their seats in loud protest. It took Frank Lawden slamming his hand against the podium to get everyone quieted down again.

"You claim you activated the music-box boon without any knowledge of its true magical potential?" he asked me.

"Yes," I said without wavering.

"Now we know he's just messing with us, Director," called a committee member. "He has figured out a way to block the truth shoe, and he's making a mockery of this committee and the very foundational rules of magic. You shouldn't tolerate this kind of behavior. We have plenty of evidence. I think we're all convinced." She looked side to side for support from the others.

My heart sank as I saw every head nodding.

Behind the podium, Mr. Lawden sighed deeply. "The committee will adjourn to the council room for final deliberation. We'll convene again once a verdict has been reached."

CHAPTER 6

I watched the fifteen committee members shuffle out of the room in single file, wishing there was one more thing I could say to convince them of my innocence. It wasn't hard to guess which verdict they'd reach. Seemed to me like most of them had made up their minds that I was guilty before they'd even met me.

I gripped the armrests of my chair, resisting the emotions that threatened to overtake me. I actually thought I was alone in the big room until Mr. Lawden stepped in front of me.

Wordlessly, he dropped to one knee and pulled the magical shoe off my foot. I secretly hoped that my sock stunk, and that he had to smell it. Then, to my surprise, I felt him sliding on my ordinary shoe.

Frank Lawden rose slowly, his knee cracking as he sighed wearily. "I don't think they'll be long," he said. "Can I get you a glass of water?"

"Not thirsty," I spat.

"Maybe something from the vending machine?"

"Why are you being nice to me?" I asked flatly.

He turned to look at me, dark eyes frightfully sincere. "It's what Magix stands for," he said. "We're servants of goodness. Servants of the magic." As he spoke, he stepped over to the large thermometer standing on the pedestal in the center of the floor.

"I think that thing's broken," I said.

"Oh?"

"If it were thirty-five degrees in here, we'd all be freezing," I pointed out.

Frank Lawden smiled. "This thermometer doesn't measure the temperature." He ran his hand carefully along its edge. "It's a boon."

"Neat," I said sarcastically, hoping I sounded as uninterested as I really was.

"It measures the level of the magic core," he said. "Little acts of goodness around the world cause the level to rise bit by bit. Ordinary people, Ignorant of magic, being kind to one another, helping each other, creating amazing things . . . those are what fuel the magic core deep under the earth's surface."

"And then an awful criminal like me comes along and probably makes the level drop," I said bitterly.

"No, actually," he said, "the magic core can't go down. It can only rise. Sure, there are plenty of bad people in the world, doing horrible things. But the bad going on out there doesn't diminish the goodness in the world. Goodness stands on its own, and it will always cause the magic to rise to the boiling point."

"Technically, it can't," I said. "Water boils at 212 degrees Fahrenheit, and your little thermometer only goes up to 140." I smirked at him. "Even criminals can pay attention in science class."

"The boiling point is just an expression we use," said Lawden. "The magic core will rise until it reaches 140. Then it'll be ready to spill out into the world."

"And that's how more boons are made?" I said, checking him against what Avery had told me.

Mr. Lawden nodded. "At 140 degrees, the magic is ready. The next person out there in the world to commit an act of pure goodness will cause the magic to come out. It'll trickle down through that person's past, filling up objects that they've touched. Objects that once meant something special to them. A music box, a shoe . . . I've learned not to judge what items held value in a person's life."

"Right," I said. "You just judge the person."

"That's not my job," he said. "I merely presented the facts as we understand them. The committee is responsible for determining what happens next."

"But what do *you* think?" I asked. "Do you really think I'm guilty? Do you really think I could pull off the biggest magic theft in twenty years when I didn't even know about magic? I'm thirteen years old. What does your gut tell you?"

Frank Lawden didn't say anything for a moment, seeming deep in thought. When he finally turned to answer, he was interrupted by the chamber door opening on squeaky hinges. Mr. Lawden closed his mouth, tucked the magic shoe under one arm, and took his place at the podium.

I remained in my seat, watching the fifteen committee members file in and sit down. When they were settled, Mr. Lawden raised his voice.

"The senior-most committee member is selected as spokesperson," he said, gesturing to a woman with gray hair to match her suit. "Ms. Harmon. The floor is yours."

The woman stood slowly and made her way down the stairs until she stopped beside the boon thermometer.

"For the record," she began. "On this day, the thirteenth of May, at seven forty-five in the evening, the Magix Committee finds Mason Mortimer Morrison . . . *guilty.*"

The word was like a giant sledgehammer pounding me down into my seat. I wanted to jump up and run out of there. I wanted to scream in her face defiantly. Instead, I just trembled, shaking like the room really was 35 degrees.

"The evidences provided against him are plentiful and conclusive," continued Ms. Harmon. "From the complete theft of the boon facility to the transportation of his entire class using an illegal music box, Mason Mortimer Morrison has proven himself a cunning and dangerous criminal. As such, we, the Magix Committee, find it necessary to conduct a full and total memory wipe."

"What?" I yelled, leaping to my feet. "What does that mean?"

"Please be seated," said Mr. Lawden.

"No way!" I screamed. "What does that mean?"

"It means we will use a special boon to erase all of your memories, starting at birth to the present day," said Ms. Harmon. "You will retain many of your basic abilities—motor skills, speech—but you will have no recollection of who you were. An accident will be staged, after which you will wake up in a hospital. We often assign new identities in these situations, but we will allow your mother to claim you, although you will not remember anything about her."

"You can't do this!" I cried. "It's not fair!"

"It's a completely painless process," she said. "Or so I'm told."

"Have you done this to a lot of people?" I asked, horrified to hear the answer.

"Magix performs memory wipes around the world on a weekly basis," she answered. "Most of those are done on Ignorant civilians who accidentally notice an Educated activating a magical boon. In such cases, the memory is isolated and can be removed individually."

"Then why won't you do that to me?" I begged. "Back up to last month. To the day before the boon church was robbed. Just erase my memory up till then."

"That option was discussed among the committee," Ms. Harmon said. "However, we have no way of knowing when you first gained knowledge of true magic. And with your criminal record, we cannot release you back into the world with the possibility that you could strike again. A full and total memory wipe is the only way to be sure you will not continue your life of crime."

"That's insane!" I called. "You people are all insane!" I whirled on Frank Lawden, but he was staring down at his feet uncomfortably. "You're so proud of your organization being founded on goodness. But this is pure cruelty!"

"This is necessary to preserve the future of magic," snapped

Ms. Harmon. "You should be grateful that we're releasing you at all. That we're not keeping you locked up in the basement like—"

"That's enough, Linda," Mr. Lawden finally spoke. "When will the procedure take place?"

"Nine thirty tomorrow morning," said Ms. Harmon. "We'll take the boy to the laboratory on the third floor."

I suddenly felt dizzy, and I slumped back into my chair. Was this really happening? Why? How?

Ms. Harmon turned and made her way back up to her seat on the raised platform.

"We'll have security escort you to a holding room," Mr. Lawden said to me. He slapped his hand against the podium. "Dismissed."

CHAPTER 7

THURSDAY, MAY 14
7:30 A.M.
HOLDING ROOM B, MAGIX HEADQUARTERS

The holding room at Magix Headquarters was *way* nicer than my room at home. It had a king-size bed, a couch, a huge TV, a microwave, a mini-fridge, a table, and some chairs.

But it didn't have a window, and the door had been locked every time I'd tried it, so escaping wasn't really an option.

I hadn't slept much during the night, lying awake and thinking about all the memories I'd miss. I wondered if I would be able to make new memories, or if I'd be a blank slate forever. I had showered off the jungle mud last night, surprised that there'd been no sign of Agent Clarkston's blue marker on my forehead.

Now it was seven thirty in the morning, and I was dressed

in some fresh clothes that I'd found in a closet. They were comfortable and just my size. I sat on the edge of the bed, rubbing my stiff leg. I think most people would have sore muscles after running through the jungle and jumping off a cliff, but it was actually my bone that ached. It got like this sometimes. Falling off the roof and breaking my femur three years ago was one memory that I wouldn't be sad to lose.

There was a sound outside my door. I sprang to my feet, heart racing. Were they coming to get me already? That wasn't fair! I deserved two more hours to stare at the empty wall and feel sorry for myself.

The door swung open, and I braced myself to see the face of my soon-to-be memory executioner.

"Avery Lobster?" I cried, my voice cracking.

"Hurry," she said, one hand plugging her nose. What was that about? Did she always enter a room like that? "We don't have a lot of time."

"What are you doing?"

"I'm here to break you out," she said, waving me over to the door. "Unless you *want* all of your memories scrubbed. And plug your nose!"

I obeyed, staggering toward her. My feet felt like bricks, weighed down by my astonishment. When I got to the doorway, I caught a glimpse of the hallway. Two guards in gray suits were lying still on the floor.

I gasped. "What happened?" My voice sounded funny with my nose plugged.

"They didn't let me past when I asked nicely," she said as we moved into the quiet hall.

"Are they . . ." I couldn't bring myself to say *dead*. It was hard to imagine Avery going full-on assassin.

"Of course not," she whispered as we stepped past the nearest guard. "I used a boon to knock them out." She pointed to a stout candle on the floor at the end of the hallway. I could see the little flicker of flame on the wick. "Scented candle," she explained. "It puts anyone who smells it to sleep."

"Where'd you get it?"

"My house," she answered, pausing at the corner to peer around. "Sometimes I use it in my room when I'm having a hard time falling asleep. My parents come in later to blow it out."

"Your parents know about magic?" I asked, obediently tagging along as she slipped around the corner.

"Yeah," she replied.

"And they let you keep cool magical items in your bedroom?" I was officially jealous. "For years, I've been trying to convince my mom to let me have a Batman throwing star."

"That's a terrible idea!" she replied. "You'd put a million holes in the walls."

"Gee . . . that's exactly what she said."

"Listen, it's not like I get special privileges just because my parents know about magic," Avery continued. "I got into the apprentice detective program on my own."

We rounded another corner, and she unplugged her nose. Hoping it was safe, I did the same, sniffing to help my nose feel normal after pinching it so tightly. We reached a closed door at the end of the hallway, and Avery pressed her ear against it.

"Why are you helping me?" I asked quietly.

Without answering, she pulled a piece of paper from her pocket and passed it to me. I unfolded it and read the message written inside, the handwriting small and compact.

The boy is NOT guilty. You can find proof of his innocence at the High Line. Talk to the bird artist.

"I found it in my locker when I got to headquarters this morning," Avery explained, opening the door she'd been listening through. Beyond, I saw flights of stairs leading upward.

"You have a locker here?" I asked, following Avery up the stairs. The apprentice detective training program was sounding a lot like school. "Who put the note in there?" Our footsteps echoed, and I peered over the railing to see that the stairs continued up and up. The building we were in must have had nearly twenty stories.

"I don't know," she answered, taking the note from my hand and stuffing it back into her pocket. "But whoever it was knew that I'd help you."

"Why?" I asked.

Avery paused on the stairs to look back at me. "Because I believe you're innocent."

I felt a flood of relief pass over me. Someone believed me! And now, that "someone" was helping me escape. I took a deep breath. The hopelessness I'd been feeling moments ago vanished entirely.

"How do we get out of here?" I asked.

"Through the front door," Avery replied as we resumed our climb up the stairs.

"Isn't there, like, a back door?" I suggested. "Or somewhere less obvious?"

Avery shook her head. "There's only one way in or out of Magix Headquarters . . . it's complicated."

I'd just have to trust that she knew what she was doing. "Are we almost there?"

"We have to make another stop before we leave," she said.

"What?" I cried. This sounded like the worst escape plan ever. "Shouldn't we hurry? What if somebody notices those sleeping guards outside my door?"

"If we get lucky," said Avery, "the scented candle boon will knock out anyone investigating before they think to plug their nose."

I was glad I'd listened to her strange instructions.

"But even with that candle boon," Avery went on, "sooner

or later, people are going to realize you've escaped."

"Then what are we doing?" I asked, trying to keep my voice under control.

"Look," she snapped. "You're currently Magix's most wanted criminal. And even though *I* believe you are innocent, it doesn't change the fact that *someone* raided that boon church and framed you to take the fall for it. I plan to find out who it was and bring them to justice. But the minute we break out of here, every Magix agent in the organization will be looking for us." She finally stopped at a door leading out of the stairwell. "We're going to need some equipment to stay ahead of them."

She listened at the door before cracking it open and peering out.

"Looks like the coast is clear for the moment," she whispered. "There's a boon armory at the end of this hallway. Don't stop until we reach it."

"Armory?" I squeaked.

"It's a room where they store boons that are prepped and ready for agents to take out on missions," Avery explained.

"I know what an armory is," I retorted. I'd played enough video games to figure that out. Avery took off running and I followed right behind, regretting the way the door banged shut behind me. Luckily, no one investigated the sound, and we reached the entrance to the armory, breathing heavily.

The door to get in looked like solid metal. There was a little shelf on the wall beside it, but the only thing on the shelf was a blender, like the kind my mom used to make smoothies.

"That's weird," I said, but Avery didn't think so. She stepped right up to the blender and took a deep breath.

"What are you doing?" I asked.

"Opening the door," she answered, pushing the blender's buttons in a specific order like she was entering a code.

"With a blender?"

"It's a boon," she told me. "Put in the right code and the door opens."

"What happens if you put in the wrong code?" I asked.

Avery paused, her finger hovering over the *on* button. "The blender blades fill the hallway and chop us into tiny bits."

"Yikes!" I yelped. These Magix people didn't mess around. "Are you sure you have the right code?"

"Ninety-nine percent sure." Avery pushed the button.

I flinched, but the blender blades of doom did not come flying at us. Instead, they began to twirl inside the blender, which seemed to power the huge metal door as it slowly swung open.

"How did you learn that code?" I asked.

"Good detective work," she replied. "I figured out a lot of things that apprentice detectives aren't supposed to know—the aliases of several undercover Magix agents, the location of the black site where they hold unstable boons . . ." She pointed at the blender. "That was the director's own master code. Now that I'm sure it works, we can use the same one to unlock the blender at the front door."

"There's *another* blender?" I croaked.

"Technically, it's part of the same one," Avery said, waiting for the door. "A few years back, some agents came across a single blender that had become a magical boon. The people at Magix were able to remove the buttons and install a few of them onto regular blenders, extending the magical effect to all of them."

"They can do that?" I asked.

"Oh yeah," she answered, leading us into the armory. "Boon manipulation. Magix has an entire department for it, remember?"

I'd seen a lot of armories in video games, but nothing that looked like this. Instead of heavy weaponry hanging on the walls, it was just a bunch of random objects scattered throughout the room.

"How do we know what to take?" I asked, inspecting a rusty teapot next to a velvet coin purse. With determination, Avery moved toward a set of shelves against the back wall, where I saw at least a dozen black top hats.

"Hey," I said, "those are just like the ones Agents Clarkston and Nguyen were wearing when they found me."

Avery reached onto the shelf and pulled down one of the hats. "These top hats are standard issue for agents in the field," she said, trying it on. It looked a little large on her head, falling almost to her eyebrows, but she nodded like she'd found the perfect treasure.

"They have huge storage capacity and come stocked with all the essentials an agent needs for a mission," she explained.

I took one down from the shelf. "Are they all the same?"

"Each one will hold different boons," she said. "I've memorized some of the standard items, but there will probably be some surprises, too."

I glanced back at the shelf. "That's a lot of magic hats."

"Manipulated boons," explained Avery. "Like the blender. The hats aren't actually magic. It's the hatband—that black ribbon." She pointed to the wide ribbon tied around the base of the stovetop hat, just above the flat brim. "A whole roll of ribbon turned magical when its owner did something purely good. Magix found it and discovered that anything the ribbon wrapped around hugely increased its storage capacity."

"And they chose to wrap it around *top hats*?" I could think of a dozen things more convenient and less conspicuous.

"This was almost two hundred years ago," Avery said. "Top hats were all the rage back then."

"Magix has been around that long?"

"Oh yeah," said Avery. "This organization started clear back in the eighteenth century. But people have known about magic forever."

"They've never updated the hats?" I asked, turning mine over in my hands.

"The ribbons are fused on," she said. "Peeling them off the hats would cause them to lose their magic."

I shrugged, finally trying it on. It wasn't as uncomfortable as I'd thought, but it did make me feel a little top-heavy.

As I turned away from the rack of hats, something familiar caught my eye on one of the shelves. It was the same dirty black sneaker that I'd agreed to wear during the trial last night.

"Hey," I said, pulling it down. "Should we take this?"

"What is it?" Avery asked.

I tossed her the shoe. "It makes the person wearing it tell the truth," I answered. "Could be helpful in our search for answers."

Avery nodded, stuffing the truth shoe into her top hat and moving over to another shelf that was labeled *Boon Detectors*.

"Knowledge is power. Power is magic," she recited. "Even though our hats are full of boons, we won't know how to use any of them unless we have a detector."

"What's that?" I asked.

"It's a specific type of boon that detects and identifies other boons," she explained. "It's how we get the knowledge we need to operate new magical items."

"I activated the music box without knowledge," I reminded her.

"No," she said. "That's not possible. Somehow you had the knowledge. Maybe the memory was just blocked or something. Add it to the list of things we need to figure out once we escape."

As I turned my attention to the shelf of boon detectors, Avery reached out and picked up a little pet collar. It was bright red with a silver buckle and a few tiny brass bells. There was a small card tied to the collar, which Avery turned over and began reading out loud.

"Attach this collar around the neck of a living creature, and the animal will become an active detector," she read. "One use only. The magic will expire when the collar is removed."

Avery glanced over at me. "Seems too complicated if we have to find an animal."

I nodded in agreement. "Let's check out those sunglasses. Or that clock-looking thing."

But before Avery could put the collar back on the shelf, an alarm blared through the armory. I screamed, grabbing the brim of my top hat to keep it from falling off as I jumped with fright.

"Warning! Warning!" a robotic voice blared through intercom speakers in the ceiling. "Prisoner has escaped! Prisoner has escaped!"

Avery turned to me, her eyes wide. She stuffed the pet collar into her pocket. "Time to run."

CHAPTER 8

I ran faster than I'd ever run before, my aching leg not even slowing me down with all the adrenaline I was feeling. We left the door to the armory wide open and made for the stairs at the end of the hallway. Avery yanked open the door but reeled backward, bumping into me.

"Toothpaste!" she cried.

"What do you mean, *toothpaste*?" I leaned past her and peered into the stairwell. It was filling up with something foamy and white. It actually did look like toothpaste—after brushing and spitting.

"It's a security boon," Avery explained, quickly shutting the door and heading down a different hallway. "There are pasted

75

toothbrushes positioned along all the interior doors of head-quarters. All an agent has to do is flick the bristles, and the doors and stairways fill up with foamy toothpaste. Impossible to get past."

"So we're trapped on this floor?" I wailed. As we moved around the corner, I saw a large floor-to-ceiling window on the right. Like all the other windows I'd seen in Magix Head-quarters, the glass was frosted and opaque. It let enough light through that I knew it was a sunshiny morning outside, but I couldn't really see out.

"A window . . . ," I muttered under my breath. Sure, we were on the ninth floor, but Agent Clarkston had used a magic pillowcase to carry us safely to the bottom of a cliff. Between my new hat and Avery's, I figured we could find *something* that would work. I just needed to break the glass first.

I skidded to a halt beside the window, yanking off my top hat. I shoved my hand into the opening, but instead of feeling the top of the hat, my hand kept going. Soon, I was in up to my shoulder, feeling a bunch of random objects at my fingertips. It was like the hat was a giant bag, but I had to select the item I wanted strictly by feel.

"What are you doing?" Avery shrieked, turning back when she realized I wasn't following.

"I have an idea." My fingers closed around something that

felt like a baseball bat. I whipped it out of the hat, discovering that it was actually one of those carved posts that belonged in a banister along stairs.

"We have no idea what that thing does," Avery said.

"I don't need it to do anything magical," I replied. "I just need it to be a club." I stuck the top hat back on my head and, gripping the banister post with both hands, wound up for a mighty baseball swing.

"Mason!" Avery said, her voice suddenly urgent. "The window isn't—"

I swung with all my strength. The end of my wooden club struck the window with an insane amount of force that could only be described as magical. The frosted glass shattered, and I saw our way out.

But it wasn't at all what I'd expected.

I leaped back from the broken window, dropping the banister post and gripping my hat in astonishment. This couldn't be the ninth floor. Based on what I was seeing, it was more like the *nine-millionth* floor!

The ground was so far away that I thought we must be higher than the clouds. But it didn't make sense, because I glimpsed other buildings—*huge* buildings—that rose so high into the sky above that I couldn't see their tops.

"Where . . . ," I stammered. "Where are we?"

"I'd say we're in a city," said Avery, her voice twinged with annoyance.

"Why's it so . . . *big*?"

"It's not," she answered. "We're actually very tiny."

Just then, a person walked by outside the window. But the pedestrian was giant. Our window was roughly at the level of his hand, and the man's pinkie fingernail was bigger than a football field!

"Why are we so tiny?" I whispered, my back against the opposite side of the hallway, as far from the open window as I could get.

Avery sighed. "Magix Headquarters is a boon. This entire facility is housed inside a diamond. Someone we call the Doorman is wearing the diamond on a ring. That's why the front door is our only option. When I put in the right code, it'll send a signal to the Doorman so he can open a door for us. When his diamond ring makes contact with a regular doorknob, that ordinary door becomes our only way in or out of headquarters."

"And if we jumped out that window?" I asked, hesitantly pointing at the shattered glass.

"Besides falling for a *very* long time," said Avery, "we'd be stuck in the real world as microscopic people."

"Okay," I said, courageously stepping closer to the open window so I could pick up the wooden banister post and drop it back into my hat. "The window was a bad idea."

"And that breaking glass was sure to get someone's attention," Avery said, taking off down the hallway at a run.

"I don't know," I said, sprinting after her. "There doesn't seem to be anybody else on this level."

Just then, a classroom door flew open and a janitorial cleaning cart came sliding into the hallway. Avery was moving too quickly, and she crashed right into it. The cart went over sideways and I crashed into Avery, causing her to land spread-eagle in the hallway.

But I got the worst of it. My top hat came off, landing upside down on the floor. I fell backward, taking a hard seat directly on the magical hat.

Something sharp stabbed me and I let out a howl, hopping straight back to my feet like a cartoon character. As it turned out, that wasn't the only cartoon thing about my injury. My top hat was smashed, but apparently, one of the boons hidden inside it was a potted cactus.

I could see the poky green plant sticking up through the hat's flattened opening. But most of the needles were missing from the plant because they were stuck in my backside!

I wanted to scream again, but I held it back, whimpering instead. Carefully reaching back, I felt a couple of sharp points piercing through my pants. I plucked one out, but I had a feeling this wasn't going to be an easy task.

"Is that Avery?" said an elderly voice. The custodian emerged from the classroom, grunting as he tipped his cleaning cart back onto its wheels. He had extremely thin gray hair and deep wrinkles at the corners of his mouth. He was wearing jeans and a long-sleeved Magix-gray shirt.

"What are you doing up here?" the old man asked. "Didn't you hear the alarm? There's a prisoner loose in headquarters."

Avery set her top hat on her head and shot me a glance. "Hi, Mr. Albrecht. My friend and I were just delivering a message to Agent Nguyen. Have you seen her?"

"Not on this floor," he said, picking up a pair of fallen spray bottles and a roll of paper towels. "I was just vacuuming this classroom when the alarm went off. Thought I heard some glass break out here—"

"Oh no!" Avery cried, drawing his attention to a mess on the floor in the hallway. Through my pain, I glimpsed a half-eaten milkshake spilling from a white foam cup.

"Ah, my breakfast," he said, sounding rather devastated.

"This is breakfast?" she asked. "A little early for ice cream, isn't it?"

He chuckled. "Never too early for my pineapple Oreo shake."

"That sounds like an exciting flavor," Avery said, positioning herself between the custodian and me before he got a good glimpse at my face and realized that *I* was the escaped prisoner. I mustered all my strength to bend down and pick up my smashed top hat.

Mr. Albrecht licked his lips. "It's the only flavor, in my opinion."

I tucked myself around the corner, finally examining my hat. It felt strangely heavy, with the cactus stuck in the opening. As I tried to straighten out the brim, I saw something that made my heart drop. The black ribbon hatband had separated from the silky hat, trailing off like a limp tail.

"Well, I'm sure the prisoner won't bother us up on the ninth floor," I heard the custodian say to Avery. "Still, you and your friend should probably close yourselves in one of the classrooms until they give the all-clear sign."

"Good idea," Avery said. "Sorry about your milkshake."

"Luckily, I've got the supplies to clean it up," he replied.

With the conversation over, Avery suddenly ducked around the corner. "That was close," she whispered as we set off again. "Are you okay?"

She must have noticed me hobbling along beside her. "Not really. No." I held out the top hat for her inspection.

"Oh, great," she moaned, taking it from my hands. She only looked at it for a second before tossing it through the open doorway into a classroom we were passing.

"Hey!" I protested. "My hat!"

"Broken," she said. "There's no way to reattach the ribbon. The hat's useless now. That cactus got stuck in the opening."

"But, but . . . ," I stammered.

"I get it," she said. "Your butt."

She kept running.

"Where are we going?" I asked.

"The elevator," she answered.

"Wait. There's an elevator?" I grumbled. "Why'd we take the stairs all the way up here?"

"It was too risky," Avery said. "If someone had gotten on, they could've stopped us."

"You don't think they'll stop us now?" I asked.

"When that alarm went off, headquarters went into lockdown mode," she explained. "The elevator can only be operated by a specific boon."

"Do you have something in your hat that'll work?" I asked.

She shook her head. "It takes a special cork from a wine bottle. There are only seven of them."

"Who has them?" I asked.

"Director Lawden has one," she said. "And the head of each department in Magix." She smiled and held up a cork. "And the custodian, Lionel Albrecht."

"Did you steal that from the old man?" I cried. "You're way more criminal than I am!"

We reached the elevator, and Avery used the cork to press the button with the down arrow. Not only did the button light up, but the cork began to glow like a little light bulb.

Avery and I looked over our shoulders nervously until the elevator doors finally opened. Once inside, I inspected the numbered buttons on the panel.

"There are sixteen stories to this place?" I asked.

"It's a sixteen-carat diamond," replied Avery, like that was supposed to make sense.

The elevator doors closed, and Avery pressed the glowing cork against the first-floor button. In silence, we watched the numbers on the digital display go down as we descended.

"We can expect the first floor to be crawling with agents," Avery said as we dropped past the third level. "The moment this door opens, we run for it. Don't stop running until we reach the end of the hallway." I tensed as the digital display turned to number one.

But the elevator didn't stop.

"What the . . . ?" Avery whispered.

"We're still going down," I said. "Is there a basement?"

"No, no, no, no, no," Avery began to mutter, a hint of panic in her voice. She pressed the glowing wine cork against the first-floor button again, but the elevator didn't stop. Then she began frantically jamming the cork against any other button, desperate to get the elevator to reverse direction.

"Avery!" I said, pulling her hand away from the panel of buttons. The cork was glowing brighter than ever between her fingers, and it was starting to smoke. With a yelp of surprise, she dropped it to the floor, and it exploded like a firework.

"This is bad," Avery was mumbling. "So bad. We can't go to the basement. Bad, bad, bad."

"Why?" I asked. "What's down there?"

"It's not *what*," she said. "It's *who*."

The elevator finally came to a stop, and the door rumbled open.

CHAPTER 9

When the elevator doors opened, I saw a room that I wasn't expecting. It was probably the fanciest place I'd ever laid eyes on. It looked like a millionaire's suite that belonged on the top floor of some New York City high-rise, not in the basement of a weird diamond-ring office building.

The floor was hardwood, with massive soft rugs covering large areas. There was no shortage of comfortable places to sit, with overstuffed couches and armchairs surrounding a glass coffee table. In one corner was a grand piano, and in another was a spacious kitchen, with an island bar that had a granite countertop and three barstools tucked under it.

There were no windows down here, but the entire far wall

was a giant fish tank illuminated with soft blue lights. A glittery chandelier hung from a high ceiling, and a glass staircase rose to an overlooking loft area above us.

I stepped forward, but Avery caught my arm. "Maybe we should just wait in the elevator. Eventually, someone will call it back up."

"And we'll be sitting ducks," I said, tugging away and moving into the suite, a few remaining cactus needles poking me with each step. "At least down here, we might have a chance to hide for a while."

Reluctantly, Avery followed after me, the elevator doors closing behind us.

"Well, this is an unexpected visit," a woman's voice sounded, smooth and confident. My eyes darted around the spacious room until I spotted her descending the glass stairs.

The woman was about my mom's age, wearing a baggy pink sweatsuit over her thin figure. Her black hair was pulled into a ponytail, and she had on a surprising amount of makeup for someone who looked like she didn't have anywhere to go.

"I've either been locked up for a lot longer than I thought," the woman said, "or the Magix guards keep getting younger."

"We're not guards," I replied. "The elevator malfunctioned and brought us down here. Do you have a key—or a cork, I guess—that could help us go up?"

Avery smacked me across the arm with the back of her hand as though I'd requested something highly inappropriate.

"Why don't you have a seat?" asked the woman, reaching the bottom of the stairs.

"No," Avery said flatly. But I thought it seemed like a good idea to take advantage of this woman's hospitality. Magix might not expect Avery and me to be down here, but if they did send someone to check the basement, we didn't want to be standing right next to the elevator doors.

Besides, I really needed a mirror so I could pluck out the rest of the cactus needles in my rear end. I stepped forward.

"Mason," hissed Avery. "We shouldn't be down here. This is . . . She's *Lina Lutzdorf*!"

"Who?" I asked.

"Lina Lutzdorf." The woman introduced herself, moving toward the kitchen. "Magix's most wanted criminal."

"Wait," I said. "I thought I—"

"Well, I *was*," she corrected. "I suppose I'm Magix's *least* wanted criminal now. Can I get you some breakfast? Coffee?" Lina held up a pot.

"We're not staying," Avery announced.

"And where are you planning to go?" she asked with a patronizing tone as she poured herself a mug and added some sugar and cream from fancy little china dishes. "Your friend just explained that the elevator won't go up. I'm guessing that's due to the lockdown. Oh, don't look so surprised. I may be shut away down here, but I know enough to realize that something tripped the alarm." She sipped her coffee. "Magix believes there's a prisoner loose, and the agents probably think it's me."

"You're a prisoner down here?" I asked in disbelief, still staring around the huge suite.

"Going on two years now," she said. "I had committed an array of magical crimes—illegal boon manipulation, intentionally exposing Igs to magic, using boons with malicious intent, theft . . . I was creating quite a name for myself in the magical community."

"You were creating a lot of problems!" Avery snapped. She turned to me. "She was building a network of criminals who were willing to do all kinds of crazy things for her. Because they believed her. They really thought she was a . . . a . . ." Avery didn't seem to be able to bring herself to say it.

"A human boon," finished Lina Lutzdorf.

"Wait. What do you mean?" I asked.

Lina spread out her arms, a smile on her face. "I am a magical human being."

"It's a lie," Avery cut in. "No living creature can become a boon."

"Why not?" asked Lina. "When someone does an act of

pure goodness, the magic core boils over and infuses certain items with magical abilities. Why couldn't one of those items be me? Plenty of people have touched me, and it would only require one of them to do something great with their life."

"That's not how it works!" Avery said. "There has never been a living boon. Never an animal, and definitely never a human being!"

"There's a first time for everything, dear." Lina took another sip.

"What can you do?" I asked. "What's your magical ability?"

"I'm a living immunity boon," she said. "No one can use magic on me, or against me."

"It's a scam," Avery said. "She figured out some way to trick our boon detectors. Maybe it's her perfume. Or the shampoo she uses . . . But it isn't *her*."

"Why would I do that?" she asked. "You think I *like* being imprisoned down here?"

"Well, it *is* pretty nice," I said, glancing around.

"Magix is an organization that believes in goodness," Lina said, copying almost the exact same phrase I'd heard from Frank Lawden. "When they discovered that they couldn't do a full memory wipe on me, they had to figure out something else to do. They made me this suite and locked me up down here. Sure, it's nice. I don't have any boons, of course. This place is so covered in magical sensors that activating the tiniest boon would bring a host of Magix agents through the elevator doors in the blink of an eye. But Magix treats me fairly. To support their cause of goodness, they bring me almost anything I ask for. But what I really want is my freedom."

"Then let us do a memory wipe!" said Avery.

"I would if I could," she said. "But you can't take the magic out of a person."

Avery shook her head, muttering something under her breath as Lina Lutzdorf set down her coffee and crossed the room to the grand piano. Standing behind the padded bench, she lifted the cover to expose the black-and-white keys.

"As you can imagine, I have unlimited free time," she said. "I've learned Italian and Spanish, mastered origami and yo-yo. A few months ago, I asked Magix to bring me a piano. I'm self-taught, but it's coming along nicely." She turned to Avery and me. "Do either of you play?"

"Nope," I said. "But according to what they told my mom, I've been taking nonstop piano lessons since yesterday."

Lina chuckled. "Then you better have something to show for it. Come have a seat. I'll teach you a simple song that will truly wow your mother."

I winced at the thought of sitting on my cactus-studded pants. "I don't think I'll be having a seat anywhere for a while.

In fact, do you have a bathroom I could use?"

"Come on!" she pressed. "Let's see what kind of natural talent you've got."

"I really need to take care of something before I sit anywhere," I said.

"All right." She pointed up the glass staircase. "Bathroom's the first door on your right, through the walk-in closet." She smiled warmly. "We can work on the solo when you get back."

I began moving for the stairs, but Avery caught my arm. "Be careful up there, Mason," she said quietly.

"You too," I replied. "You know, down here."

Lina Lutzdorf didn't seem particularly dangerous, but she'd already admitted to being a criminal, and Avery obviously had concerns about being here.

I made my way up the stairs and into the most amazing bathroom I'd ever seen. There was a large mirror that went all the way to the floor, which made it quick and easy to pull out the few remaining cactus needles.

Ah . . . sweet relief! My rear end was finally starting to feel better. At this rate, I'd be back to sitting in no time.

I dropped the dangerous bits of cactus into the toilet and flushed them down. Wow. Even the toilet seemed to flush in a fancy way! I wondered what a person like this would keep in her closet?

Quietly, I cracked the closet door beside the sink. There were a few folded towels and toiletries on an upper shelf, and at least a dozen outfits hanging from a rod. They were organized by color, with a handful of long dresses hanging almost to the floor. Reds, greens, blues . . . What were these gray clothes? They didn't match the rest of Lina's colorful wardrobe.

I pushed aside some purple clothes to get a better look. Gray suits! Three of them. These looked just like the ones worn by everyone I'd seen working at Magix. What was Lina Lutzdorf doing with these?

Hmm. Maybe she'd stolen them. It would be hard to know who they really belonged to, since all the suits looked so much alike. . . .

I suddenly had such a good idea that I gasped out loud. I snatched two of the suits off the hangers—just the jackets, leaving the pants behind. Then I dashed out of the bathroom, calling to Avery from the top of the stairs.

"Use your top hat!" I shouted. "Pull something out. Anything!"

"What?" Avery said, watching me come down the stairs, trailing the gray suit jackets.

"Activating a boon in my suite will bring the Magix agents straight to you," said Lina, turning away from the piano.

"That's what I'm counting on!" I said. "Trust me, Avery. Just do it!"

Lina Lutzdorf lunged at Avery as she pulled the hat off her head. The two of them tumbled sideways, crashing into the back of the couch, the top hat flying across the room.

"You're trying to get me in trouble!" Lina cried.

Picking up Avery's fallen top hat, I plunged my hand through the opening, feeling around all the way up to my armpit. I grabbed onto something that felt like a water bottle and yanked it out of the hat. I had no idea what this new bottle boon would do, but I didn't actually need to use it. Reaching into the magical top hat had already tripped a new set of alarms that instantly started blaring through Lina's suite.

The woman abandoned her wrestling match with Avery and turned to me. "Magix will think it's my fault that you're down here," she said, slowly walking forward. "They'll blame me and take away my privileges!"

"Magix won't even know we were here." I dropped the water bottle into the hat and donned one of the gray suit jackets. "We'll slip back into the elevator disguised to look just like every other agent in this weird building." I turned to Lina. "And if you're smart, you won't say anything to incriminate yourself." I tossed the second jacket to Avery.

Lina smiled at me. "You're a clever one. I can tell. Let's

strike a deal. I won't tell Magix you're down here if you'll just have a seat at the piano and play a few notes." She crossed to the instrument.

"What?" I said, backing away from her.

"Don't do it, Mason!" said Avery, who was on her feet again, the large gray jacket hanging loosely across her shoulders. "It's got to be a trap."

"No traps," said Lina Lutzdorf. "I just get so lonely down here. I want to hear a song, a single note . . . anything." Stooping over the keyboard, she played a chord.

Avery and I had reached the suite's exit, and we paused next to the doors. I heard the elevator descending, rumbling through the shaft.

"You're bad to the core, Mason," said Lina, releasing the chord she'd been sustaining. "I know a criminal when I see one."

"I'm not," I said. "Unlike you, I'm actually innocent."

"Everyone is guilty of something. Nobody's truly innocent," said Lina. "Those who say they are just haven't been caught yet."

The elevator chimed and a voice from inside shouted, "Ready!" I flinched as the doors rolled open. At least a dozen agents in gray suits and top hats flooded into Lina Lutzdorf's suite, Frank Lawden at the lead.

"What did you do this time, Lutzdorf?" he bellowed. The woman dropped to her knees on the plush rug, interlocking her fingers behind her head. Avery and I didn't get the chance to hear her response. Disguised as two small-statured agents, we ducked into the elevator just as the doors were closing.

This time, our elevator rumbled upward, Avery and I riding in silence. It stopped on the first floor, and we emerged into a hallway swarming with people in gray suits. We blended in quite well, walking toward the front door with our heads down.

At the end of the hallway, I saw our way out—a regular-looking heavy door, like the ones that led into my school. Two guards stood watch behind a desk on the side, and I saw the magic blender in front of them.

"Distract the guards," Avery whispered.

"What?" I said. "How?"

"I don't know," she said. "Just tell them who you are."

That seemed like a dangerous idea, but Avery had trusted my plan earlier. Now it was my turn to trust hers.

I stepped up to the desk. "Hi there, fellas," I said, looking directly at the guards. "I thought I'd stop by and introduce myself." I hadn't even mentioned my name, but they must have recognized me anyway, because both of them reached up for their top hats.

At the same moment, Avery pounced over the desk, tipping back the blender and punching in the master combination. Like before, I braced myself for the possibility of twirling death blades, but Avery must have done it correctly because the front door suddenly swung open.

At last . . . the way out of Magix Headquarters. The way to freedom.

CHAPTER 10

The open door didn't look like it led outside, so I hoped this was really an exit. Avery and I ran for it anyway, the Magix guards leaping after us, pulling boons from their hats.

"Close the door!" Avery screamed as we stumbled over the threshold and into the room beyond. There was a man standing beside the door, holding it open for us with his hand on the knob. Unlike everyone else involved with Magix, he was wearing a navy blue suit, but his tie was that same drab gray. There was no top hat on his head, but I saw a huge diamond ring on the hand holding the door open.

He looked surprised when he saw us, but he promptly responded to Avery's demand, slamming the door shut and letting go of the knob.

We were standing in a small bakery. Through the window, I could see that we were in the heart of a big city—bigger than any I'd ever been to. Countless pedestrians hustled down the sidewalks, and a line of cars clogged the street, their occasional honks echoing against the tall buildings outside.

As stunned as I was to have just appeared through the front door of a bakery, the three other customers and two employees inside looked even more shocked. The man with the diamond ring turned to us.

"What's going on?" he asked. "That was the director's emergency signal. You better have a good reason for tumbling through like that. I didn't even have time to find a private door." To prove his point, he gestured around the bakery to the five people still staring at us.

Suddenly, his diamond ring started to sparkle. At first, I thought it might have been the sunlight glinting on the huge gemstone, but I realized that his hand was in the shadows. And the sparkling effect was much too bright.

He glanced down at his hand and moaned. "Magix is going to have quite the morning wiping up these memories," he said, reaching for the doorknob again.

"Thanks, Doorman!" Avery shouted, diving in front of him to grab the handle first. She yanked open the door and I flinched, expecting it to lead back into Magix Headquarters. Instead, it opened to the busy street I'd seen through the window.

Of course! The door only became a portal into Magix Headquarters when the Doorman touched the knob with his magic diamond ring. To everyone else, it was just an ordinary door.

"Run!" Avery whispered, pushing me through the door.

"Run where?" I asked.

"Doesn't matter," she replied, leaving the bakery door ajar and sprinting down the crowded sidewalk. I cast one quick glance at the bewildered Doorman and then headed after her.

By the time we finally stopped running, I thought my lungs were going to explode. Avery had led us into a narrow alleyway between two buildings that towered like mountains. It was a little quieter here, with a puddle at our feet that reflected the line of blue sky that could be seen between the buildings.

"Where are we?" I gasped.

"Looks like New York," she answered, adjusting her top hat.

"As in, New York City?" I cried. I'd never left Indiana in my entire life. Actually, I couldn't remember ever being more than an hour's drive from home.

"Why?" I asked. "How? What are we doing in New York City?"

"Well," Avery answered, "Magix Headquarters can techni-cally be anywhere in the world. Wherever the Doorman's ring goes, that's where Magix will be. He's been spending a lot of time in New York City lately, which is good for us."

"How is that good?" I asked, trying to digest all of this. "How do we get back to Indiana?"

"Indiana?" Avery repeated. "You can't go home yet."

"I'm not talking about going to my house," I said. "Now that I've escaped magic jail, we can go free my dad."

"But isn't he in jail?" she checked.

"Exactly!" I cried. "That's why we have to free him. I could tell in the video they showed me—he didn't actually rob that bank. He was set up . . . like me."

Avery was studying me with one eyebrow raised. Then she sighed. "Sorry, Mason, but there's nothing we can do for him."

"But you've got a hat full of magic tricks." I pointed. "There's got to be a boon in there that would help him escape."

"We can't go around freeing criminals," she started.

"He's not—"

"You don't know that," Avery cut me off. "Your dad's situation is totally non-magical. If we interfere with that, we could get in big trouble."

"Bigger trouble than we're already in for breaking out of Magix Headquarters?" I asked her.

"That's different," she said. "This is a magical case. It's what I've been training for. If we can find out what's really going on . . ."

"Then I can be found innocent and go home with all my memories," I finished as she trailed off.

Avery nodded. "We have to clear your name. We find evidence that you didn't actually steal the boons from the church. And if we're lucky, we find out who really did."

"Where do we start?"

"With the note," said Avery, pulling it from her pocket.

"Right," I said. In all the excitement of escaping Magix Headquarters, I had almost forgotten about the note.

"The boy is NOT guilty," Avery read aloud. "You can find proof of his innocence at the High Line. Talk to the bird artist."

"Okay . . . ," I began. "What's the High Line?"

"It's here in the city," Avery answered. "It's like a big park built over an old rail line."

"This is good," I said. "We've got to go there. Talk to the artist . . ."

Avery tucked the note back into her pocket. "Of course. But whoever this bird artist is, there's a good chance he's associated with Magix. Or at least, he probably knows about boons. We need to get our detector set up so nothing takes us by surprise."

"You're talking about that little red collar you swiped from the armory?" I asked. "Didn't the instructions say we had to put it on an animal and it would become a boon detector?"

"Technically, no," said Avery, pulling the collar from her pocket. "A living creature can't become a boon."

"Except for Lina Lutzdorf," I pointed out.

"No. She . . ." Avery trailed off, flustered. "Lina Lutzdorf is a liar and a criminal. Of course she's not a boon. She's just figured out a way to trick everyone into thinking she is."

"Maybe she was wearing something like a magic collar," I said, taking the red collar from Avery's hand. "Could that turn someone into a boon?"

"Not exactly," she said. "It could give the wearer magical abilities—like how you teleported when you opened the music box—but it doesn't turn you into a boon. And besides, Lina Lutzdorf isn't wearing any kind of boon. Magix investigators have done plenty of checks for that."

"Maybe she has a magical boon under her skin."

Avery shot me a strange glance. "That's just creepy. How would that even work?"

I shrugged. "Maybe she found a magical needle and poked it under her skin."

Avery shuddered.

"Or maybe she ate some magical food," I said, offering a less morbid hypothesis.

She shook her head. "That's not possible. As soon as a magical boon enters the body, it loses all of its magical powers. It's one of the basic rules of magic."

"So, no magic food?" I said. I'd been having high hopes for

a magical slice of pizza that could make me fly.

"There's no reason a piece of food couldn't become a boon. You might even be able to access its magical powers if you hold it just right, or shake it, or something. But as soon as it goes inside your mouth, it loses all of its power." Avery yanked the collar out of my grasp. "Don't try to figure out Lina Lutzdorf. There's a reason Magix has her locked away for life. Let's just make sure you don't end up the same way."

"Locked up in Magix's secret basement?" Maybe that would be better than a complete memory wipe.

"They were never going to lock you up," Avery said. "I just mean—let's make sure you're not found guilty." She narrowed her eyes at me. "Unless you really are . . ."

"Seriously?" I cried, my voice echoing down the alley. "Don't you think it's a little late for you to be questioning that?"

"It's just . . . after we raided the armory, you . . ." She trailed off. "Oh, never mind."

"Hold on," I said. "You can't start a sentence like that and not finish it." I folded my arms. "After we raided the armory, I *what?*"

"There's just something . . . suspicious about you," Avery said. "The windows in Magix Headquarters are nearly invincible. Yet you shattered that one on the ninth floor like it was regular glass."

"It was that wooden banister post," I explained. "I guessed that it was a boon that gave me extra strength, or something."

Avery nodded unconvincingly. "Yeah, okay. I suppose that makes sense."

"Right," I said, pointing at the collar. "So now we need to find an animal who can wear that thing?"

Avery held the collar in front of her, sizing it up. "Technically, a human is an animal, right? Let's save ourselves some hassle."

She reached up and tried to clasp the collar around her neck. It was clearly too small, even when she pulled so tight that it made her cough.

"Okay. Maybe you should try it on," she said, passing it to me.

I didn't think my neck looked much skinnier than hers, but I gave it a try.

"This definitely wasn't made for a human neck," I said, rubbing at my throat after nearly choking myself. "Maybe it would fit a baby."

Avery took the collar back. "I think it'll be easier to find a pet."

CHAPTER 11

THURSDAY, MAY 14
11:42 A.M.
THE PETHOUSE PET STORE, NEW YORK CITY

The pet store smelled funny. It was cramped and dim, with animal cages stacked on top of each other.

"Welcome to the Pethouse," muttered a pimply teenage employee without looking up from his phone. Other than him, Avery and I were the only two humans in the store.

It had taken us hours to find this place—a task that would have been so simple if I'd had my phone. Avery had claimed to know her way around New York City, but this was an area she wasn't very familiar with. Apparently, she and her parents lived on the Upper East Side.

"Does it matter what animal we choose?" I asked quietly as we moved past a row of chirping and squawking birds.

"It shouldn't," she answered. "As long as the collar fits."

"What about that dog?" I asked, pointing to a little pug who was staring through the bars with big dark eyes.

"Look at the price tag on that guy!"

"We have to buy it?" I asked.

"Unless you plan on stealing," she replied. "You're already Magix's most wanted criminal. Let's not give the NYPD a reason to arrest you, too."

"So, we're looking for a cheap small pet," I said. "But not too small, because that collar is way too big for a hamster or a rat."

"And hopefully a pet that's easy to feed and likes being carried, so it can keep up with us."

"A lizard?" I asked.

"Yuck," Avery said. "I hate reptiles."

"A cat?" I suggested.

She shook her head. "I'm allergic."

"Well, I'm out of ideas," I said, studying the fish tank. She gasped behind me.

"Here we go." Avery dropped to one knee. I came up beside her to inspect the animal she was considering.

"A bunny?" I asked.

"Why not?" Avery opened the cage and reached in. "People already think that bunnies go along with magicians. This way, if she does anything strange when we put the collar on her, people might think it's just a magic trick."

"Isn't that exactly what it'll be?" I said.

"There's a difference between a trick and *real* magic," said Avery. "Besides, I like her."

"She has red eyes," I pointed out. "Makes her look kind of . . . evil. Like a demon bunny."

"Pinkish-red eyes are common with white rabbits," replied Avery. "I think she looks friendly."

"She looks like a fluffball," I said. The rabbit was little more than a puff of white fur with a face and a set of ears poking out.

"Don't be shy," Avery said in a sweet voice, managing to scoop up the bunny even though the animal had retreated to the far corner of her cage. I closed the cage door as Avery carried the trembling bunny to the front desk.

"You have money, right?" Avery whispered, nudging me with her elbow as the employee gave us the total.

"Me?" I said. "I've got *some*."

"Well?" she urged.

I dug in my pocket and fished out a small wad of cash, feeling grateful that I'd remembered to take it from the jeans I'd been wearing when I was arrested.

I handed her the amount we needed and let Avery handle the transaction. A moment later, the two of us were outside again, this time with the fluffy bunny tucked under Avery's arm. We walked down the busy street until we came to a metal bench.

Avery sat down, depositing the rabbit next to her. I wasn't comfortable enough to sit. Not with so many strangers walking past. Any one of them could be a Magix agent in disguise, and I needed to be on my feet in case someone jumped out and tried to grab me.

"Can you hold her steady?" Avery asked, struggling to get the red collar around the bunny's neck.

"I'm not very good with animals," I warned, reaching down to hold the rabbit. "What do you think we should name her?"

"I think you already did," Avery said, finally managing to clasp the collar in place. "Fluffball."

"Fluffball?" a deep voice rumbled. I let go of the bunny, staggering backward and glancing around the street for the person who had spoken.

"Fluffball?" the voice said again. "What kind of a stupid name is Fluffball? It's insulting. It's demeaning. It's downright shallow. There's so much more to me than my fur. You know that, right?"

The words kept coming, and my eyes grew big as I realized exactly who was speaking.

"Avery!" I whispered, pointing at the animal on the bench

beside her. "The . . . the bunny is talking."

"*Bunny?*" cried our new pet. "That's *rabbit* to you, smelly human."

Avery reached out and stroked Fluffball's head. "Sorry about my friend's terrible manners," she said. "He isn't really used to magic."

The rabbit seemed to purr softly, his red eyes squinting closed. "Oh yeah, sister. That's the spot."

"I was wondering if you could help us out?" Avery continued. "What do you see when you look at my top hat?"

Fluffball cracked open one eye and peered at the black hat on the girl's head. "Boon," he said in his rumbly voice. "Definitely a nip."

"What's a nip?" I asked.

Fluffball started to laugh. "What a noob . . . He doesn't even know what a nip is?"

I felt my face turning red. "Demon bunny," I muttered, embarrassed about getting embarrassed by a rodent.

"*Nip* is slang for a ma*nip*ulated boon," answered Avery. "Fluffball can tell that the ribbon was cut and sewed onto the hat, manipulating it into having magical properties." Avery turned back to the rabbit. "Can you tell us what the hat does?"

The bunny sniffed at the air. "Tell smelly boy to back away."

"What?" I cried. "I'm not smelly! I just showered last night."

"Apples and oranges, kid," said Fluffball. "You're smelly to me."

Avery gave me an impatient look, and I suddenly realized that she expected me to do what the bunny was demanding.

"You've got to be kidding me." I sighed in annoyance, taking a large step back.

"Ah. That's better," said the rabbit, his nose bouncing as he actively sniffed. "The top hat allows you to safely store other boons inside it. Even items that should be too big to fit."

Avery looked at me with excitement in her eyes. "I think we've got our detector, Mason."

"Don't call him that," said the rabbit. "If he's going to call me Fluffball, I'm going to call him Stinky."

"Look," I said. "I'm sorry I named you Fluffball. That was before I knew you could talk. Why don't you just tell us what you'd like to be called?"

He turned up his pink nose, flipping his ears back. "If you really cared, you wouldn't have to ask."

I groaned. "Fine. Fluffball it is."

Avery scooped the rabbit into her arms. "I'm Avery," she introduced. "And this is Mason Morrison. He's been accused of a crime he didn't commit. We'll fill you in on the way to the High Line. We just need you to keep an eye out—or a nose— or whatever—for any potential boons we might come across on

110

the way. Magix will be looking for us. Possibly setting traps."

"I'll do it for *you*," Fluffball said. "But I gotta know. Why are you helping him?" He flicked an ear at me.

"It's my duty," she said, "as an apprentice detective. I made a promise to uphold the law and the truth."

"And now you're on the run with a criminal?" Fluffball said. "Doesn't sound like upholding the law to me."

Avery glanced at me, then back at the bunny. "He's innocent. I got a note that said—"

"But you could have taken that note to anyone," I cut in. The bunny had touched on a good point. One that I'd been too hasty to think much about so far. Why was Avery *really* helping me?

"Why didn't you tell anyone at Magix about the note you found in your locker?"

Avery fidgeted, straightening her top hat with the hand that wasn't holding Fluffball.

"I was afraid they wouldn't believe me," she finally answered. "I didn't want anyone to think that I'd written the note myself, just because I *believed* you were innocent."

"Did you?" I asked. "Did you believe I was innocent *before* you got that note?"

"Does it matter?" she said, suddenly moving away. "Come on. We've got to find that bird artist."

CHAPTER 12

I'd never been to a park like the High Line before. It was elevated about thirty feet above the city streets, built on the remains of an abandoned rail track. As we walked along the long, narrow park, I could catch glimpses of the old train rails running through the grasses and flowers that'd been planted to make it look nice.

We were snacking on some big salted pretzels that I had bought from a street vendor. They tasted good, but they had pretty much bankrupted me.

"Dry," said Fluffball. "If you give me another piece of that dry pretzel, I'm gonna choke and die."

It made me nervous to have the bunny speaking out in the

open, but the people of New York didn't seem to pay attention to anything going on around them.

"Sorry," Avery said. "I guess we should have bought a salad for you."

"Now, that would've been much more thoughtful," grumbled Fluffball. "With a light vinaigrette dressing on the side."

"Were you always this picky?" I asked. "Or did that just happen when you got a voice?"

"Were you always this stinky?" he replied. "Or did that just happen when you rolled around in the garbage?"

"I'm curious, too," Avery said, backing me up. "What was life like in that cage in the pet store?"

"I'll just say, I don't exactly remember," answered Fluffball. "Life in the cage was . . . like an old dream. I know it happened, but I can't remember what it was about."

"So the collar was an upgrade?" I asked.

"Now, I wouldn't go that far," he said, "since it means I have to hang around with you."

I was quickly learning to shrug off his insults. He was an ornery little bunny. He obviously liked Avery more than me, although I couldn't figure out why.

"There." Avery pointed ahead. A portion of the park walkway was covered, and I could see a gathering of artists with small tables set out to sell their work.

I drew in a deep breath. "Let us know if you see any boons, Fluffball," I said as we drew closer.

"That's what I'm here for," he groaned.

"And maybe don't talk for a while," I added. "We don't want people to grow suspicious."

"Okay, smarty-pants," said the bunny. "How am I supposed to tell you if there's a boon if I'm not allowed to speak?"

Hmmm. Good point. "Maybe flick your ears or something," I suggested. "Yeah. Point at the boon with your ears, and thump your back foot to make sure we notice."

"Why don't I jump up and do a little tap-dance routine while I'm at it?" said Fluffball.

"Or we could always take off the collar . . . ," I threatened.

"You wouldn't dare," the rabbit said. "Take off this collar, and the boon loses its power. And I don't think you'll make it very far without a detector."

"Might be worth the risk," I said.

"All right, all right. Fine." The rabbit sighed. "I'll do the ear thing."

As we drew closer, I could start to see how talented these street artists were. There was a guy wearing a dust mask, wielding two cans of spray paint. Somehow, the colors were turning out to look like an amazing view of outer space.

Another artist had pencil drawings of different buildings in New York City. Another had scenic nature landscapes in

114

watercolor. One artist had a psychedelic array of artwork made from geometric shapes in bright colors.

And then there were the birds.

The table was covered in paintings and drawings, prints and sketches. All of them depicting a wide variety of birds. There was no question that we were in the right place.

"Do you see something you like?" asked the artist, looking up from her phone. She was seated cross-legged on the ground behind her table, but she popped up to her feet with ease. Her matted dark hair looked unwashed, a wide cloth headband tying it back. A twinkle on the side of her nose revealed a small gemstone stud, and her pierced earlobes had been stretched to hold large wooden plugs. The woman's sleeves were rolled partway up, and her jean overalls were smudged with paint.

"Your work is nice," Avery said. "Is it all birds?"

"Mostly," she answered. "I've always wanted to fly. Painting them might be the closest I get."

I was going crazy with this small talk. If this painter lady had proof that I was innocent, I needed to see it. But how was I supposed to bring up the topic?

"I'm Mason," I said, offering my hand to shake. "Mason Morrison."

"The name sounds familiar," replied the painter as we shook.

"We're in a bit of trouble," Avery dared. "We were told you might be able to help us out."

"Ah, I think I know what you're after," said the painter. She turned around to shuffle through some of her prints. She had only flipped through two or three of the matte-framed pictures when she lifted her phone, fingers flying across the screen as she typed something. Then she picked a print and turned back to face us.

"The hummingbird is one of my favorites to paint," she said, holding out the artwork.

Hummingbird? This wasn't helpful at all! How was a tiny hummingbird supposed to prove my innocence?

Her phone chimed, and a text message notification lit up the screen in her other hand. I wasn't trying to be nosy or anything, but a certain word instantly caught my eye as she lifted her hand and swiped the notification away.

The word was *Mason*.

A secret text about me? Something didn't feel right. I reached out, taking the hummingbird painting with such enthusiasm that the edge of the frame clipped the woman's phone and knocked it out of her other hand.

"Sorry!" I cried as it clattered across the table and fell to the ground. I quickly stooped to retrieve it, my eyes reading the text message conversation that she had just opened.

From the painter: They are here.

One minute later, another text from the painter: Where are you? Can't stall them much longer.

The reply was what had caught my eye, sent from a contact named *Wreckage*. It said: Almost there. Don't let Mason get away!

My heart was pounding as I stood up, holding the phone facedown as if I hadn't seen the screen. Who was Wreckage? And how did he know my name when the painter hadn't mentioned it in her text? I swallowed against a lump in my throat as I realized what this meant.

This was a setup. *Don't let Mason get away!* The painter wasn't here to help us!

"I just remembered we don't have any money," I said, setting the hummingbird painting on the edge of the table. "And we're going to be late for a thing we were supposed to do, so . . . We should probably be going."

"Umm. You guys?" said Fluffball, breaking his vow of silence. "I'm detecting some major boons!"

"You were supposed to tell us if she had—"

"Not her," interrupted the rabbit. His back foot started thumping against the crook of Avery's arm, and his ears pointed frantically. "Behind you!"

CHAPTER 13

I whirled around to see what Fluffball was warning us about. A figure was striding toward us through the narrow park. The sight of him made my blood run cold.

He was tall and broad across the shoulders, like somebody who had dedicated his life to lifting weights. His face was completely hidden behind a dark welding mask with the protective shield down, but I could see that his dark hair was trimmed short.

He was wearing heavy black boots that laced up halfway to his knees, and his belt buckle was big and shiny. The man's wide chest was draped in a reflective yellow vest—the kind I'd seen crossing guards wear when helping people walk across busy streets.

118

His hands were covered with thick leather gloves, and he gripped two ordinary-looking items: a single wooden drumstick in his right, and a trailing red-white-and-blue jump rope in his left.

I was willing to guess that this was Wreckage. And I didn't think he was here to play jump rope with us.

"Run!" I shouted, taking off down the High Line. Avery was at my side in a second, carrying Fluffball in the fold of her elbow like a quarterback running a football downfield.

I risked a glance over my shoulder just in time to see Wreckage bring the drumstick down. The wooden tip struck the ground with a deafening *boom*. At the same moment, shockwaves of sound rippled out from the stick, catching Avery and me in the back and throwing us face-first into a flowerbed.

As I rose to my knees, I realized that we weren't the only ones who had been knocked down. The blast from the drumstick had rippled out in all directions, sending a dozen innocent park-goers tumbling to the ground.

Screams and cries for help sounded all around, but Wreckage didn't seem worried. He continued his determined stride toward us, his face unseen behind that welder's mask.

"This guy's loaded with boons," said Fluffball, who had tumbled from Avery's arms and was shaking a bit of soil off his white fur. "His mask is a detector, so he's going to know exactly what we've got as soon as he sees it." The bunny squinted one red eye at Avery. "I'm assuming you *do* have some useful boons inside that fancy top hat of yours?"

"Yes . . . ," she said, picking up the hat from where it had fallen to the ground. "Maybe . . . I just grabbed a hat that was stocked and ready for a field mission. I don't know exactly what we ended up with."

"Oh, you guys are going to go far," Fluffball said sarcastically. "I've never met a pair of innocent criminals more ill-prepared than—"

Mid-sentence, Avery snatched the bunny by the neck and stuffed him straight into the black top hat.

"Find something useful!" she ordered, withdrawing her hand and leaping to her feet at my side.

There was a cracking sound like an exploding firework and suddenly, I was yanked off my feet again. This time it was the jump rope, which had somehow grown almost ten times its length and lassoed around my ankle.

Wreckage had both feet planted as he reeled me in like a fish. The magical jump rope was shortening itself as he pulled on it, dragging me kicking and screaming toward him.

"Mason Mortimer Morrison," he said, his voice gruff and cold. "You will come with me."

This was bad. This was very bad. What was this freaky supervillain going to do once he had me?

Luckily, I didn't have to find out.

Avery sprang forward with a battle cry, grabbing the jump rope with one hand. I saw that her other one was holding a credit card, which she wielded like a knife.

With very little resistance, the edge of the plastic card sliced through the jump rope. The sudden release of tension sent Wreckage stumbling a few steps backward, while the severed piece of rope around my ankle seemed to disintegrate into ash.

"You had a credit card?" I cried, staggering to my feet. "Why'd you make *me* buy Fluffball?"

"I hear you, Stinky Boy!" came the rabbit's deep voice from Avery's hat perched on her head. "And I ain't nobody's property."

"I don't think it actually works for buying stuff," said Avery, holding up the credit card. "It's a boon my dad gave me. It can cut through almost anything."

"Your parents trust you with that?" I cried. "You've got a razor-blade credit card and I can't even get a Batman throwing star?"

"Really? Again with the throwing star?" Avery said, exasperated. "My card isn't dangerous. It only cuts when I hold it just right and slice with the edge."

"Can it cut through *him*?" I asked, noticing Wreckage moving toward us again.

"Nope," Fluffball's voice answered. Avery's hat tipped back, and the bunny's head appeared above her forehead, peeking out. "That guy's covered in boons. His yellow vest is an immunity boon. It'll protect him from direct strikes from other boons. That's why he's not getting leveled by his own drumstick."

As though in response to Fluffball's comment, Wreckage crouched, striking his drumstick against the ground once more. Again, the shockwave leveled everyone within fifty feet, Avery and myself included. I grunted, gripping my scuffed elbow and trying to get up quickly.

"I was trying to tell you . . . ," said Fluffball, who had tumbled out of the top hat as it fell from Avery's head again. "You've got to jump when he hits the drumstick. The shockwave won't knock you down unless you're touching the ground."

"That would have been helpful ten seconds ago," I said, watching the bunny dive headfirst, disappearing into Avery's hat as she snatched it up again.

There were sirens sounding on the streets below the elevated park, and I figured the police had been notified about the madman with the jump rope.

"We've got to get out of here before the police come," Avery said.

"Why?" I asked. "We didn't do anything wrong. Talking to bird painters isn't against the law."

"If we get picked up by the police, Magix will know exactly where to find us," she explained. "We'll be back in headquarters by dark, and you can say goodbye to your precious memories."

Avery was right. Best not to get caught. But I was worried about her escape plan. She had run to the edge of the park, peering over the railing to the street far below.

"We have to jump," she said.

"What?" I shrieked, pushing past some shrubs to join her. I almost tripped as I crossed the old metal train tracks that ran down the side of the park.

"No way!" I said, backing up the moment I reached her. It was at least thirty feet down to a street crammed with moving vehicles. "This is way higher than the roof of my house, and that was bad enough."

"What are you talking about?" she asked, boosting herself up onto the railing. "I think we can land it. Maybe Fluffball will find a boon that'll help."

"Have you ever broken your femur?" I snapped.

"No," she answered.

"Well, I have. And it's not pleasant." I grabbed her arm and pulled her back to solid ground. "The stairs we used to get up here aren't far away. We can make it if we—"

"Mason Mortimer Morrison!" Wreckage called again, causing me to whirl around. Did he have to use my middle name? I mean, I knew he was talking to me. "Come with me now, and no one has to get hurt."

"I already got hurt!" I yelled back, pointing at my scuffed elbow. Besides, I was pretty sure that was something only lying bad guys ever said.

"The Mastermind wants to speak with you," called Wreckage. "You would be wise to come willingly."

Mastermind?

"Not going to happen!" I shouted back. As I glanced toward our enemy, I saw him raise the drumstick.

"Jump!" I shouted to Avery.

We both leaped in the air as the drumstick hit the train track. The shockwave passed beneath us, and we landed on our feet. I liked to imagine that Wreckage's face was totally surprised behind that black welding mask.

Suddenly, Avery's top hat tilted back and Fluffball's white paws stretched out, clutching a light bulb. "It electrifies anything it touches," the rabbit's deep voice hurriedly explained, giving us the knowledge we needed to use the boon's true magic.

"But the vest . . . ," I said.

"We can't electrify him with the boon directly," said Avery. "But that doesn't mean he can't be electrocuted by something else."

I had no idea what she was talking about, but Avery seemed to have a plan. She drew in a sharp breath and snatched the light bulb from his paws.

"Give up!" Wreckage shouted. "There is nowhere you can run. Nowhere you can hide—"

Avery bent over, touching the fragile light bulb to the train track. Blue bolts of electricity streamed out of it, connecting to the metal rail and traveling the distance to where Wreckage stood with one foot on the track.

The electricity surged into the big man, his body jolting and spasming until he finally fell to the ground.

Avery pulled the light bulb away from the rail, and the blue bolts vanished as quickly as they had appeared.

We didn't wait to see if Wreckage recovered. We didn't wait to see if the police would arrest him. We ran, finally reaching the stairs and moving down to the New York City streets, leaving the High Line and the traitorous bird artist behind.

CHAPTER 14

"**O**ur only clue was a trap!" I wailed as soon as we had found another quiet alley to hide in.

"Not necessarily," said Avery.

"What do you mean, *not necessarily*?" I cried. "The bird artist texted that guy—Wreckage—and told him to get us!"

"I'm going to side with Stinkbug on this one," said Fluffball, who was sniffing around behind a dumpster. "The bird lady was bad news."

"I'm just saying that the actual clue might have been fine," continued Avery. "We were told to find a bird artist at the High Line, and we did. But we have no way of knowing if that was the *right* bird artist."

126

"You think there might have been two?" I said. "And we just happened to pick the one who wanted to get us killed?"

"Technically, captured," said Fluffball. "If that Wreckage guy had wanted to kill you, it wouldn't have been very hard."

"Thanks for believing in us," I said to the bunny. Then I turned back to Avery, who was peering around the corner, where police had swarmed the elevated park. "You want to go back and find the right bird artist?" I asked.

"I don't think there are two," she replied. "And it was definitely a trap."

"But you just said—"

"What if someone knew about the note I received?" Avery said, looking back at me. "What if they sent a woman to replace the real bird artist and lay the trap?"

Hmm. I hadn't thought of that.

"I mean, we never actually saw that lady paint anything," continued Avery. "Maybe she was a fraud."

"But how did Magix find out about the note in your locker?" I asked.

"Magix?" Avery wrinkled her forehead. "Magix had nothing to do with that trap up there."

"But Wreckage was using magical boons," I pointed out.

"That's exactly how I know he didn't come from Magix," said Avery. "They would never reveal magic in such a careless way. What Wreckage did up there"—she gestured over her shoulder toward the park—"goes against everything Magix stands for. In fact, the Magix agents are going to have a month's worth of work tracking down exposed Igs and trying to alter their memories."

"But if Wreckage didn't come from Magix," I said, "then who sent him to get us?"

"The Mastermind," said Avery.

"Who's that?" I asked.

"I have no idea," she replied. "I just heard Wreckage mention him."

"Do you realize what this means?" I whispered.

"Does it mean you're going to buy me a salad now?" Fluffball asked.

I ignored him, talking only to Avery. "It means Magix isn't the only group looking for us." I slumped against the wall and slowly lowered myself until I was sitting in the alleyway. "I'm Magix's most wanted criminal, there's a crazy supervillain after us, and we don't have a single clue to help prove that I'm innocent. We should just go free my dad, and he and I can live out our days as fugitives together."

"We might not have a clue," Avery said, "but we've got plenty of leads."

"*Leads?*" I repeated.

"It's something we talk a lot about in detective training," she said. "A lead is something that can *lead* us to a clue."

"Well, I knew that." I'd picked up on a lot of legal and investigative terms during my dad's trial. "But what leads are you talking about?"

"If we're going to solve this case," said Avery, "we're going to have to start thinking like detectives. This whole thing started with that music box. Where did you get it?"

I shrugged. "I told my mom I needed one for a book report. I think she borrowed it from somebody."

"I'd call that a lead," Avery said. "And during your trial, they showed you pictures of some stolen boons from the church that were found in your room."

"I'd never seen them before," I said. "I definitely didn't take them to my room."

"But someone did," replied Avery. "And that's another lead."

"So, how do we investigate?"

"We need to go to your house," said Avery. "Question your mom and see if we can find any clues."

"My house is in Indiana," I reminded her. "It'll take us forever to get there."

"Not if we have a transportation boon," said Avery. "That seems like an essential thing to keep stocked in the top hats for Magix field agents." She knelt down in the alley and lifted

129

the hat from her head. "Fluffball?"

The rabbit glanced over, a look of annoyance on his face. "Whaddaya want?"

"We need to get a list of all the boons in this top hat and what they do," she said.

"How am I supposed to make a list?" he asked. "I can't write with a pencil. I've got no thumbs." He waggled a paw in our direction.

"You don't have to write anything down," Avery said. "Just tell us about every item that's in there."

The rabbit sauntered over, grumbling under his breath and rolling his reddish eyes. "Okay, but you've maxed out your favors for the day." He rose onto his back legs, front paws resting on the brim of the black hat. "It'll take me a while to sort through everything. And I ain't doing nothing else until I get a salad."

Avery scooped up his back legs, and he tumbled headfirst into the hat again.

"That was good thinking with the magic light bulb back there," I said.

"I just hope it didn't hurt anyone else," Avery said. She turned to me. "Did you really break your femur?"

"Of course," I said. "Why would I lie about that?"

"I just thought maybe . . ." She shrugged. "Maybe you were just too scared to jump."

I took a deep breath. "Heights and I don't really mix. Ever since the accident."

"What happened?"

"It was about three years ago," I said. "When I was ten. I was helping my dad on the roof and I fell off."

"Ouch," she said. "Bet that hurt."

"Worst pain ever," I said. "Mom was so mad about it. She didn't want me up on the roof in the first place."

"She sounds really protective," said Avery.

I chuckled. "You could say that. . . . Speaking of my mom, how are we going to deal with her?"

"What do you mean?" asked Avery.

"Well, Frank Lawden told me that one of his agents gave my mom a boon bracelet that makes her think I'm always at piano lessons. Apparently, other people believe it without question when she tells them."

"We should be glad about that," said Avery. "The last thing we need is for your mom to file a missing persons report and have *even more* people looking for us."

"That's exactly what I'm worried about," I said. "We'll probably have to leave my house after we talk to my mom. What if showing my face ruins the magic of the bracelet?"

"Shouldn't be a problem," said Avery. "She'll just think you came home. And when we leave again, the boon will make her think you've gone back to piano lessons."

"Wait a minute." I scrunched up my face in confusion. "How can my mom be operating a boon if she's an Ig with no knowledge about real magic?"

"By the sound of it, your mom isn't the one who activated the boon," said Avery. "It was probably the Magix agent who gave her the bracelet. Your mom's more like the target."

I grimaced. "That makes me even madder at Magix."

Avery shrugged. "She's the target, so the magic is influencing her, but since she's also an Ig, she's probably getting quite a bit of good luck rubbed off in the process."

Fluffball's head popped out of Avery's top hat. "You gotta lotta good treasures in here," he said.

"How many?" I asked.

"An even nine," replied the rabbit.

"Nine isn't an even number," I pointed out. "It's odd."

"*You're* odd," snapped Fluffball. "Now, listen up, because I'm only going to tell you once."

With the speed of an auctioneer, Fluffball rattled off the nine items along with their magical powers. By the time he was finished, I could only remember two or three of them, but Avery was nodding her head.

"We can use the atlas transportation boon," she said, reaching toward her hat. "What does it feel like?"

Fluffball sighed wearily. "Just give me your hand and I'll guide it to the right boon."

She put her hand on his soft back as the rabbit ducked out of sight again. A moment later, Avery withdrew her hand, pulling out a large book.

"What's that?" I asked.

"It's an atlas, dummy." Fluffball leaped out of the hat, flicking his long ears as he landed on the street. "Weren't you listening to anything I said?"

"Yeah," I said, "but I actually don't know what an atlas is."

Avery flipped open the book, and I saw that the pages were covered in complex maps.

"It's what people used before fancy phones and GPS devices," explained the rabbit. "Road maps. This one is almost too good to be true. Magix officials are going to have their undies in a knot when they realize that you two swiped it."

"Does it have every road in the world?" I asked.

Avery flipped back to the cover, and she read the title out loud. *Atlas of the United States of America: East of the Mississippi.*

"Good enough," I said. "Find Indiana."

She thumbed through the pages before handing me the book. "You should probably . . . I don't know where you live."

It took me a painfully long time to find the page that included my suburb. Fluffball muttered something about how "kids these days" didn't know how to read old-school paper maps. I shot back that "rabbits these days" shouldn't be able to talk.

"Here," I said, pointing to an intersection on the page. "Or, maybe here." I slid my finger half an inch to the right.

"You don't know your address?" Fluffball challenged.

"I do," I answered. "It's just . . . I think this book was made before my neighborhood was built. But I think this will get us pretty close."

Avery put on her hat and scooped up Fluffball. "How do we activate it?"

"You need a pen or a pencil," he answered. "Really, anything pointy will do. When you touch it to the page, you'll instantly be transported to that location."

"Just one of us?" Avery asked.

"Anyone touching you will get pulled along. And anyone touching them," explained Fluffball. "Like a chain reaction."

There were some obvious similarities to the music box, only that one transported anyone who was simply *looking* at me. The atlas seemed much better, and more controlled, since we'd be able to choose where we were teleporting.

"Something pointy . . . ," mused Avery.

"Will this work?" I asked, spotting a toothpick beside the dumpster. I stepped over and scooped it up.

"Ugh!" Fluffball cried. "You're just gonna pick up a nasty old toothpick? You've got no idea whose teeth that was picking." He shuddered. "No wonder you smell like a wet shoe."

I held back an angry response. "Will it work, or not?" I nearly shouted.

"Yeah, yeah," he said defensively. "It's gross, but it'll do the trick."

Avery suddenly reached out and touched my shoulder. And since she was holding Fluffball, he would be coming as well. Too bad, really. If the bunny weren't so valuable, I'd have loved to leave him behind.

With the open atlas in my left hand, I touched the point of the chewed toothpick to the intersection on the road map, and the three of us instantly disappeared from that New York City alleyway.

CHAPTER 15

THURSDAY, MAY 14
2:48 P.M.
MASON'S NEIGHBORHOOD, INDIANA

Teleporting didn't *feel* like anything strange, just like when I'd used the music box. In the blink of an eye, we found ourselves standing on the street corner of a familiar neighborhood. Well, familiar to me, at least.

"My house is just a couple of blocks away," I said, shutting the atlas and flicking the toothpick into the road.

Avery took her hand off my shoulder, and I handed her the book of road maps. She pulled off her top hat and dropped it in.

As we walked, I wondered if the neighbors would notice my new friend and her talking bunny. Over the last year—since my dad's arrest—I'd had the constantly growing feeling that people were watching my mom and me. I'd heard their whispers more than once, but I didn't need to know what they were saying to read the looks on their faces.

It was stuff like: "There goes that poor Morrison boy."

Or: "Can you believe his dad would try to rob a bank? Did he seriously think he would get away with it?"

Or: "It would have been better if the man had just pleaded guilty. Pretending to be innocent gives his wife and boy false hope."

It wasn't false hope for me. My mom and I had been going to a therapist for months to talk about it. Mr. Morano had been trying to help us accept that my dad was guilty. I went along with everything he said, but there was always a little piece of me that just couldn't believe it. And I was more sure of it than ever, now that Magix had found *me* guilty of a magical crime I hadn't committed.

"Home sweet home," I said, pausing on the sidewalk and pointing at my house.

The houses in this neighborhood weren't very big, and they all looked pretty similar. They were packed close together, and everybody had a fence as if trying to defend what little land they did have. Mom did a good job caring for our small front yard. She'd planted some tulips last year, and lots of them were still in bloom.

"Anything special we ought to know about your old lady?" asked Fluffball.

For a moment, I thought about telling him that she really

didn't like animals. "She's nice," I said instead. "Works hard for our family. I guess I should mention that Mom's been a little paranoid since, uh . . . since my dad was arrested."

"Paranoid?" asked Avery.

"Well, she installed a security system on the house a few months ago. And she always keeps the front door locked."

"But you've got a key, right?" Fluffball asked.

"Yeah," I said. Then I grimaced. "With my cell phone, in my backpack, at my school."

"Nice work, genius," the rabbit said. "How are we supposed to get inside?"

"I know the garage code," I replied, grateful that my house wasn't as high security as Magix Headquarters, so there was no risk of getting blended up if I entered the code wrong. "Or we can just ring the doorbell," I continued. "It's Thursday, so Mom should be home."

Avery started up the walk, but I grabbed her sleeve.

"Fluffball's got to be quiet from here on," I said. "We have one of those fancy doorbells that takes video of everyone who comes onto the porch."

"And you're ashamed of me?" Fluffball retorted. "Is that it? You're ashamed to be seen coming home with an Angora rabbit? It's because I talk, isn't it."

"Well . . . yes, actually," I answered.

Fluffball grunted and lowered his ears as we moved onto the porch. Avery pressed the doorbell, and I stared at the little camera right above it.

"It's me, Mom," I called. "I guess I lost my key."

There was a moment of silence, and then I heard both deadbolts unlock and the door whipped open.

"Mason!" she cried, gesturing Avery and me inside. "What are you doing here? You're supposed to be at piano lessons."

My eyes fell to the bracelet on her right wrist. It was made of thin braided pieces of leather, with a few beads set in the middle. Not really my mom's style at all. She definitely would have taken it off if she hadn't received magical instructions not to.

"I had to run home to ask you a question," I replied. "I'll go back soon." Didn't she think it was strange that I'd been at piano lessons since yesterday?

"And who's this?" Mom asked, turning to Avery.

"Avery," the girl answered. "Avery Lobster." Then she added, "Ma'am."

"Avery and I take piano from the same teacher," I said, hoping it would explain why we were together.

My mom was about to close the front door behind us when Fluffball wriggled in the crook of Avery's arm.

"Mason!" Mom shouted, as though I'd done something

terrible. She jerked the door all the way open again, pointing out to the front yard. "You *know* how I feel about pets in this house!"

I *did* know. And it wasn't good.

"Pet?" Fluffball suddenly yelled back, his ears standing straight up. "Watch who you're calling a—"

Avery wrapped her hand around the bunny's entire head, muffling his voice.

"What did you say, Mase?" Mom asked. Did she really think *I* had such a deep rumbly voice?

"Nothing, Mom," I said. "We're happy to stick the bunny outside."

Avery moved onto the porch, whispering something to Fluffball before setting him on the ground. Then she stepped back inside, and Mom finally shut the door.

"If it's okay, we have a couple of questions for you, Mrs. Morrison," said Avery as Mom led us into the kitchen.

"This sounds like an interrogation." Mom laughed. "I'd say we've had enough of those in our family."

Sometimes Mom joked about Dad. Our therapist told me it was just how she dealt with the stress, but it made me a little sad. Like Mom didn't believe Dad was innocent anymore. Like she had finally given in to what society had told us to believe.

"Nah, Mom," I said casually, taking a seat on a barstool at

the counter. "We just wanted to know where you got that music box for my book report."

"How did that go?" Mom turned to the dirty dishes in the sink.

"Umm . . . good. I think." And by *good*, I meant horribly terrible, leading me to become the most wanted criminal in a secret magical organization.

"We want to take the music box back to whoever you borrowed it from," Avery said.

"It's all the way across town," Mom answered, rinsing a plate and placing it in the dishwasher. "Don't worry about it. I'll just take it to work with me tomorrow."

"We don't mind," I replied. "My piano lessons are all the way across town, too, and we're headed back there. I'd like to personally return the music box. Say thanks for letting me borrow it."

I saw a smile cross Mom's lips. "That's very thoughtful of you. I borrowed it from Tom Pedherson. I'll text you his address."

"Actually, could you write it down?" I asked. "I accidentally left my phone at piano lessons."

"Sure," she said.

"How did you know Tom Pedherson had this particular music box?" Avery asked.

"Remember when I went to that work party last month?" Mom asked me. I nodded. It had been a memorable night for me, too. I'd eaten two microwave dinners and played a lot of video games while she'd been gone. "Tom won the music box at the party. He was very happy about it."

"Where do you work?" asked Avery.

"True Cost," said Mom. "It's a billing company. We call people who haven't paid their bills."

"And how exactly did Tom win the music box?" Avery asked. I was worried she was going into full detective mode, but my mom didn't seem to notice.

"It was a raffle," she answered. "They had lots of prizes. I won that gift card to Smoothie Palace."

"Interesting," Avery said. "I was wondering if you could give me a list of everyone who has entered your house in the last week."

Mom paused, a dripping bowl hovering above the open dishwasher as she glanced suspiciously at the girl out of the corner of her eye. Okay. Avery had obviously gone too far with the questioning.

"Can I borrow your phone, Mom?" I cut in, hoping to break the tension. "I wanted to text Hamid and tell him I don't have my phone."

Hamid was a few years younger than me, but he was the

only kid in the neighborhood willing to hang out with me after my dad's arrest.

"It's over there by the toaster," Mom said, finally loading the bowl.

I jumped up and snatched the phone as Avery followed me out of the kitchen.

"Why were you questioning her like that?" I hissed once we were in the living room. "My mom's not a suspect!"

"Of course she is," Avery answered. "She gave you the music box that linked you to the theft at the boon church."

"Are you serious?" I cried. "My mom didn't frame me for a crime. That's ridiculous."

"I admit that it seems unlikely," said Avery. "But a good detective considers *every* possibility. That includes your mom. And anyone else who entered your house earlier this week who could have planted those stolen boons in your bedroom."

"Interrogating her isn't the best way to see who's been in my house." I held up my mom's phone.

"The doorbell camera?" A hopeful look spread across Avery's face.

I nodded. "I think it stores ten days of footage in the cloud. It'll just take a minute to load. Let's go up to my room to look for more clues while we wait."

CHAPTER 16

"Someone's definitely been here," Avery said, scanning my messy bedroom. The dirty clothes strewn across the floor and the books and papers on my nightstand were probably going to make it hard to spot any useful clues.

"They didn't just plant those boons," Avery continued. "They must have been looking for something."

"How can you tell?" I asked.

"Look at this place," she said. "Somebody trashed your room."

I chuckled, feeling my cheeks turn red. If I'd known my bedroom was going to be a crime scene, I would have at least made my bed. "Umm . . . ," I stammered. "Actually, my room always looks like this."

144

I saw Avery shudder. At least Fluffball wasn't here to tell me what he thought about my living conditions.

"You should have seen it a few months ago," I said, kicking a pair of dirty underwear out of sight.

"It was worse than this?" Avery asked skeptically.

"It was bright orange," I answered. "When I moved upstairs two years ago, my dad thought it would be cool to paint the new room my favorite color. It was like living inside a pumpkin."

"Was your dad a painter?"

"No way." I laughed. "The first time he used the roller, it splattered paint all over my room." My laughter petered out. Even good memories of Dad were kind of painful. "Mom and I painted it white a few months ago."

"Not a fan of orange anymore?" she asked.

I just shrugged. Too hard to explain.

"Well, does anything look out of place?" Avery nudged aside a pair of jeans with her toe. "I mean, more out of place than usual?"

I scanned my room. Same lamp. Same cluttered dresser. Same closet gaping open. Same mess.

"I used to have a poster for *Battlefield 900* on my wall," I said.

"Is that a movie?"

"Video game," I responded.

"What happened to it?" she asked.

I shrugged. "It disappeared a couple of weeks ago. I figured my mom took it while I was at school. She doesn't like that game."

I glanced at my mom's phone and saw that the video footage from the doorbell camera was ready to view. Grateful for the distraction from my personal things, I gestured Avery over to check it out.

The two of us sat side by side on the edge of my bed as I scrolled through the last few days. "This is a lot of video," I said. "Where should we start?"

"The only footage that matters will be from Tuesday and Wednesday," Avery said.

"What makes you say that?"

"Well, Magix arrested you on Wednesday," she said. "That was the day of the book report, when you used the music box. And we know agents searched your room that day, which means the boons had to have been planted earlier that morning or the day before."

"Okay," I said. "Let's start with Tuesday."

I tapped on the video and it started to play. The first thing I saw was myself, leaving the house wearing my backpack at 7:13 a.m.

"That's me going to school," I explained. "I catch the bus just down the street."

"I have a feeling this is going to take a while," Avery said. "Any way you can fast-forward?"

"Don't need to," I said. "The camera has a motion sensor. It only records when there's movement on the porch."

The next clip happened at 7:40 a.m. A large robin flew into view, vanishing into the porch rafters out of the camera's angle. The movement was followed by lots of chirping and tweeting that caused me to turn down the phone's speaker.

"Sounds like she's got a nest on your porch," said Avery.

"And babies," I said.

We continued watching the clips, quickly growing bored with what we saw.

7:43 a.m.: Bird left the nest.

7:56 a.m.: Bird came back.

8:17 a.m.: Bird.

8:22 a.m.: Bird.

8:39 a.m.: Bird.

9:07 a.m.: Dog.

"Ooh," I said sarcastically. "I didn't see that coming."

The dog was a floppy-eared brown cocker spaniel that belonged to a walker who could barely be seen on the sidewalk. The curious canine had wandered onto the porch, sniffing, before the walker had called it back.

9:40 a.m.: A woman rang the doorbell. She was wearing dark blue coveralls, and I could see her van parked in the driveway with *Skyline Appliance and Repair* painted on the side.

"Finally something interesting," Avery said. "Who's that?"

"She looks sort of familiar," I answered.

"Thanks for coming," my mom said on the recording. "I'm hoping you can repair it, but it's an old dishwasher, so . . ." Mom invited the woman inside.

"What was wrong with your dishwasher?" Avery asked.

"It only worked half the time." I tapped my chin. "Who *was* that lady?"

"Umm . . . the dishwasher repair person." Avery pointed out the obvious.

I nodded. "I guess that's why she looks familiar. Mom's had a couple of people check it out lately."

Avery gestured to the screen. "When does your mom go to work?"

"She works a short afternoon shift at the grocery store on Tuesdays," I explained. "Monday, Wednesday, and Friday, she's at the billing call center. And she does Thursday nights and all day Saturday and Sunday at the grocery store."

"Busy woman," said Avery.

"That's Mom," I said.

The repairwoman moved between her van and the house a handful of times before she left for good at 10:38.

10:54 a.m.: Mom pulled out of the driveway.

"She's off to the grocery store," I narrated.

Footage of the mama bird continued until 3:17 p.m., when I got home from school.

"Okay," Avery said. "What did you do after school that day?"

"Same thing I always do," I said. "Had a snack and started on my homework."

"You were home alone?"

"Fine!" I said. "You caught me. I played video games until I heard my mom open the garage door." Wow. Avery *was* a good detective.

3:52 p.m.: Hamid stepped onto the front porch and rang the doorbell.

"Who's that?" asked Avery.

"My friend Hamid," I replied. I turned up the volume on the phone so we could hear a replay of the conversation, hoping that Hamid and I hadn't said anything embarrassing.

"Hey," said Hamid.

"Hey," I said.

"What are you doing?" asked Hamid.

"Nothing."

"Cool."

"Wanna play Xbox?" I asked.

"Okay."

Then Hamid came inside.

5:55 p.m.: Mom pulled into the driveway.

5:57 p.m.: Hamid went home.

6:04 p.m.: Mrs. Damakis rang the doorbell.

"Who's that?" Avery asked.

"Our neighbor Mrs. Damakis."

"Shh," Avery hushed me as a conversation started between my mom and the neighbor.

"Hi, Susan," Mom said.

"Thank you so much, Tamara," said Mrs. Damakis as my mom handed her something. I squinted at the small screen.

"Onion," I said.

"Making something delicious, I'm sure," Mom said.

"Dolmas," said Mrs. Damakis. "Nothing fancy."

"Fancier than what we're having," Mom said. "Good ole mac and cheese."

They talked about the weather for a moment, and then Mrs. Damakis asked how I was doing. My mom said, "Just fine," and then Mrs. Damakis was gone.

6:09 p.m.: Bird.

6:11 p.m.: Bird.

7:04 p.m.: Someone I didn't recognize rang the doorbell. He was dressed in a collared shirt, and he had a messenger bag slung over one shoulder. The sun was starting to set behind him.

"Are you the owner of the house, ma'am?" he asked.

"I am," answered my mother.

"I can see you keep a tidy home. Do you mind if I ask what kind of cleaner you use?"

I heard my mom sigh. "Are you selling cleaner?"

"Yes, ma'am. We have three different products, all of them completely eco-friendly and—"

"I'm going to stop you right there," Mom said. "I'm really not interested in buying any sort of cleaner today. I don't mean to be rude, but we haven't even had dinner yet, and my son just informed me that he has a book report due tomorrow and he doesn't have anything prepared for it."

The salesman tried to convince her a few more times, but I knew firsthand how stubborn my mom could be. He left by 7:06.

"You didn't tell your mom about the book report until the night before?" Avery said.

I shrugged defensively. "I knew she'd spend the rest of the night trying to help me. And I really didn't know what the book was about, so I was just making stuff up to satisfy her."

I hadn't expected any more video for Tuesday, so I was surprised when someone showed up on the step at 10:22 p.m. I had already gone to bed by that time.

I didn't recognize the figure as he knocked on the door, but I certainly recognized the item in his hands.

The music box.

"Hi Tom," said Mom as she stepped onto the porch. "Thanks for bringing this so late."

"Hey, no problem. I know how kids can be." Tom Pedherson looked like he was in his late forties, maybe ten years older than my mom. He handed her the dreaded music box.

"He's going to bomb his report anyway," Mom said. Ouch. Thanks for the confidence boost, Mother. "I'm pretty sure he didn't even read the book. But it had a music box on the cover, and he thought a good visual aid would at least give him something to talk about."

"Hopefully this does the trick," Tom said. "See you at the office tomorrow."

Tuesday's videos ended.

"Okay," said Avery, who had scrounged up a pad of paper and a pen from my nightstand. "Let's write down Tuesday's suspects."

"Tom," I said.

She shook her head. "Start at the beginning. Your mom." She wrote it down. "Then the dishwasher repairwoman. Then Hamid."

"Hamid didn't frame me," I protested. "He's only ten."

"*All* the suspects," Avery said. "Then there was Mrs. Damakis. Then the cleaner salesman and then Tom Pedherson."

"But none of them came inside," I said, "so they couldn't have planted the boons in my room."

"Your mom and Hamid came inside," Avery corrected.

I scoffed. "But they didn't do it. Besides, if someone had stashed those boons in my room on Tuesday, I would have noticed them later that night."

"Really?" Avery said, glancing up at me. "In *this* junk heap?"

I sighed. Fair point. Maybe I wouldn't have seen a few extra items cluttering my room that night.

"Let's watch Wednesday," said Avery.

I tapped on the video of the fateful day of my arrest. The first thing I saw was the robin leaving the nest at 6:59 a.m.

Then I saw myself leave for school at 7:12.

"You're not holding the music box?" Avery asked.

"It was in my backpack," I explained. "I didn't want to look like a total dork carrying around a cute little wooden box."

"Then when was the first time you actually opened it?"

"During my book report," I answered.

"You weren't curious that morning?" asked Avery. "You didn't crack open the lid to see what kind of song it played before presenting it to your whole class?"

"My mom opened it at breakfast," I answered. "I heard the song. . . . It wasn't as cool as I'd hoped it would be, but it was all I had for my book report. After breakfast, Mom stuffed it into my backpack."

8:04 a.m.: Mom backed out of the driveway.

"Where's she going?" Avery checked.

"She's off to her other job," I answered. "The call center."

The next clip was at 11:12 a.m. The FedEx guy pulled up to the curb and dropped a big box on the front porch.

12:05 p.m.: My mom pulled into the driveway.

"She's home from work already?" questioned Avery.

"She must have come home for lunch," I said.

"Does she do that often?"

"No," I said, inwardly admitting that it did seem a little strange.

12:07 p.m.: Mom collected the package off the front porch.

12:26 p.m.: A pizza delivery guy rang the doorbell.

"What?" I cried. "Mom ordered pizza on her lunch break? She never orders pizza when I'm home!"

"Sounds like suspicious behavior for our suspect," Avery said, squinting at the phone screen. There wasn't much to see on the porch. The pizza delivery guy looked like he was in his early twenties, with three boxes balanced in his hand. His silver truck made a loud putter as it idled at the curb, the magnetic logo of Patrick's Pizza Place on the driver's door and a bunch of stickers in the back window.

"Here are those pizzas you ordered," said the delivery guy on the recording.

My mom stepped out onto the front porch, and I saw a

half-eaten sandwich in her hand. "I didn't order any pizza. You must have the wrong address."

The delivery guy checked a piece of paper and read aloud the address he had listed.

"Next street over." Mom stepped forward to point, and for a second we saw nothing but a close-up view of her ham-and-Swiss sandwich.

"Thanks, ma'am." Then the pizza delivery guy left.

"She should have claimed it," I muttered. "I could have had leftover pizza for dinner."

"Except you never came home from school that day," Avery reminded me.

12:48 p.m.: My mom left for work again.

"Do you notice something different about this day?" Avery asked, gesturing to the screen. She didn't leave me much time to think about it before saying, "No bird."

"Hmm." That was a good observation. "Maybe a cat got her."

3:10 p.m.: Four figures in gray suits moved onto the porch. I tensed. I instantly recognized the two in the lead—Agent Clarkston and Agent Nguyen.

"Magix agents," Avery said. "By this point, you'd already been arrested and taken back to headquarters. They've come to search your room."

Suddenly, the video stopped, a spinning circle appearing in

the middle of the screen to show that the feed was buffering. When it started again, the four agents were headed away from the house and more than a half an hour had passed, the time displaying 3:48 p.m.

I could barely hear Agent Nguyen's voice as she moved down the steps. "Let's find the mother and get the bracelet on her quickly . . ."

"Wait!" I cried, trying to back up the video. "What just happened?"

"Magic," answered Avery. "The agents must have used a boon to get into your house. As you know, regular cameras can't capture magical effects. All we know is that they were in your house for thirty-eight minutes."

"Supposedly, they raided my bedroom and found boons. But they're not carrying anything away," I pointed out.

"Top hats," Avery said. "They could have easily loaded those stolen items into their hats so they wouldn't draw attention when they left."

"If they're worried about attracting attention, they shouldn't wear suspicious gray suits and two-hundred-year-old hats," I said.

4:33 p.m.: Hamid rang the doorbell. He rocked back on his heels, whistling a video-game theme. "Mason," he muttered under his breath in a pretend scary voice. "You are no match for me. Prepare to burn." Then he picked his nose for a second.

"I don't think he knew he was on camera," Avery said.

I shut off my mom's phone. "So the FedEx guy and the pizza delivery guy are our only new suspects from Wednesday," I said.

"And the Magix agents." Avery added to her list. "We have to question everyone." At least she wasn't playing favorites. My mom and Avery's agents were on the same chopping block.

"But again, neither of Wednesday's suspects actually came inside," I reminded her.

"We don't know that for sure," she replied. "The Magix agents and the repairwoman were the only ones to enter through the front door." Avery stood up abruptly. "We should check your window."

"Good idea." I pushed aside an overflowing laundry basket with my knee and moved around my unkempt bed. I was walking close against the wall, almost to the window, when my foot suddenly crashed through the floor.

I grunted, catching myself on the side of my bed and gritting my teeth against the scrape on my ankle.

"You okay?" Avery asked.

I looked down at the floor to see what possibly could have happened. My foot was ankle-deep in the heater vent. One of my shirts had been draped across the hole like a simple pit trap for a wild animal.

I pulled my foot out of the duct. "Just the heater vent," I explained.

"You know, people usually put a cover over those," Avery said. "For safety."

"I thought I had one," I said. But then again, my room wasn't exactly in great condition. Who knew how long that had been missing?

"The window's locked," I said, checking it.

Avery nodded as though she expected it. "Still, we can't rule it out. There could be a magical boon to bypass locks. Or let people pass directly through the glass. Maybe we should sneak Fluffball up here and see if he can detect any traces of lingering magic."

"I don't think that's a possibility," I said, staring down into the yard from my upstairs window, my stomach sinking at what I was seeing.

"Why not?" Avery asked.

"Because Fluffball just ate my mom's tulips!" I cried. "We've got to get out of here before she kills him!"

CHAPTER 17

Luckily, I caught my mom in the kitchen before she had a chance to look out the window and notice the hungry rabbit's path of destruction through her flowers.

"Thanks," I said, handing her the phone.

"Tom's address is on that sticky note." She pointed, and Avery snatched it off the edge of the counter. "But his shift at the call center doesn't end for another hour or so."

"Okay," I said, moving backward to the front door. "We'd better get back to piano lessons." I paused. "Be careful, Mom."

"What do you mean?" she asked.

I shrugged, trying to chuckle it off as a joke. "It's dangerous work, ringing up people's groceries." But I was actually nervous

159

for her. I didn't like the idea of those Magix agents tricking her into wearing that boon bracelet. What if they came back to bother her? Or worse, what if Wreckage came sniffing around my house?

"One more thing, Mrs. Morrison," Avery said. "Did you get a FedEx package in the mail earlier this week?"

Mom raised her eyebrows. "Your friend sure asks a lot of questions, Mason."

"We, uh, saw the box in the garage," I lied. "Avery wondered what you got." My mom did a lot of online shopping, so it didn't seem suspicious to me. Still, I guess it was good to ask.

"Clothes," Mom answered. "And another pair of shoes." She waved her hand at me defensively. "What? It was a good sale."

"And when was the package delivered?" Avery continued.

"It came on Tuesday," Mom replied. "I saw on the doorbell camera that it had been delivered, so I decided to come home for lunch that day and bring it inside."

"That'll be all," Avery said. "For now."

Sort of embarrassed by her interrogation of my mother, I followed Avery onto the front porch, quickly pulling the door shut behind me.

"You really need to lighten up on her," I said. "She's going to be suspicious of you."

"Then I guess it'll go both ways," Avery remarked.

We reached the bottom of the porch steps. "Fluffball!" I whispered anxiously into the garden of downed tulips.

"I'll admit, I was mad at first," said the bunny, hopping into view through the floral carnage. "But I must say, this place is paradise."

"No!" I scolded. "Look what you did to my yard! Bad bunny. Very bad bunny!"

"If I wasn't so stuffed right now, I would bite your finger for that insult!"

"*I'm* not the insulting one!"

"Hey," interjected Avery. "I'm ready to go whenever you two are done bickering."

"Okay," I said. "But we'll need to use the atlas to get across town."

"We're not going to Tom Pedherson's house yet," she said. "Your mom said he wouldn't be home from work for another hour. Besides, we've got other suspects in your neighborhood that we need to question."

"We do?" I said.

"Mrs. Damakis and your 'friend' Hamid." She did little air quotes with her fingers when she said friend. "Who lives closer?"

"Mrs. Damakis," I said. "But she's not—"

"Let's go," Avery cut me off. "Or do you still want to be

161

standing here when your mom comes outside and sees the state of her tulips?"

"It's this way," I said, practically running down the sidewalk, Fluffball hopping along to keep pace.

"Anything we should know about this Damakis woman?" Avery asked.

I shrugged. "She and her husband are friendly. Nice retired couple."

"Specifics," Avery said as we made our way up their walkway.

"Umm . . ." I tried to think of something that would be useful to a detective. "Mr. Damakis mows his lawn three times a week in the summer. Mrs. Damakis has a new car, but she refuses to drive it."

Avery reached down and lifted Fluffball as I rang the doorbell.

"I know, I know," said the rabbit. "I won't say a word."

The door swung open. "Hi, Mr. Damakis," I said.

"Mason," the man replied cheerfully. He was heavyset, with a gray mustache. Today he was wearing a comfortable-looking sweatshirt and a pair of jeans. The fuzzy socks that covered his feet were blue with little polka dots on them.

"Is Mrs. Damakis home?" I asked.

"Sure thing," he said. "Come on in. I'll find her."

"Before you go," said Avery, "I was wondering if we could talk to you for a moment."

I shot her a puzzled look as we stepped inside. So, Mr. Damakis was a suspect now, too?

"My name is Avery Lobster," she said. "I'm a friend of Mason's. He tells me your wife makes delicious Greek food."

"That's right," he said.

"Does she ever make dolmas?"

Finally, I saw where Avery was going with this. But I didn't understand why it was necessary.

"Oh," Mr. Damakis said, "she hasn't made dolmas in months."

Wait. Mrs. Damakis had borrowed an onion from my mom just the day before yesterday. To make dolmas.

"What did you have for dinner on Tuesday night?" I asked. I realized it was a strange question to ask your neighbor, but he humored me with an answer.

"Chinese takeout," he said. "We were watching the football game."

Avery shot me a victorious glance. "Thanks," she said. "We'd love to talk to your wife now."

He bid us farewell and headed out of the room.

"So they had Chinese instead of dolmas," I said quietly. "It doesn't mean anything."

"It means Mrs. Damakis lied to your mom," said Avery. "It means she didn't really need an onion."

"Or it means that Mrs. Damakis changed her dinner plans," I said.

"We'll find out," whispered Avery as Mrs. Damakis entered the room.

"Hello, Mason," she said. "Your mom told me you were at piano lessons."

So, she'd talked to my mom since the bracelet went around her wrist yesterday afternoon.

"Remember when you borrowed an onion from my mom on Tuesday?" I asked bluntly. "What did you have for dinner that night?"

Mrs. Damakis shifted uncomfortably. "I made dolmas."

"Interesting," said Avery. "Then why did your husband say you had Chinese takeout?"

She sighed, as though she'd finally been caught. "Tony bought it on his way home from playing golf," she admitted. "I didn't know he was bringing it."

"Then why were you sticking to the dolmas story?" Avery asked. I thought she was pressing the old woman unreasonably hard.

"I didn't want to say anything because, well . . ." Mrs. Damakis stammered. "I should have brought the onion back.

But I kept it." She backed up toward the kitchen. "I'll go get it, Mason. You can take it home and tell your mother I'm sorry I didn't return it sooner."

Mrs. Damakis ducked around the corner, but Avery headed for the front door.

"I think we've heard enough," she said to me.

"You think she's innocent?" I asked, following her.

"I haven't decided yet," said Avery. "They teach us in detective training not to rule anyone out until you figure out the whole truth." She pulled open the front door. "We're just gathering data right now. We'll come back to Mrs. Damakis if we find out anything new that might involve her."

"But shouldn't we wait for the onion?" I asked, shuffling my feet in the doorway as Avery moved down the sidewalk.

"I hate onions," Avery called over her shoulder.

Awkwardly, I pulled the Damakises' door shut and ran to catch up to Avery and Fluffball.

"I'm guessing you use onions as deodorant," Fluffball said to me, free to speak now that we were out of the house.

"That's not even funny," I said, instinctively sniffing at my own armpits to be sure he was lying.

"Where does Hamid live?" asked Avery.

"This way." I moved across the street and veered down the sidewalk.

"What can you tell me about your friend?" she asked.

"Well, he loves video games," I began. "His parents moved here from England when he was a baby, but he doesn't have an accent." What else did I know about Hamid? "He once ate a whole bag of potato chips without taking his hands off his Xbox controller."

"Respect," muttered Fluffball.

"Do you have any reason to suspect that Hamid is only your friend so he can gain access to your house?"

The question took me by surprise. It was tough to say how and why Hamid and I were friends. A lot of the kids from my school and neighborhood stopped hanging out with me after my dad went to prison. They each had their excuses, but it wasn't hard to see the truth—their parents didn't want their kids spending time with me. Maybe they thought jail time was contagious. Or that I was a criminal, too. It never made sense to me.

But Hamid showed up the day after my dad went away and wanted to play video games. We didn't talk about personal stuff much, making him just the friend I needed.

"He might be using me," I said, finally answering Avery's question as we approached Hamid's house. "I *do* have a bigger TV than he does."

Hamid answered the door without a word. He wasn't very tall, even for a ten-year-old. His black hair was a little longer than mine and swept to the side. Hamid's dark eyes darted from me to Avery, and finally to the ball of white fur in her arms.

"Is that an Angora rabbit?" he asked.

"Yep," I said.

"Cool."

"I'm Avery," she said, seeming annoyed that he hadn't asked. "Can we come in?"

"Why?" asked Hamid.

"We have a couple of questions for you," she replied.

"Is this, like, an interrogation?" he said. "Can't I answer your questions out here?"

Avery raised an eyebrow in my direction. Well, Hamid was sure making himself sound suspicious. But she didn't know him like I did. He was sort of a strange kid. It didn't mean he'd committed a magical crime and framed me for it.

"Fine," she said in a no-nonsense tone. I could tell Avery was going to interrogate him hard, clearly unintimidated by a kid who was younger than she was. "Where were you on April third, at eight o'clock in the evening?"

That was the day and time the church had been raided and the boons stolen. But it was over a month ago. Hamid wasn't going to remember—

"I was at Game Net in the mall," he said. "There was a video game competition happening that evening. Over a dozen people can confirm that I was there."

Wow. That was a surprise. Hamid was taking this very seriously.

"How familiar are you with music boxes?" Avery asked.

"I've seen a few in my time," he replied melodramatically.

"Have you ever seen one with a fox that chases a goose inside?"

"Maybe."

"Just answer the question," said Avery.

Hamid folded his arms. "You can't get me to talk."

I rolled my eyes. Hamid loved dramatic games and movies. He was always muttering one-liners like that under his breath.

"We have ways," Avery said, taking off her top hat.

"Believe it or not," I cut in before things could escalate further, "Avery's questions are actually very important. Have you ever seen a music box that plays a happy little tune while a fox chases a goose?"

"Do they go around and around in a circle?" he asked.

"Yes," I said, encouraged that he might have a clue for us, but fearful that he might actually be involved.

"If they're going in a circle," Hamid said, "then how do you know it's not the goose chasing the fox?"

Avery sighed in annoyance. "I think it's time for the shoe."

"The truth shoe?" I clarified. I had almost forgotten that we'd stolen it from the armory. "But it's a boon. We'd have to tell him the truth—give him knowledge—for it to work," I muttered. "We can't risk involving him more than he already is. Let's just go, and we can come back later if we think of more questions."

Avery narrowed her eyes at Hamid. "This isn't over." She placed the top hat back on her head.

"I'll be waiting," he said. "You can torture me, starve me . . . I'll never betray the others."

"Others?" Avery said. "What others?"

Hamid unfolded his arms, his dramatic demeanor falling away. "I don't know. It just sounded good." He turned to me. "She's kind of crazy, Mason. But that was fun. It was like a real-life movie scene." He snarled. "I'll never betray the others," he quoted himself.

By this point, Avery was halfway down the walk. I turned to catch up to her, but Hamid had one more thing to say. "Are you going to be home later? I thought we could team up to take on that double-barreled tank in the brickyard."

I shook my head sadly, wishing that a video game tank was my biggest worry. "I'll be at piano lessons."

"Cool," he said. "For how long?"

"I dunno. Probably a couple more days." Then I dashed to catch up to Avery and Fluffball.

CHAPTER 18

"You did a great job keeping your mouth shut, Fluffball," I said once Hamid's house was a safe distance behind us. He was hopping along the sidewalk to stretch his legs after being in Avery's arms for so long.

"And you did a great job questioning our first two suspects," replied the bunny.

"Really?" I said, surprised by the compliment. "Thanks!"

"No. I'm just kidding. Your questions stunk like the rest of you," Fluffball said. "The girl is much better at interrogation than you."

I felt my face go red as the compliment turned into an insult. "Well, she's had training," I justified. "I'm new at this. I'll do better when we get to Tom Pedherson's house."

"It's a quarter to five," Avery said, checking her watch. "I think we better give him a little more time to get home from work."

"So, back to Mason's house?" suggested Fluffball with excitement.

"I don't think that's a good idea," I said. "At least, not until my mom has had a chance to come to terms with the tulips."

"Mmmm . . . ," Fluffball muttered. "The red ones were my favorite. Crisp and juicy, with just a hint of sweetness."

I resisted the urge to kick the bunny.

"I've got something in mind." Avery had stopped on the sidewalk. Her hat was off, and she'd just pulled out the transportation atlas. "We should go examine the crime scene."

"What crime scene?" I asked.

She paused thumbing through the map book to give me an incredulous stare. "Umm . . . the crime you were arrested for?"

"Oh, right. Good idea." I peeked over her shoulder at the book. "Mr. Lawden said that the boon church was at an undisclosed location in the eastern United States."

"I know right where it is," she said, tracing her finger over the roads in a Kentucky suburb.

"But he said it was undisclosed . . ."

"I know lots of things I'm not supposed to," said Avery.

"The location of the black site for unstable boons, the undercover aliases of several Magix agents—"

"The director's master code for the blenders," I finished. "Yeah. I remember. You've bragged about this before."

"There," Avery said, pulling a pen from her pocket. "Grab Fluffball."

I stooped down, and he looked away in disgust. "I will *allow* you to pick me up, human," he said disdainfully.

With the cantankerous rabbit in one arm, I touched Avery's shoulder with the other. She put the tip of the pen against the page and *poof*, we were standing somewhere new.

Avery's pinpoint with the atlas had been very accurate this time, and we were standing on the sidewalk directly in front of the Church of the Faith. I immediately recognized the place from the camera footage during my trial. But unlike in that grainy nighttime security video, I could now see the entire church and property.

The grass was green and well trimmed. There was a big tree shading half the building from the left side, and several concrete steps ran onto a covered entryway. Four white pillars held up a triangular gable with a tall steeple and cross at its pinnacle. The rest of the building was bright red brick, with plenty of arched windows along the sides.

Avery headed toward the front door, but I stopped her.

"During the trial they told me there were two guards inside. Whoever robbed this place knocked them both out with a boon of some kind. There aren't any cameras in there, but both guards identified me afterward."

"I know," she said. "I reviewed every detail of your case, remember."

"Then you should know we can't go inside."

"Of course not," she said. "They've been restocking the church since the theft. There will definitely be Magix people inside."

I shuddered. "Maybe this wasn't such a good idea. Maybe we should go."

"Let's just have a look around outside," she said, moving up to the steps.

"Why don't you set me down for a breath of fresh air," Fluffball said from the crook of my arm. I lowered him to the ground and caught up to Avery.

"What exactly are we looking for?" I whispered, my eyes on the front door, fully expecting people in gray suits and black top hats to come flooding out and surround us.

"Clues," she said. "Any evidence of who might have actually been here that night."

"It was over a month ago!" I said. "Don't you think the clues will be long gone?"

"The first thing they teach us in detective training is to be thorough," Avery said. "Let's try to re-create the security footage as accurately as we can."

"Good idea," I said sarcastically. "Let's try to make myself look as guilty as we can."

"You've already been tried and proven guilty," said Avery. "And then you committed a bunch more crimes while escaping Magix Headquarters. We can't really make you look *more* guilty."

"That's not helping," I said.

"Get up on the top step and pretend like you just came out of the church," she said, pointing.

"I don't like this," I grumbled. But Avery was the professional here, so I did what she said, skipping up to the covered porch as quickly as I could.

"Okay," said Avery, "what's different about this from the security footage?"

"Well, for starters, everything," I said. "I've never been here before."

"Your clothes are different," she said. "And when you stole the boons, you had on a huge hiking backpack."

"I didn't steal the boons," I reminded her.

"We're going to talk like you did for a minute," she said. "Because it certainly looked like you in the video. Another difference—your hair isn't combed today."

"Oh, sorry I didn't do my hair before you unexpectedly broke me out of a high-security building at seven thirty in the morning."

"Time of day is different, too," mused Avery, glancing up at the sky. "It was dark at the time of the theft."

"Does any of that matter?" I asked.

"It might," she said. "Now come down the stairs looking nervous."

That wouldn't be too hard. I started down, but Avery stopped me with a wave of her hands.

"No, no. You have to come down the *left* side of the handrail," she said like a movie director. "And pretend to grip the backpack straps." She demonstrated, her arms bending like she had chicken wings. "That's how it was in the video."

Okay. Avery was getting overly picky about this. I pretended to grab the backpack straps and moved down the stairs on the correct side of the handrail.

"Now pause at the bottom of the stairs," she said. I did. "At this point, you looked left and right. So, do it." I did. "Then, for some reason you moved off to the right, going around the corner of the church and disappearing from the camera angle. Let's check it out."

I followed Avery around the corner, discovering that Fluff-ball was already there, sniffing around the bushes that grew along the church's side.

"Are you detecting anything?" Avery asked the rabbit.

"Hard to tell," he said. "There's so much residual magic from all the boons that were stored inside the building. It's throwing off my sniffer. I think I see something in this bush, though." He pointed with his ears.

Avery parted the branches and reached down. When she stood up again, she was holding a can of spray paint.

"It's empty," she said, giving it a shake and hearing the ball rattle inside. "And the lid is missing." She turned it over, giving it a close inspection. "The color is brick red. And it hasn't been here very long."

"How can you tell?" I asked.

She pointed to a few little specks of rust around the spray nozzle. "And it would be in a lot worse shape if it had spent the winter in this bush. The label is barely even wrinkled."

"It's not a boon," said Fluffball.

"I thought your sniffer was broken," I said.

"I can see it clearly now that it's not in a bush," said the rabbit. "Trust me. It's just a regular can of spray paint."

"But the color matches the church's bricks," she said.

"Maybe someone was just touching up the walls," I said. "Or covering graffiti."

Avery took off her hat. "We'll keep this as possible evidence." She dropped the empty can into the top hat. "Let's head back around to the front of the church."

"What?" I cried. "Why? Weren't we lucky enough not to get noticed the first time?"

"We're re-creating the security video," said Avery. "You came out of the church and went around the right side of the building. Then a moment later you came back into the camera view."

I followed her back to the front of the church, muttering, "*I* didn't do any of those things."

"From here, you walked down the sidewalk," said Avery, leading the way. "You were clearly holding the music box. You paused in the middle of the street and glanced up at the security camera before heading off into the storage units over there." She pointed across the street.

"Where *is* the camera?" I asked.

"The Magix agents took it down after the theft and logged it into evidence," Avery explained. "They checked to see if it had been magically tampered with in any way."

"Had it?" Fluffball asked.

"No," answered Avery. "And, honestly, I'm surprised they haven't hung it back up yet. The camera didn't actually belong to Magix. It was the property of Total Storage across the street."

She turned and looked back at the church, holding up her hands with her thumbs touching. She squinted one eye as though sighting through a camera lens.

"Based on the angle," Avery continued, "the security camera would have been hanging there." She turned back around, pointing at the light post that stood over the driveway entrance to the storage units.

"So, whoever stole the boons from the church fled under the light post and into the storage units?" I said. "Magix didn't recover all the stolen boons, did they?"

"No," said Avery. "Only the handful that turned up in your bedroom."

"Maybe the thief stashed the rest in one of those storage units!" I cried.

But Avery shook her head. "That was the first place the Magix agents searched. They didn't find anything magical."

"Then why did the thief come back to the front of the church just to run off in this direction?" I asked. "Why risk getting picked up by the camera again?"

"Maybe that was the whole point," said Avery. "Whoever did this wanted it to look like you. By running right under the security camera, it gave everyone a clear view of your face."

"That stupid camera!" I said. "Why did it have to be pointing at the boon church?"

"It wasn't, really," said Avery. "The church happened to be in the background, but the camera was actually pointing at the road so Total Storage could see who was coming and going."

"And to catch the occasional car crash," said Fluffball, hopping over some debris in the gutter and landing next to the base of the light post.

I stepped over to him, the soles of my shoes crunching over bits of broken glass. As the afternoon light reflected on them, I realized that they were actually pieces of shattered mirror. Probably a car passing too close to the light post and clipping off the side mirror. My mom had done that once, backing out of the garage.

I watched Fluffball circle the post. "Nothing unusual here," he said. "Just a little bit of dog urine." It seemed like we had come up empty on clues.

I looked over to see that Avery already had the atlas open to my city. The sticky note with Tom's address was stuck to the opposite page, and the point of her pen was hovering above the road map.

"Grab my arm," she instructed.

Fluffball hopped onto my foot, and I reached out and touched her. Avery's pen came down, and we were instantly back in Indiana.

CHAPTER 19

"What's our plan when we see this guy?" I asked, staring at Tom Pedherson's house from the sidewalk.

"We ask him if he noticed anything unusual about the music box he won at the work party," said Avery. "That was a few days after the church was robbed, but there's still a chance he was involved."

"Billing people on the phone by day, magical criminal by night," I said.

"I think you're joking, but that could easily be the truth," said Avery. "A lot of people that work for Magix also have regular day jobs. They just keep the magic secret so the Igs can benefit from it."

"So do we think this guy's an Ed?" I asked.

"That's the first thing we have to find out."

We were on the porch now, and Avery knocked on the front door. A moment later, it swung open to reveal the man we'd seen in the doorbell cam footage. He was very tall and somewhat round in the middle. His hair hadn't gone gray yet, but it had receded almost halfway across his scalp.

"Tom Pedherson?" Avery checked.

"That's me," he said, his voice friendly. "What can I do for you kids?"

"My name is Mason Morrison," I cut in. "I believe you know my mom?" Avery cast a glance at me like she didn't know what I was doing. But I kept going. "I wanted to thank you personally for letting me use your music box for my book report."

"Glad to be of help," he said. "How did that go for you?"

"It was . . . unbelievable. My teacher is holding on to the music box for a day or two while she finishes grading the report," I lied. "Do you mind if we come inside for a minute? Ask you a few follow-up questions about it?"

"Of course not," he said, but I thought he seemed uneasy. Tom led us into his living room, inviting us to take a seat on the couch. But I was too stunned by what I saw to sit down.

Music boxes.

The living room was full of them. They filled a bookcase,

lined shelves, and covered the mantel above the fireplace. There must have been almost a hundred of them—some wooden, some metal, some glass. Most of them were open to display the wide variety of figurines inside, but there was no music playing.

"That's a nice rabbit there," Tom said, gesturing to the creature in Avery's arms.

I waited for Fluffball to say something rude, but he actually held his tongue for once. Maybe it was because Tom didn't say "pet" or "bunny."

"What breed is it?" asked Tom, seating himself on a padded armchair.

"Annoying," I said.

"He meant Angora," corrected Avery, still glancing around the room. "This is quite a collection of music boxes."

"Eighty-eight of them," he answered proudly. "Well, eighty-seven, since I let you borrow one."

"My mom said you won a music box at the work party last month," I said. I'd assumed that was why she'd reached out to him. But maybe she knew about his collection. He could have lent me any one of these. . . . "Which one did you win?"

"The one I let you borrow, actually," answered Tom.

"Can you tell us exactly how it came into your possession?" Avery asked, her tone very businesslike.

Tom chuckled, as if amused by such a professional attitude

in someone so young. "Like Mason said, it was at a work party for True Cost—Mason's mom was there, too, sitting right across the table from me."

"What do you do for True Cost?" Avery asked.

"I just make phone calls," he said. "Tell people to pay their bills."

"Go on with the work party," Avery said, waving for him to continue.

"Everybody took a raffle ticket when they got there," Tom went on. "At the end of the night, they drew tickets from a bowl. If the numbers matched, you won a prize."

"And the music box was your prize?" I clarified. That seemed awfully lucky. Maybe he'd touched the boon earlier in the night, and a bit of good fortune had rubbed off on him.

Tom fidgeted for a second before nodding. "I was excited about it. As you can see, I'm a collector."

"Did you display that particular music box after winning it?" Avery asked.

He nodded, pointing to an empty space in the center of the mantel. "Cleared a prime spot for it."

"Did you notice anything unusual about that music box?" she pressed.

"It was probably my favorite song of the bunch," he said. "It would get stuck in my head when I opened it. Helped make the

183

workday go by a little quicker if I had that tune in my mind."

Avery and I shared a quick glance. If the magic was rubbing off on him—and it sounded like it had been—then Tom Pedherson had to be an Ig.

"If that particular music box was precious enough that you cleared a prime spot on the mantel for it," Avery continued, "then why were you so willing to lend it to Mrs. Morrison, knowing that her thirteen-year-old son would be taking it to his middle school, where it could easily be broken, smashed, or ruined?"

Tom's fidgeting was very noticeable now. "Wait a second," he muttered. "Did something happen to my box?"

"It's in perfect condition," I answered. Or at least, it had been the last time I'd seen it, flying off the edge of a cliff to land in a raging muddy river.

"Could you answer the question, please?" Avery pressed. I was surprised by her boldness. I had a hard time standing up to kids my own age, let alone adults I didn't know. "Why did you lend out the music box?"

"Your mom is a friend of mine," Tom said. It didn't take a skilled detective to see how uneasy he was. "She called me because she knew I had a collection of music boxes . . ."

"Exactly. You could have let her borrow any one of these"—Avery motioned around the room—"but you picked the one that played your favorite song, and personally delivered that particular box to the Morrison household, all the way across town, after ten o'clock at night. Why?"

Tom Pedherson took a deep, steadying breath. "I think it's time for you kids to go." He stood abruptly, and something seemed to catch his eye out the living room window. Following his gaze, I glimpsed a pair of pedestrians down the road. I felt my body go tense, my heart beginning to pound.

Agents Clarkston and Nguyen were coming down the sidewalk toward Tom's home!

They were still several houses away, but their gray suits and top hats instantly gave them away. Avery must have seen them, too, because she gasped and took a step away from the window.

"How did they find us?" I hissed, joining her on the other side of the room.

"I don't know," answered Avery. "But we can't let them see us." She whipped off her top hat and reached inside.

"Excuse me?" Tom said. "I asked you to leave."

Avery pulled out her hand, and I saw that she was holding the familiar truth shoe.

"What?" I cried. "Are you sure that's a good idea?"

"We're already the two most wanted criminals on Magix's list," she said to me. "Exposing an Ig isn't going to make things worse for us. Besides, we have that memory boon notebook in the hat that Fluffball told us about."

"What on earth are you kids talking about?" Tom asked.

"Would you do us a favor and put on this shoe?" Avery held it out, as though it were enticing.

"What?" cried Tom. "I don't think so—"

"Look, Mister," Fluffball suddenly chimed in, his deep voice clearly irritated. "The girl was asking nicely, so put on the shoe!"

Tom Pedherson swore.

"And watch your language in front of the kids," Fluffball added, shaking a paw at the man who stood rooted in place, staring at the talking bunny with wide, disbelieving eyes. Fluffball pointed at the item in Avery's outstretched hand. "The shoe?" he grumbled impatiently.

Wordlessly, Tom Pedherson took the dirty sneaker and dropped into the armchair, slipping the shoe onto his stocking foot.

"This shoe is a magical item called a boon," Avery explained. Was she really doing this? "It makes the person wearing it tell the truth."

"Okaaaay?" said Tom.

"Were you aware that the music box you won at the work party was a magical boon capable of transporting the person who opened it along with anyone looking at them?" Avery asked.

Tom shook his head. "Nope. I just liked the song it played."

186

"Then why were you so willing to give it to my mom?" I asked. "Why did you lend me that particular music box when you had so many others to choose from?"

"Because it should have been hers to begin with!" Tom cried. Then he gasped and covered his mouth, as though surprised that he'd spoken the truth.

"What?" I muttered.

"Explain yourself," Avery demanded.

"Your mom was supposed to win the music box in the raffle," he said. "The announcer read the number on her ticket, but she wasn't paying attention. I reached across the table and switched our tickets so I could claim the prize."

"Why?" I asked.

He pointed around his living room. "Hello?" he said. "I'm a collector."

"You already felt guilty about winning the music box," Avery summed up. "And when Mason's mom asked to borrow one, the guilt was too much and you were willing to drive all the way across town to give her the box she should have won."

"That's not all," said Tom. "The woman calling the numbers . . . she must have wanted Tamara to win the music box, because the drawing was rigged."

"What do you mean?" I asked.

"When I was leaving the party, I passed by the bowl with

187

the remaining tickets—the numbers of all the people who didn't win anything." Tom looked right at me. "Your mom's number was in there—sitting right on top."

"I don't understand," I whispered.

"That means the person calling the numbers cheated, too," said Avery. "They said your mom's number to make sure she would win the music box, even though they didn't draw her ticket."

"I don't know why they wanted her to win," said Tom sincerely. "Everybody knows that *I'm* the one who loves music boxes."

"So you stepped in and claimed the prize meant for my mom," I said.

Out the living room window, I saw Agents Clarkston and Nguyen heading up the walk toward the Pedhersons' front door.

"We've got to get out of here," I started, but Avery wasn't finished.

"I'm going to need the name and address of the person who called the numbers," she said to Tom.

"It was Cheryl Denton," he answered. "I can give you her address, but you won't find her there."

"Why not?" she followed up.

"She's in Hawaii with her whole family," said Tom.

"Honestly, I don't know how she's affording it. Cheryl's always complaining about how tight money is . . ."

"I bet someone paid her off," Avery guessed, "for reading your mom's raffle ticket even though she drew a different number that was supposed to win the music box."

There was a knock at the front door.

"We have to get out of here," I whispered again. "Get out the atlas."

Avery took off her top hat, but Fluffball shouted, "Wait! The atlas puts off a unique signature. Magix could be tracking it."

"Of course!" said Avery to me. "It's the same way Magix tracked you when you used the music box. They must have picked up the magical signature when we used the atlas to leave New York. Then they focused on it when we transported to the church and back, tracking us here." She held her hat out for the rabbit. "Find that memory boon notebook—quick!"

Fluffball jumped into the top hat, disappearing from view with an audible gasp from Tom.

"Is there another way out of here?" I asked.

"You can go out the back door," suggested Tom, obviously still under the influence of the truth shoe. "The backyard borders up against a little creek."

Another knock from the people at the front door. This time

Agent Nguyen's voice called out. "Hello? This is . . . the police. We're looking for two runaway children, thirteen years of age."

"Here," whispered Fluffball, whose head suddenly poked out of Avery's top hat. She pulled out the bunny, who was holding a small notebook between his front paws.

"What is that?" Tom asked.

"The childhood journal of someone named Angelica Gutierrez," answered the rabbit.

"Who's that?" Tom cried.

"I don't really know," answered Fluffball. "But she must have done something really good with her life because her journal is now a memory boon."

"Listen up," said Avery. "Every time you rip out a page of the journal, any person who hears the paper tear has the last fifteen minutes of their memories erased."

That was the way Fluffball had described it to us when he briefly listed the boons in the hat.

"Tom should rip it," I said. "That way we can plug our ears."

"If we give you this notebook, will you rip out a page?" Avery asked him.

He nodded anxiously. "I'd be more than happy to forget about that bunny. He's the stuff of nightmares."

Fluffball hissed at him, baring his buckteeth and bulging his reddish eyes.

"We should probably take the shoe back, too," I said.

Tom reached down and yanked it off. Avery handed him the notebook, and we both plugged our ears. I hummed a little, just to make sure I couldn't hear.

I saw him rip out the page, his face wrinkling with confusion the moment it was done. "Who are—" he began.

"Thanks," Avery cut him off, snatching the book out of his hands and racing for the back door. I grabbed the shoe and followed, rounding the corner just as I heard the Magix agents push open the front door.

We burst into the backyard, sprinting until we were safely hidden in the dense trees that ran along the little creek.

"I think we can cross off Tom Pedherson as a suspect," I said. "He's a selfish Ig, but he didn't frame me for a magical crime."

"But he *did* give us some useful information," added Avery.

"Not really," I said. "With that Cheryl lady in Hawaii, there's no way we can question her. Even if we dared to use the atlas, it only covers the eastern US."

"Think about what else we learned," she said as we moved quietly along the creek. Avery had set Fluffball on the ground, and he seemed quite happy to be exploring nature, nibbling at the greenery.

"A lot of people cheated at my mom's work party," I said.

"Exactly," said Avery. "Why?"

"To make sure my mom won the music box."

"And why did they want her to have it?"

"So I would use it," I said. "To frame me for stealing the boons from the church."

"But when your mom didn't win it," replied Avery, "whoever was framing you had to take a different approach to getting the music box into your hands. They needed you to ask for it. Why?"

I snapped my fingers. "For my book report!"

Avery nodded. "What was the book?"

"It was called *The Music in the Box*," I said. "It had a robot music box on the cover."

"Where did you get the book?"

I thought back to two weeks ago. "The school library."

"Did you pick it randomly off the shelf?"

"No," I said, trying to remember details that hadn't seemed important at the time. "Somebody gave it to me and suggested that I read it."

"Do you remember who?"

"The usual school librarian was absent that day," I said. "There was a substitute. Charity Vanderbeek's mom. She was the one who gave me the book."

"And what did she say about it?"

The memory was actually pretty clear in my mind. "She said I might like it. She said all I'd need for my book report was a good-looking music box and I'd probably get an A." I sucked in a sharp breath of surprise at what this all meant.

Avery grinned. "I think it's time to pay Ms. Vanderbeek a visit."

CHAPTER 20

Charity Vanderbeek was in my third-period class, and I actually knew where she lived, but it took Avery and me a long time to get there since we didn't dare use our magical atlas. We caught a bus that took us back to my side of town, and then we went the rest of the way on foot. By the time we arrived in the right neighborhood, the sun was setting.

"That's the house," I said, pointing through the twilight. "Are we just going to ring the doorbell again?"

Avery shook her head. "We probably shouldn't have risked such a direct approach with Tom Pedherson. Let's peek through a window and see what we might be up against."

"What if the neighbors notice us?" I asked. "They could call

194

the Vanderbecks. Or worse . . . the police."

"Let's creep into the backyard, then." Avery veered off the sidewalk.

We moved in total silence, hopping over the low fence that sectioned off the Vanderbeeks' backyard.

"This window isn't shut all the way," Avery said, inspecting one she could easily reach from the patio.

"Shh!" I hissed. "Someone might hear you."

"I'd say there's no one here to hear," said Fluffball.

"What do you mean?" I asked, annoyed that he wasn't even whispering.

"Come on, kid," said the rabbit. "Look around. Nobody's home. There aren't even any lights on inside."

I hated to admit it, but he was right. It wasn't totally dark yet, but if someone was inside, they probably would have turned on a light by now. "Maybe it's a trap," I tried. "What if that substitute librarian is just sitting in the dark, waiting for us?"

"The garage was empty," continued Fluffball. "No cars."

"How do you know?" Avery turned on him.

"Oh, you two didn't notice that?" asked the bunny. "I caught a quick peek in the garage window as we snuck past. Fun fact: rabbits see best in dim lighting like twilight and dawn."

"Why didn't you say anything?" I cried.

If a rabbit could shrug, that was what he did. "You're the

195

detectives. I'm just along for the ride."

I looked at Avery. "I guess it's safe to go inside and have a look around, then."

"After you." She gestured to the window she had pried open.

But I hesitated. I'd never broken into someone's house before! This was real criminal stuff and I had a bad feeling about it. With my heart in my throat, I stepped up, putting my knee on the sill and ducking my head inside.

All was dark and quiet. Nobody home. Just like Fluffball had guessed.

"All clear," I whispered back to Avery as I slipped into the house. I fumbled along the wall until I felt a light switch.

"Nice place," Avery whispered as the room brightened. We were standing in a large room with a couple of couches, a big TV, and a fireplace. The kitchen was divided by a little half-wall, but I could see well enough to know that no one was hiding there.

"What are we looking for, exactly?" I asked.

"Clues," Avery said. "Anything that might tell us if this Vanderbeek lady was involved in framing you."

"Well, she probably wouldn't leave important evidence lying around in the front room," I said. "Should we head upstairs?"

"Come on, Fluffball," said Avery. "We need you to sniff out any boons."

The rabbit twitched his ears from his perch on the window-sill. "I was going to stand guard at the window and warn you if the family comes home."

"More like, jump out the window and run away at the first sign of trouble," I said.

"Suit yourself," said Fluffball, hopping down. "Don't blame me if you're stuck upstairs when the evil Ms. Vanderbeek shows up."

I moved toward the staircase. I was almost there when Fluffball snapped at me. "Not another step, kid! That scarf's a boon!"

"What scarf?" I asked, freezing anyway.

Fluffball used his ears to point to a plaid scarf draped over the railing at the bottom of the stairs. As I watched, it slowly slipped off, falling to the floor. The minute it touched the car-pet, something terrible began to happen.

It was just like the game everyone plays as a kid—the floor turned to lava.

It started at the spot where the scarf landed, spreading quickly toward us. Fluffball and I scrambled backward to avoid the bubbling orange liquid.

"Nice job, Skunk Boy!" cried Fluffball, bouncing across the room and leaping back onto the windowsill.

"What happened?" asked Avery, climbing onto the low

hutch against the wall where the TV was mounted.

"I didn't do anything!" I replied, springing onto the couch. "I didn't even know what that boon could do."

"You didn't need to," answered the rabbit. "That's what I was trying to tell you. The scarf boon was manipulated to take action if an Ed so much as approached the stairs."

"Wait!" I gasped. "Maybe that's how the music box activated. What if someone had manipulated it to activate for an Ig like me!"

"Not likely," said Fluffball. "Didn't you say your mom opened the music box before you? And Tom Pedherson? Nothing special happened to them."

The lava had boiled right up to the feet of the couch, and my perch was starting to sink. I ran across the cushions and sprang to the loveseat, realizing I would soon be marooned.

"Mason!" Avery suddenly shouted, nearly giving me a heart attack. "Do you know who this is?" Crouched on the TV hutch, she was holding out a framed picture that she'd taken from the shelf next to her.

I squinted to see what she'd found, but it was just a picture of Ms. Vanderbeek with her two daughters, Charity and the older one I didn't know.

"Is this really the time to look at family pictures?" I shrieked, the loveseat tilting sideways as the lava ate away at its feet. I didn't know why Avery seemed so surprised to see Ms. Vanderbeek's picture. We were in her house, after all.

"Don't you recognize her from somewhere?" Avery cried, still holding the frame insistently.

"Yeah," I said, moving to the back of the loveseat to get to higher ground. "She was the substitute librarian who gave me the *Music in the Box* book." We'd already been over this.

"That's not all," said Avery. "She's also the repairwoman who fixed your mom's dishwasher on Tuesday morning!"

"*That's* why she looked so familiar!" I called back. "Oh, we're onto something now. I bet Ms. Vanderbeek doesn't even know how to fix—"

My loveseat jolted, dumping me off the back. I managed to spring to the side table, but it was small, bobbing precariously in the sea of red and orange.

"You've gotta jump!" Fluffball yelled from the windowsill.

"To where?" I shrieked. The nearest surface that wasn't being flooded by lava was Avery's hutch. But even she was cornered, probably only a few seconds remaining until she got fried.

Then I remembered something. I hadn't seen the boon, but Fluffball had mentioned it briefly when giving us his list from the top hat. "Avery!" I called. "Toss me the hat!"

"What?" she cried.

"Just do it!"

With a deep breath, she pulled it off her head and threw it across the room like a Frisbee. I caught it just inches above the lava, my sweaty hands almost slipping on the black fabric. I plunged my hand into the opening, feeling for what Fluffball had described.

Baseball!

I pulled it out of the hat, holding it up victoriously as my little table dipped lower into the lava.

"Throw it!" Fluffball shouted.

I didn't need him to remind me how it worked. He'd already given me the knowledge in that New York City alleyway.

I stuffed the hat onto my head so my hands would be free. Then I pulled back my arm and hurled the baseball at the middle of the staircase. The moment it struck the step, I was transported to that exact spot, landing on the sixth stair from the bottom.

"Where are you going?" cried Fluffball. "We've gotta get outta here!"

"That scarf was guarding the stairs," I said, bending down and picking up the baseball. "That means she must be hiding something up there!"

I dropped the baseball back into the hat and tossed the whole thing across the room to Avery. I didn't even have time to see if she caught it because the lava suddenly gurgled up over the bottom three steps, heating my toes.

"Yikes!" I cried, turning frantically to sprint up the staircase. "I didn't think it would follow me up!"

"That's what happens when you don't bother to ask the expert!" griped Fluffball.

I didn't look over my shoulder, but I knew the lava was rising quickly behind me. I could feel its heat nipping at my heels.

I reached the top stair and spun on the newel post, racing down a hallway. There were doors on my left, probably leading into bedrooms, but I didn't want to corner myself now that I didn't have a single boon to help me escape.

There was a closed door straight ahead. I could barely see it in the reddish glow of the lava chasing behind me. If I could get into the room and shut the door, it might buy me a few seconds to think while the lava ate through the door.

I grasped the doorknob desperately, my hand slipping once before I flung it open. I threw myself headlong through the doorway, only to discover that it was nothing but a coat closet.

I slammed into a couple of stacked cardboard boxes, the contents spilling around me as I staggered backward, falling right into the lava.

Except it wasn't lava anymore.

The floor behind me had returned to regular carpet, soft enough that I hadn't even hurt myself as I fell.

I gasped for breath, my heart bouncing around inside my

rib cage. "What did you do?" I sputtered. But no one was there. I glanced back through the empty hallway just in time to see Avery reach the top of the stairs. Her sprint slowed to a walk when she realized that I was okay and the lava was gone. Then she slid her hand along the wall until she found the light switch, bringing the hallway into full view.

"How did you stop it?" she asked.

"I . . . no," I stammered. "I didn't do anything."

She looked at me, confused. "What happened?"

"I don't know," I answered. "One minute the floor was lava, and then it was back to normal."

"Fluffball!" Avery shouted over her shoulder. "The coast is clear. Get up here!" She stepped over and offered a hand. I accepted, letting her pull me up onto my shaking legs.

"You were trying to hide from the lava . . . ," she said, "in a *closet*?"

"I thought it was a bigger room," I admitted.

My sudden impact had made the closet virtually explode. Several of the boxes had popped open, papers and clutter now spilled all over the floor.

"This looks familiar." Avery tugged on the corner of a dark blue piece of cloth sticking out of one of the boxes. As she pulled it free, I realized that it was a mechanic's jumpsuit with the *Skyline Appliance and Repair* logo embroidered on the front.

"Well, well, well," I muttered, pulling down the entire box.

It was mostly papers inside, but I quickly spotted a Skyline Appliance name tag. It had Ms. Vanderbeek's picture on it, but the name underneath was *Janet West*.

"She *was* a fake!" I exclaimed. "But wait a minute . . . It seems like she really fixed our dishwasher. At least, my mom was loading it when we saw her."

"Maybe it was never actually broken," Avery said, riffling through a stack of papers from the box.

"It definitely was," I said. "Hasn't worked right for a month."

"Since April fourth," Avery said, holding up the paper. "These are all the service dates when Skyline repair technicians visited your house. Looks like that first visit was supposed to be a free tune-up."

"April fourth," I said. "That was the day after the boon church was robbed."

"It's all connected," said Avery. "Maybe the 'free tune up' was actually meant to break your dishwasher so they'd have a reason to get into your house again. And Ms. Vanderbeek wouldn't really have to know how to fix it since she could have just repaired the dishwasher with a boon."

"We should probably go," I said. "There's no telling when Ms. Vanderbeek will be home."

As I stepped forward, my foot sent some clutter scattering and my toe clanked into something hard. "Whoa . . . ," I muttered, stooping down to pick up the metal item.

"A vent cover?" Avery said.

"Not just any vent cover," I said. "The one from my bedroom!"

"How can you be sure?"

I tilted the metal grate toward her so she could see the droplets of bright orange paint that my dad had spilled across it in his haphazard remodel of my room. "Why would she take this?"

"It's got to be a boon," she said. "Fluffball? Where are you?"

"There was a boon in my room?" I mumbled, cradling the metal vent cover. "For how long?"

"When did your dad paint your room?" she asked.

"At least two and a half years ago," I said. "After I got the cast off my leg, so I could go upstairs again."

"You know what this means?" she asked. "Whoever organized all this—the Mastermind—has been targeting you for a long time, Mason."

I felt my blood run cold. The vent in my hands felt like ice. "Why me?" I wondered aloud. "Why would anyone want to target me? I'm just a regular kid. An Ig."

"What if they needed an Ig for their plan to work?" Avery mused.

"But why *me*?" I repeated.

"Hmm. Maybe you have something the Mastermind wants . . . ," suggested Avery.

"What could I possibly have?"

"A boon that you didn't know about?"

"But that doesn't make sense," I said. "The Mastermind has already proven that he can break into my house and leave boons to frame me. If I had something he wanted, why not just steal it?"

Avery quietly took the boon vent from my shaking hands. "I don't know why they targeted you," she said. "But we're going to find out." She took off her top hat and dropped in the metal vent cover.

It didn't fit.

I watched her struggle with it for a moment, the vent cover fitting through the hat's opening but clearly hitting the inside.

"What's wrong?" I finally asked.

"It's not . . ." She whispered something under her breath, then withdrew her magic credit card from her pocket. Holding it carefully, she slid the edge along the carpet.

Nothing happened.

"The boons," she said, panic sneaking into her voice. "They're not working."

Finally, Fluffball appeared at the top of the stairs, hopping casually toward us. "Great timing," I said. "Something's wrong with Avery's boons."

Fluffball turned, sniffing around a doorway into one of the bedrooms.

"What are you sensing?" Avery asked. "Are you picking up a magical signature?"

Fluffball pooped. A handful of little brown pellets that stood out against the beige carpet.

"I don't like Vanderbeek, either," I said. "But that's just low, Fluffball. Even for you."

"Mason." Avery took a step closer to the bunny. "I think something's wrong with him."

"That's not new," I said.

"No. I mean, his collar." She took a knee and stroked his fluffy white fur. "He's just a regular rabbit."

"Did it come unclasped?" I asked.

She checked the collar. "It should be working," she said, "but it's broken, just like all the other boons. There must be something around. Something dampening the magical effects."

"That's why the lava suddenly stopped," I said. Then I saw the vent cover in Avery's hand. Could it be?

I reached out and took it. "Maybe we should put this back in the closet," I said. "So Vanderbeek doesn't know we were here."

She noticed me studying the vent cover. "You don't think . . . ?"

I shrugged. "A dampener boon? It could make sense. Especially if the Mastermind wanted to make sure I never came into contact with other magical boons."

"Until the day he wanted to frame you," finished Avery. "Which was why Ms. Vanderbeek was at your house on Tuesday. Maybe she really did fix the dishwasher, but I'm guessing her main purpose for going to your house was to steal this from your bedroom."

With a clunk, I tossed the vent cover back into the clutter surrounding the hallway closet. "No way to know what it really does, since it shut down our detector." I stepped over and picked up Fluffball. "Let's get out of here."

"Wait," said Avery, staring at a fresh stack of papers that had scattered when I'd dropped the vent cover. "Look at this." She bent down and picked up a handwritten note scrawled on a paper napkin.

"What does it say?" I asked.

Avery read aloud. "'My friends, by this time tomorrow, the boon church will be ours. I'm putting my neck on the line (again), and I'm counting on the two of you to follow up. Talbot—meet me at the rendezvous point with your truck. Vanderbeek—stand ready to enter the Morrison house at the Mastermind's orders.'"

"Whoa," I said. "This is . . . this is . . ."

"The evidence we've been looking for," said Avery. "It proves *you* didn't steal the boons from the church."

"I don't know if Magix would call this proof," I said.

"Okay. Maybe not quite, but it's certainly getting us closer to the truth," she said. "So, this note was written the day before the boons were stolen from the church. We know who Vanderbeek is—"

"'Enter the Morrison house,'" I repeated from the note. "That must have been to break down our dishwasher, since that happened just two days later."

"But who's Talbot? And who's the Mastermind?"

"And who wrote this message?" It sure would have been nice if the criminal had signed it.

"Hold on a second . . ." Avery reached into the pocket of her jeans and pulled out a crumpled note. As she unfolded it, I realized that it was the anonymous note she'd received in her locker.

"Check it out." She held the two papers side by side. "Same handwriting."

"You're sure?" They certainly looked similar, but so did lots of handwriting.

She nodded. "Handwriting identification is a basic in detective training. Look at the words that are the same." She started pointing them out. "*The, you, line . . .*"

"You're right," I said. Those few words were basically identical.

"This is bad," she whispered.

"I don't understand."

"This means that the same person who stole the boons from the church tipped me off with a note that said you were innocent," she began. "It means that whoever set this up wanted me to help you escape. The High Line was definitely a trap, and . . ." Avery took a deep breath. "It means that the same person had access to my locker inside headquarters." She looked at me, her dark eyes wide. "The Mastermind has a spy inside Magix."

I swallowed hard. "What can we do?" I asked. "We can't really call and warn them."

Avery sighed. "We keep going. Hopefully, in the process of proving you innocent, we can also figure out who the traitor is inside Magix Headquarters."

She carefully folded the two notes and reached back to slip them into her pocket.

"Wait." I caught her arm. "That napkin." Now that she had folded it, I could see something printed on the other side. "Gran's Kitchen," I said, reading the name of the restaurant. "It's a diner downtown. This note could have been written there."

Avery nodded. "It's worth checking out in the morning."

"We can make it tonight if we hurry," I said. "Gran's is open late." I started down the hallway. "Besides, I'm starving."

CHAPTER 21

We were on the bus headed downtown when Fluffball suddenly blurted out, "I'm aliiiiive!"

The few people on the bus glanced at Avery and me, but there was no way they could have known it came from the bunny. They probably thought we were playing a video on a phone with the volume up too high.

"Keep your voice down," I said, holding the rabbit close against my chest. "And I never thought I'd say this, but I'm glad to have you back."

"Pass me over to the girl, kid," Fluffball said. "One more second in your arms and I'll have to take a shower."

As I let him hop into Avery's arms, I noticed that she was

210

reaching into her top hat, well past her elbow, silently letting me know that it was working again.

"What happened, anyway?" Fluffball asked. "I saw the lava chasing you upstairs. I heard a big crash and then . . . well, that's the last thing I remember."

"What do you know about dampener boons?" Avery asked him.

"Yeah. They're freaky," he replied. "They can completely shut down other boons that are nearby."

"We think we found one at Ms. Vanderbeek's," I explained.

Fluffball's pink nose bobbed against Avery's hand. "I'm getting a whiff of residual dampener magic, for sure."

"But we left it in the house," I said. "Why did it take so long for you and the other boons to work again?"

"A powerful dampener can soak into boons around it," Fluffball explained. "The effect lasts even after the dampener is gone. How long was I out?"

"Almost an hour," Avery said as the bus came squealing to a halt.

"This is our stop," I said, catching a glimpse of Gran's Kitchen through the fingerprint smudges on the bus window.

As we approached the diner, Avery took a moment to fill the bunny in on what we'd found in Vanderbeek's upstairs closet. My stomach rumbled at the smell of greasy fried food wafting down the street. The lighted sign above the door had a few letters burned out, so it looked like *Gra Kitch*.

I glanced at Avery and pointed to a notice taped on the door. It read "No pets allowed."

"Hey," Fluffball interjected. "You know I can read, too."

"And we don't consider you our pet," Avery said delicately, "but we also don't want to get kicked out of this place."

"Fine," the rabbit muttered. "Stow me away. Stick me in the magic hat like some common boon."

Gently, Avery lowered Fluffball into the top hat and propped it on her head.

"It's for the best," I whispered to her.

A bell chimed as we stepped inside, and someone shouted for us to take a seat wherever we'd like and they'd be right with us. This late at night, I only counted three other people seated at the long counter with tall stools rising from a dingy black-and-white checkered tile floor. Avery and I picked one of the booths against the window, the red vinyl seats surprisingly bouncy.

"You've still got some money left?" she asked me quietly.

"I grabbed some cash when we were in my room. Just don't order anything over ten dollars."

Our waitress appeared, an older woman with bleached hair and a wrinkled tattoo of a leaf on her forearm. A pin with the name Kathy was fastened to her stained red apron. She placed a couple of menus in front of us and poured two glasses of water.

"What can I get ya started with?" Kathy asked.

"What's good?" Avery asked.

The waitress rattled off a half a dozen menu items, but it didn't seem like Avery was really listening.

"You seem to know the menu pretty well," Avery said. "Have you worked here a long time?"

Kathy smiled. "Oh, honey. I was working here since before you were born."

"I bet you get to know a lot of folks," she continued. "See a lot of interesting things . . ." I realized what Avery was doing now. Winning over the waitress was probably lesson one in detective training.

"Somebody ought to write a book about it," Kathy said. "'Cuz I've seen some straaaange things going down."

"Any secret meetings?" I asked, hoping it wasn't too obvious.

"All the time," said Kathy.

"We're looking for somebody that might have passed through here a month or so ago," said Avery.

Kathy held up her hands. "We get a lot of customers, sweetheart."

"I figured it was a shot in the dark," said Avery, taking a sip of her ice water. "His name is Talbot?"

"You talking about Steve Talbot?" Kathy said. "He's come in on and off for years. But he's been a regular for nearly two months now."

Avery and I glanced at each other. We didn't know about a first name, but the timing lined up with the robbery of the boon church.

"If it's the same Talbot I'm thinking of," said Kathy, "he always sits in that corner booth by himself. Next to the window."

"Did you ever see him meet with this woman?" Avery asked, suddenly holding up the Skyline Appliance badge with Vanderbeek's picture and the name *Janet West*. I hadn't realized Avery had taken it from the house.

Kathy studied the badge. "I remember her. She came in dripping wet, but it wasn't raining. Would have been about a month ago."

"April second?" I asked.

Kathy shrugged. "Seems about right. She met with your friend Talbot."

I grinned at Avery. By the sound of it, we'd found the right man.

"But the meeting didn't look romantic, if that's what you're wondering," said Kathy. "Nah. It was too serious. But Steve

Talbot's always got a serious edge to him."

"What else can you tell us about him?" Avery asked.

"Quiet fellow," said Kathy. "But always respectful. I think he's a fisherman. At least he's got a lot of fishing stickers on the back of his truck."

"Truck, you say?" asked Avery, clueing me in that the detail was important. Of course! The note had told Talbot to bring his truck to the rendezvous point.

"Big silver truck," Kathy said. "A diesel, by the sound of it."

"I'll have the country fried steak," Avery said so abruptly that it seemed like she was speaking a foreign language.

Kathy jotted it down.

"And I'll have the . . . uh . . ." How had Avery even had a chance to look at the menu? They had a ton of options. "Cheeseburger and fries."

"It'll be right out." Kathy topped off Avery's water before sauntering away.

"Steve Talbot," Avery whispered across the table to me. "He must've been the pizza delivery guy."

"The one from the doorbell camera?"

Avery nodded. "The one who *accidentally* came to your house during your mom's lunch break on Wednesday."

"What makes you think that?"

"The silver truck that was idling on the curb was loud like

a diesel," she explained. "And I could see stickers in the back window, but I couldn't make out what they were from the doorbell camera."

"But he didn't come into the house," I said. "My mom talked to him on the porch."

"Still," she said, "it's important. We need to find out where he lives so we can snoop around."

"Hopefully there won't be any lava this time," I added.

Kathy walked past and Avery held up her hand. "Excuse me. You wouldn't happen to know Mr. Talbot's address, would you?" Avery asked.

"I don't," said Kathy. "But if you're looking to talk to him, I'm sure he'll be in tomorrow morning. Eight thirty sharp. Five days a week."

Avery looked back at me as Kathy moved on. "Maybe we don't need to snoop around his house. We'll just grab him at his morning coffee and find out what we need to know."

"Isn't that going to be . . . dangerous?" I asked.

Avery gestured around the restaurant. "It's a public place. And we *need* answers."

"Okay," I said. "We'll come back here first thing in the morning. My mom could drop us off on her way to work."

"We can't stay at your house tonight," Avery said. "Now that Magix knows we're back in Indiana, your house will be under close supervision."

"We could probably stay at Hamid's house," I suggested.

"And if he's working for the Mastermind?" Avery said. "They'd have us exactly where they want us."

"Then where are we supposed to sleep?" I cried. "On the street?"

Avery smirked, reaching up to tap the side of her hat. "I think we've got the perfect boon in here for that."

CHAPTER 22

FRIDAY, MAY 15
8:42 A.M.
GRAN'S KITCHEN, INDIANA

We had slept in a tent in Colter Park downtown. It hadn't been an ordinary, uncomfortable tent like the one my dad and I had used on a camping trip before I broke my leg. This was a boon tent. And it had been manipulated, spliced with another boon—a bit of mesh screen—to make it twice as nice.

When it was zipped closed, the tent became invisible to everyone on the outside, while the inside turned into a luxurious room way nicer than any hotel room I'd ever seen. There had been a bathroom, a small kitchen, and two beds that were far enough apart that I'd barely been able to hear Avery snore. It was actually amazing.

218

But now we paused before the entrance to Gran's Kitchen. The diner looked even more rundown in the morning light.

"Steve Talbot is probably going to recognize you," Avery said to me. "But *I* shouldn't be familiar to him."

"What are you saying?" I asked.

"Fluffball and I will go in first with the element of surprise and secure him in the booth," she said.

"How exactly do you plan on pulling that off?" I asked.

"With that, genius," said Fluffball, using his ears to point at an item draping between Avery's fingers. It was a long necktie, already tied in a loop to slide easily over a person's head. The pattern was bold, with large triangles of red, yellow, and blue.

I tried to think back to Fluffball's list. "I'm supposed to remember what that does?" I said.

"If the tie is put on by someone who has the knowledge of its true power, then the magic causes the wearer to be frozen in place," Avery explained.

"Can they talk?" I asked.

"Originally, no," answered Fluffball. "But the tie's a nip. Somebody cut a little bit off the skinny end, and now the person wearing it can move their head. But only their head." The rabbit chuckled, rubbing his paws together. "Pretty clever."

"Wait here," Avery instructed me, tucking Fluffball into her hat to obey the "No pets allowed" rule.

"So, you're just going to leave me out here?" I said, trying not to panic. "At least give me a boon to defend myself in case the bad guys show up."

"Here you go," shouted Fluffball from inside the hat. Suddenly, the magic baseball came flying up through the opening and I caught it in midair.

"Don't use it unless it's an emergency," Avery said. "You don't want to make a scene out here. We'll call you in as soon as it's safe." Then she turned and walked through the front door of the diner.

The moment she was out of sight, I stuffed the baseball into my pocket and moved along the outside of the building. The waitress, Kathy, had told us that Talbot always took breakfast in the same booth beside the window. If I was sneaky enough, I could watch Avery net him and then join them when it was safe to come in.

I thought I was in the right place, but sunlight was glinting off the glass, making it almost impossible to see in. I squinted, stepping into the flowerbed that bordered the diner. I tried to stay low, cupping my hands around my eyes. Then my foot caught a root and I stumbled forward, slamming my forehead against the glass.

Inside, I saw the pizza guy, Steve Talbot, just inches away from me. His eyes grew large as he recognized me through the glass. He turned away, trying to stand up. Avery was waiting for him, looping the tie around his neck before his backside had left the bouncy booth seat.

Avery stared through the window at me, tilting her head with a look of pure disapproval on her face. Her top hat was tilted back, and Fluffball's face was just peeking out under the brim. He pointed both ears in my direction and laughed rudely, his buckteeth shining in the morning light.

I peeled my face off the glass and retreated through the treacherous flowerbed. A moment later, I was inside the diner, sliding into the booth to sit beside Avery.

Across the table, Talbot didn't look too comfortable. His body was turned to the left, both hands braced on the edge of the table as though he were about to stand up. But his head was swiveling back and forth, finally stopping to focus on me.

"Mason Mortimer Morrison," he whispered.

I just sighed. Maybe I was finally getting used to this bad-guys-say-my-entire-name thing.

"You really think you can get away with this?" he asked quietly. "You're Magix's most wanted criminal. And if they don't get you, the Mastermind will."

"Who is he?" I asked, leaning across the table. "Who is the Mastermind?"

Talbot turned his face away from me, eyes closed, nose up in disdain. "You think I'll talk?"

"Yeah," said Avery. "We know you will." She held up the

truth shoe. "Will you do the honors?" she asked me.

I took the shoe and ducked under the table. Luckily, one of Talbot's feet was hovering a few inches off the floor as if he'd been in the process of jumping up. I quickly slid off his tan shoe and put the dirty sneaker in its place.

"That shoe is a boon that requires the wearer to speak only the truth," Avery explained as I popped back up beside her. Now that she'd shared the knowledge with him, the sneaker would work perfectly.

"This is a crime," Talbot muttered. "This is against Magix code three dash two four; a boon cannot be—"

"We know the law," Avery said, even though I didn't. "But like you pointed out: we're Magix most wanted." She shrugged. "What's an extra crime or two?"

"Who is the Mastermind?" I asked again.

"Just because I have to tell the truth doesn't mean I have to speak," Talbot said. "I won't answer any of your questions." The bell on the diner's front door chimed, catching Talbot's attention. "Besides," he said with a smirk, "looks like you're out of time."

I peered around the edge of the booth and quickly drew back. "Magix agents," I hissed to Avery. Just Clarkston and Nguyen this time. I risked another peek. They were glancing around Gran's Kitchen, clearly looking for someone.

222

"I'd say *you're* out of time, too," Avery said to our suspect. "When those agents find you sitting here with a paralyzation boon around your neck, you'll be brought in for questioning. It won't take much to realize that *you're* the real criminal here."

She pulled off her top hat, and Fluffball jumped onto the table. Digging up to her armpit, Avery quickly retrieved two items. The first was the transportation atlas, and the second was an old newspaper.

"What's that supposed to be?" Talbot asked, glaring at the paper.

"Invisibility newspaper," said Avery. "Works like camouflage. All we have to do is open the newspaper and as long as we're behind it, we'll disappear."

"It also has a really interesting article about an old lady who knocked down a bicyclist with her purse," said Fluffball. "She said he was going too fast—"

"Not now, Fluffball," I muttered.

"It *talks*?" Talbot remarked.

"What . . . I've been reading it when you guys make me go in the hat." The rabbit shook his head in disappointment. "Nobody appreciates a real newspaper these days."

Avery grabbed the sides of the newspaper and unfolded it, holding it sideways to cover our booth. I assumed the three of us disappeared, but it was hard to tell. I could still see Talbot and Avery, but the newspaper in her hands was shimmering with a slight magical glow. From where I was seated, there was just enough gap between the newspaper and the back of our bench for me to see if the agents were coming our way.

"We're not worried about getting caught," Avery said to our prisoner. "You know why?"

"Why?" spat Talbot.

"Because we came prepared. That atlas will transport us anywhere in the eastern United States, but you have to be touching the person that uses it. Answer our questions, and we'll take you with us when we go. Or you can play tough and we'll leave you here for Special Agents Nguyen and Clarkston to discover."

I grinned. Avery was really stepping up her game with this new tactic. She must have aced the intimidation portion of her detective training.

"Who is the Mastermind?" I asked again.

"I don't know, okay?" Talbot said. "I've never spoken with him. I only ever communicate with the Mastermind's right-hand man."

"And who would that be?"

"I don't know his real name," said Talbot.

"Ahh, this guy's useless," said Fluffball. "Let me bite off his fingernails."

Talbot's face twisted with fear. "Everyone just calls him the Cleaner!"

The Cleaner . . . wait a minute. My mom had spoken to a door-to-door salesman on Tuesday evening. A salesman selling *cleaning* solution. She'd sent him away, but he'd seemed very interested in coming inside.

I glanced at Avery. "I think one of our doorbell camera suspects just shot to the top of the list."

"Where can we find this *Cleaner*?" asked Avery.

"I don't know where he lives," answered Talbot. "Mostly, we just leave notes. I . . . I've only talked to him once over the phone."

"We're going to need that phone number," said Avery.

"Okay," said Talbot. "It's in my wallet. You can get it out of my pocket."

I climbed onto the table and reached down, slipping his wallet free.

"There's a little slip of paper in there with a phone number on it," Talbot said as I thumbed through. "That's it!"

I examined the number. It was written on the back of a Gran's Kitchen receipt.

"The Cleaner wrote this down for you?" I clarified. "This is his handwriting?"

Talbot shook his head. "No. It's mine. I jotted that down

when I got his number from Janet."

Avery beckoned for me to hold the newspaper. It took just a second to switch seats, and then her hands were free.

"*This* Janet?" she asked, setting Ms. Vanderbeek's fake Skyline Appliance card on the table.

"Yeah," he said.

"What can you tell me about this note?" Avery unfolded the napkin message we'd taken from Vanderbeek's closet.

"The Cleaner left that for Janet and me," he said. "We thought we were meeting him here, at Gran's Kitchen, but when we arrived at the scheduled time, he was already gone. All he left was that note, and the bill for his meal, expecting us to pay for it."

"Why did you come to my house pretending to be a lost pizza guy during my mom's lunch break on Wednesday?" I asked.

"I didn't know your mom was going to be home," he answered. "I had to plant evidence in your room."

"The five stolen boons from the church?" I checked.

"Yeah."

"But you didn't come inside," I said. "We watched the video. My mom was talking to you on the porch the whole time."

"I used a speed boon," Talbot confessed. "It allowed me to run past your mom at high velocity, dump a bunch of boons out of my magic pizza box, and get back to the porch in the blink of an eye. And I knew the doorbell camera couldn't record anything suspicious since I was using magic."

"But the camera never cut out," I said. "There should have at least been a blip in the footage."

"The sandwich," said Avery. "Your mom accidentally covered the camera with her sandwich for a second."

"And a second was all I needed," said Talbot.

"How did you know your way to Mason's room?" Avery asked. "Was this your first time in the Morrison house?"

Talbot shook his head. "I was involved in the first job, too."

"Stealing the boons from the church last month?" I asked.

"No," he said. "I'm talking about the very first job. We've had Mason Morrison under surveillance for *years*."

"Why?" I shouted, the newspaper trembling in my grasp. Avery glanced around the edge of our invisibility boon to see if my outburst had caught the agents' attention.

"I don't know," answered Talbot. "The Cleaner might have answers. And the Mastermind certainly does."

I sank back on my bouncy seat, feeling violated. People with magical knowledge had been spying on my family for *years*? Maybe my mom had reason to be paranoid.

"What was the first job?" I asked, my voice low and threatening.

"The Mastermind wanted your dad out of the picture," said Talbot, "so we framed him for the bank robbery."

I felt so paralyzed that the necktie boon might as well have slipped around my own neck. It took a few long, heart-pounding seconds for the words to really make sense in my brain.

"You . . . framed . . . my . . . dad?" I felt a rage bubbling up inside me. I wanted to leap across the table and put this guy in a headlock.

"Take it easy, chief," said Fluffball, hopping onto the table and positioning his fluffy self between Talbot and me.

"Why?" Avery asked our suspect. "Why did the Mastermind want Mr. Morrison locked away?"

Talbot swallowed nervously. "It was something we picked up on our surveillance of the house," he said. "Last year, the Morrisons were getting ready for Mason's twelfth birthday. A week before the big day, Mr. Morrison came home, telling his wife that he had picked up a special present for the boy."

"What was it?" I asked. Last year's birthday had been one of the worst, since it happened to be just one day after my dad's arrest.

Talbot shrugged. "He wouldn't say. Wouldn't even tell your mother what he'd found. He was keeping it a secret from her because he said he didn't think your mom would want you to have the gift. The way he talked about it made

228

us worry that he'd found a boon."

"Why would it matter?" asked Avery. "Igs keep boons all the time. That's the whole point—to let the magic rub off on them."

"Maybe my dad is an Ed," I whispered. The thought kept me shaking, and I turned to Talbot. "Did he have knowledge of real magic?"

"No," he answered. "He was an Ig just like you and your mom. But the Mastermind *really* didn't want this reversal boon going into your house."

"Hold on, pal." Fluffball spun to look at our suspect. "You said *reversal boon*?"

"We sent in a powerful detector to examine Mr. Morrison for magical residue," explained Talbot. "The results got the Mastermind panicked. Trace amounts of magic from a reversal boon were found on both of your dad's hands and in his pocket."

"What's the big deal about a reversal boon?" I asked.

"They're powerful," said Fluffball. "And often unpredictable. They literally reverse the magical effects of any boon that is exposed to them."

"The Mastermind had people scour every inch of your house," said Talbot. "But the reversal boon wasn't there. Your dad had definitely held it, though. And it was small enough to put in his pocket. We knew he was planning on giving it to you for your birthday. The only way the Mastermind could make sure that didn't happen was to remove your dad from your life."

I looked at Avery, trying to keep my voice steady against the pure anger I was feeling. "That's all we needed," I said. "Now we know for sure that my dad is innocent. We can use the boons from the hat to get him out of jail!"

"Mason." Avery sighed. "We've been over this. If we break your dad out, he'll just be a fugitive on the run for the rest of his life."

I grimaced in frustration. "Then . . . then . . . we'll take Talbot to the police," I said. "We can make him testify that my dad is innocent."

Talbot merely laughed. "You think what I just said is going to stand up in a court of law? Talk of magic and boons?"

I looked back to Avery for support, but she shook her head. "He's right," she whispered. "We need something more concrete if we want to save your dad."

I knew she was just trying to make our case as strong as it could be, but it felt like a betrayal. After all this time believing that my dad was innocent, I was one step away from proving it.

"Guys," Fluffball said. "Those Magix agents have a detector out. They're going to spot our nifty newspaper in about ten seconds."

Avery flipped open the atlas and grabbed a toothpick from the little tray with the salt and pepper shakers.

"Wait," I said. "I've got one more question before we decide to take him or leave him."

"Well, you better hurry!" squeaked Fluffball. "They're heading this way!"

I leaned across the table. "Where can I find evidence?"

Talbot swallowed, his eyes flicking past the edge of the newspaper I was holding. "The Cleaner," he finally said. "The Cleaner was the one who robbed the bank, and he stole the boons from the church, too. If you can locate him, he'll have proof that will exonerate you from Magix, *and* your dad from prison."

Avery reached across the table and touched Talbot's shoulder. Fluffball rubbed his head against her forearm, and I lowered the newspaper and grabbed her arm.

"There they are!" shouted Agent Nguyen, spotting us.

"Take your hand away from that boon!" called Agent Clarkston. "I'm not going to tell you again, Miss Lawden."

Lawden? I shot a confused glance at Avery just as she touched the toothpick to the atlas.

CHAPTER 23

T he world around us suddenly changed. The air was hot, and we definitely weren't in the diner anymore. We were outside in a shabby-looking park with scrubby grass. Without a table or benches to support us, Avery, Fluffball, and I crumpled to the ground. Miraculously, Steve Talbot did not fall. He remained paralyzed from the necktie, seated in midair.

"We have to act fast," Avery said, yanking the truth shoe off Talbot's foot and stuffing it into her top hat. "Magix Headquarters will have picked up the atlas signal. Agents will be here any second."

"He called you Miss Lawden . . . ," I muttered, folding up the newspaper in my hands.

232

"We're somewhere in Georgia," she carried on, completely ignoring me. "We leave Talbot here, while you and I transport ourselves to a more defensible location."

"What?" Talbot cried. "We had a deal! You can't leave me like this."

"We won't," said Avery, reaching out and ripping off the necktie. He collapsed to the ground with a groan.

"As in . . . *Frank Lawden?*" I continued, my gut tightening with nerves as I dared say it out loud.

"Just hold on to me," Avery said, toothpick hovering over a new spot in the atlas. Fluffball jumped onto her foot, but I just stood there, confused. She jabbed an elbow into my side and touched the toothpick to the map.

Suddenly, we were somewhere else, a car whizzing past and honking its horn. We jumped onto the safety of the sidewalk, and I noticed that Talbot was no longer with us, left behind for Magix agents to gather up in Georgia.

"There's a bus depot not far from here," said Avery, shutting the book. "We're about fifty miles from your house. If we hurry, we can catch a bus and be gone before the Magix agents follow the atlas's signature."

"No," I said. My mind was reeling. First with the news I'd just received about my dad, and second with the name Agent Clarkston had called Avery as we'd escaped. "I'm not going anywhere until you tell me who you are."

"Oh boy," mumbled Fluffball at our feet. "Here comes the drama."

She shrugged defensively. "I'm Avery."

"Lawden," I said. "Why did he call you that?"

Avery shifted uncomfortably, glancing from side to side as if hoping for a way out of this conversation. "He's my dad," she finally said. "Frank Lawden is my dad."

I was speechless for a second. Then I said, "Ha! I *knew* your last name wasn't *Lobster*." But she looked really upset. "Why didn't you tell me?"

"I didn't want you to know," she said. "I didn't want you to think that I had special privileges because my dad is the director of Magix."

"Just because your dad is in charge, doesn't change the fact that you're a great detective," I said. "You did that on your own. The training, the apprenticeship . . ."

Avery held up her hand. "There is no apprentice detective program at Magix."

"What?" I said.

"I'm not *really* a detective." She stared off down the street, unwilling to look at me. "I don't have any training or experience."

"So, you lied to me?" I said. "You told me whatever it would take to get my trust so I'd escape with you?"

"Well, I'm sorry I rescued you from having all your memories wiped. How rude of me!"

"Uh-oh," interjected Fluffball. "She's getting snarky now."

"Why didn't you just tell me the truth from the start?" I asked. "I would have gone with you anyway."

"Listen," she snapped. "You don't know what it's like to live in your dad's shadow. I want to work for Magix Investigation when I grow up, but even if I do make it through detective training, people will just say that I got there because of my dad. Just for once, I wanted to do something on my own. Something that really mattered. When I found that note in my locker, I thought that was the answer. Freeing you and proving you innocent would show everybody at Magix that I was legit."

That stung. So it wasn't about saving me from having a lifetime of memories wiped away. It wasn't about discovering the truth to uphold justice. Avery was only using me to prove how important and smart she was. . . .

"Well, I think you got what you need," I said. "We've got tons of useful information. Isn't it time to go running back to Daddy?"

"What are you talking about?" she retorted. "I can't go back now. There's a mole at Magix Headquarters."

"Look at you, using big fancy detective words," I said. "Probably makes you feel cool."

"Really?" said Fluffball. "You don't know what a mole is?"

"Of course I do," I barked. "It's a little rodent that burrows underground."

"It means there's a *spy*," Avery said, "or someone who is on the inside but working against the organization."

"Probably your dad," I taunted, slapping the rolled-up newspaper against my open palm.

"It's not him," said Avery.

"Think about it," I said. "He's at the top of the command chain. He could have easily delivered the note to your locker, knowing that you'd chomp on the bait as hard as you could. And we know the note was written by the same person who robbed the boon church *and* the bank."

"It's not him," Avery said again, her voice growing more tense.

"Your dad was the first person I saw in headquarters, and he was the one who led the discussion in my trial," I carried on. "He could have made sure that the evidence against me looked convincing, and—"

"It's not him!" Avery bellowed.

"Just because he's your dad?" I shouted back. "If you think my mom is a suspect, then your dad should be our *prime* suspect. At this point, I don't even know if I can trust *you*. What if you're just stringing me along to look like a hero so you can get into your stupid Investigation program?"

Avery clenched her jaw, a look of obvious anger on her face.

"I risked *everything* to help you," she whispered through her teeth.

"Well, maybe you shouldn't have," I spat. "I would already have this solved if I was on my own."

She threw the magic atlas down on the sidewalk between us. "Have a nice life." Then she turned and stalked away.

I glanced at Fluffball, who looked back and forth between us, twitching his ears. "Sayonara, kid," he said, waving a paw at me. "When in doubt, a rabbit always follows the less stinky path." And with that, he hopped to catch up to Avery.

I stood there fuming for a few moments, totally expecting them to turn around. But they didn't. Without looking back even once, Avery reached the bus depot, scooping up Fluffball as she moved out of sight around a corner.

I breathed out in a slow sigh. So, I was really on my own.

I folded the newspaper one more time and stuffed it into my pocket. Stooping, I picked up the atlas, noticing the toothpick poking out the top like a makeshift bookmark. Thumbing through the pages, I knew exactly where I wanted to go. Magix agents would be tracking the signal of the atlas, but hopefully Talbot would slow them down in Georgia. Besides, it wouldn't take me long to do this. I'd been saying it all along.

It was time to free my dad.

CHAPTER 24

I waited outside the tall chain-link fence at the prison for nearly an hour before I got a glimpse of my dad. He was with a bunch of other inmates, using up their time outside.

I slowly lowered the newspaper boon I had been shielding myself with, feeling confident that even the security cameras couldn't see me while it was in use. I wondered about trying to use the atlas to get myself inside, but it wasn't precise enough. I had decided to leave the heavy book on the ground a safe distance from the fence.

My heart began to race as I thought about what I was about to do. My dad was going to be so proud of me. He probably wouldn't know what to say. I knew we'd have a lot of catching up to do, even without all the magical stuff. I had only visited my dad three times since he'd been moved to this prison six months ago. It was a far drive from our house, and Mom was always so busy with her jobs. . . .

What was Mom going to think when I showed up with Dad? She was mad at him, but I knew she still loved him, too. And once I explained about how the Cleaner had framed Dad, Mom wouldn't be able to hold anything against him.

Finally, I saw my dad move off on his own, sitting next to the basketball court while a few other inmates got a game started. Basketball was never really Dad's thing. But he did like baseball.

Letting go of the paper with one hand, I fished the baseball out of my pocket. I'd been holding it safe since Gran's. I'd have to act fast now. If everything went as planned, I could get to my dad in just two throws.

My first toss was almost straight up, hard as I could. It arched just enough, coming down on the inside of the barbed wire–topped fence.

And just like that, I was inside the fence, instantly reappearing in the spot where the baseball landed.

Scrambling, I picked up the ball once more and threw it toward the basketball court. It landed just behind my dad, and *poof.* I was standing there, feeling nervous and excited at the same time.

I quickly held up the newspaper, its magical effect

camouflaging me from unwanted eyes. "Hey, Dad," I said, trying to sound casual.

He turned, glancing in my direction. I lowered the newspaper, suddenly becoming visible to him. My dad's eyes grew bigger and bigger until I was afraid they might pop out of his head.

"Mason!" he cried. "What on earth—"

"Shh!" I said, gesturing for him to join me behind the newspaper. "I'm here to take you home."

"What?" He stood abruptly, his face twisted in confusion. "How did you get in here?"

"We don't have very long," I urged.

He finally ran forward, catching me in a huge hug. It was nice, and I felt all warm inside, but we really didn't have time for that.

I pulled away, raising the newspaper to shield both of us. "Pick up that baseball," I said, pointing at it with my foot.

"Mason, you can't be out here," he said, glancing over his shoulder. "You could get—"

"We're fine for the moment," I said. "No one can see us while we're behind this."

"A newspaper . . . ," he said skeptically.

"It's actually a magical item called a boon," I said. "That baseball is, too. It'll transport you to wherever you throw it."

He scrunched up his face, probably wondering why I was goofing around with make-believe stuff at a time like this.

"I'm serious," I said. "Try it."

Reluctantly, my dad gave the baseball a timid underhand toss. It landed a few feet away, and my dad was suddenly standing over there.

His look of surprise doubled. "What the—"

"There are lots of different boons," I said, quickly moving over to him. "I can explain more on the way." I scooped up the ball and pitched it to him. "Catch!"

I lifted the newspaper into position again as he caught it. Neither of us were transported anywhere. Fluffball had explained that the baseball didn't work if it was caught by another person. It was a fact I was relying on to get us both out. Dad would go over the fence first, then throw the ball back to me. I'd catch it and throw it over to transport myself.

Just a boy and his dad playing ball and escaping from prison. Nothing to see here.

"Come on!" I said, moving toward the fence.

"*Magic*, Mason?" My dad shook his head. "There's no such thing."

"Seriously?" I shrieked. "Didn't you just teleport? How do you explain that? And you saw how invisible I was behind this newspaper."

"I don't know." He held up his hands. "It's just a lot to wrap my head around."

"Magical items are all over the world," I explained. "It's just, most people don't know what they really are, so they can't access their power."

"So, it's only magic if you know about it?" he said.

"Yeah," I replied. "Everybody else just gets some luck rubbed off."

He scoffed. "I could have used some luck a year ago."

"You had it," I said, suddenly remembering the reason he was framed. "Up until the day before you got arrested."

"What do you mean?" he asked.

"Look, I know you're innocent. I'm working with a Magix apprentice detective . . ." I trailed off. "I guess she isn't really a detective, but I *was* working with her. And we found out who framed you."

"You did?" he cried.

"Well, we don't know who he is or where to find him," I said. "But we know he's called the Cleaner. Anyway—the Mastermind wanted to get you arrested because you had a powerful reversal boon that you were planning to give to me for my birthday."

"Mason . . ." Dad scratched his chin. "What are you talking about?"

I grunted. "It's a lot. I know. Let's just get out of here, and I can explain more once you're free."

Suddenly, my dad threw the baseball back to me. Instinctively, I caught it, letting go of the newspaper with one hand. But the look on my dad's face wasn't full of excitement like mine. In fact, he looked sad.

"I can't go with you, kiddo," he said, voice quiet.

"What?" It felt like something was squeezing around my heart. "Of course you can. We can get out of here."

He reached out and put a hand on my shoulder. "It's not that simple."

"Yes, it is. We just have to throw the baseball . . ."

"Where would we go?" he said. "I'd be a wanted man. That wouldn't be freedom. All it would do is put you and your mother in danger."

"I don't . . . I don't understand." I was fighting back tears. "You don't want to come with me?"

"Of course I do," my dad said. "More than anything, I'd love to come with you. But it's not right."

"But you're innocent!" I cried.

"I know," he said softly. "And I'm glad you know it, too. But that doesn't change what everyone else thinks."

"We can get proof," I said. "The Cleaner . . . If we can find him, we might be able to get proof that you're innocent."

He smiled sadly. "That would be nice."

I gritted my teeth. I couldn't tell if he really believed in the magic or not. Did he think I was just making all this up?

"Hey!" someone shouted from across the yard. I turned in time to see a guard moving toward us, his gun drawn. Lost in the conversation, I had forgotten to hold up the newspaper. Now my cover was blown.

"Go, Mason," Dad said. "If you find out the truth, you know where to find me."

The guard shouted at me again. "Put your hands where I can see them!"

I looked at my dad. "The present," I said. "The one you were going to give me for my birthday last year . . . What was it?"

This time there was a little happiness behind my dad's smile. "It's something you've wanted for a while. I was worried Mom wouldn't let you have it, so I had asked my buddy Carson to hang on to it until your birthday. But things changed . . ."

"Mr. Kilpack?" I asked. "What was it?"

"Carson still has it," Dad answered. "Go find out."

Another security guard was joining the first. "I'm not going to ask again! Put your hands up!" They were closing in on me quickly.

"I love you, Mason," my dad said.

"Love you too, Dad." Then I pulled the newspaper up in front of my face and heard the two guards gasp in shock at my disappearance.

I ran for the fence, keeping the boon paper between the guards and me. When I was close enough, I let go for just one second so I could throw the baseball. It landed outside the fence, transporting me away from trouble. But also away from my dad.

I picked up the baseball, scooped up the atlas, and ran, not daring to look back for fear that Dad would see my tears.

CHAPTER 25

I was out of breath by the time I got to Carson Kilpack's house. I hadn't dared use the atlas to transport myself directly to my street. Hoping to throw off Magix's trackers, I'd teleported myself from the prison to the far side of town and used the rest of my money for a bus ticket to get a few blocks from my neighborhood. I'd run the rest of the way, anxious to find out exactly what sort of present had caused such huge problems in our life.

Carson was a friend of my dad's. He lived just a few houses away from us, though Mom and I didn't see him much anymore. I skipped up the front steps and rang the doorbell, following up with an impatient knock. A dog started barking inside, and the second the door cracked open, the furry pet burst through,

246

jumping up on my leg, nipping at the large book of maps I had tucked under my arm. The dog was just a friendly little cocker spaniel, so I put my hand down and let him lick it.

"Mason!" Carson Kilpack said from the doorway. "How have you been?"

I must have grown in the last year, because I was almost as tall as he was. His sandy hair was longer than the last time I'd seen him, and he had a nice beard.

He clapped his hands at the dog. "Back inside, boy." The pet yipped once but obeyed, licking my leg once more before disappearing through the doorway.

"My dad said you were keeping something for me," I said, cutting straight to business. "A birthday present he wanted to give me?"

He looked a little confused, and I felt my hopes falling. Maybe he'd forgotten about it. Or worse, what if he'd gotten rid of it?

"Well, do you have it or not?" I asked impatiently.

"I did," he said. "But your mom was just here to pick it up less than a half hour ago."

"What?" I cried. Had she known Carson Kilpack was keeping the present all along? And if so, why had she waited until a half an hour ago to get it from him? On top of that, it was Friday morning. Wasn't she supposed to be at work?

I retreated from the Kilpacks' front door without even

saying goodbye. By the time I hit the sidewalk, I was headed for my house at a full sprint. I went straight for the garage, assuming that the front door would be locked, and I still didn't have my key.

I punched in the garage code and ducked inside as soon as the door was high enough, skipping up the stairs and bursting into the house.

Wreckage was standing in the kitchen.

He was wearing the same outfit from the High Line yesterday: black boots, yellow reflective crossing-guard vest, and dark welding mask. His gloved hand was clutching one end of that familiar red-white-and-blue jump rope. But the other end trailed out, tying up Wreckage's two prisoners.

My mom and Avery Lawden.

They were seated on a pair of dining chairs that had been scooted back-to-back. The jump rope was wound tightly around both of them, securely lashing them in place. It was even wrapped over their mouths so they couldn't shout a warning, although my mom seemed to be trying anyway.

"Mason Mortimer Morrison," said Wreckage in his raspy voice. "You have played right into my hands."

"The birthday present . . . ," I muttered.

"Yes," said Wreckage. "We didn't know where your father had hidden the reversal boon until you were kind enough to get him to blab about it."

"You were at the prison?" I said in disbelief. "Where?"

"The Mastermind has eyes and ears everywhere," said Wreckage. "Once we knew the location of your present, I sent your mother to collect it from Mr. Kilpack. I was lucky enough to find Miss Lawden here, interrogating her prime suspect— your mom."

I didn't feel any anger toward Avery anymore. In fact, I was embarrassed that I ever had. It didn't matter if she wasn't a *real* detective. She was a smart kid. And my friend. I was the one who had messed everything up by going to the prison. Now everyone was in danger and Wreckage had my birthday present.

"Where is it?" I asked boldly.

"Oh, you mean this?" With his free hand, Wreckage reached into his vest and pulled out a small, thin box covered in green wrapping paper. "The Mastermind will be happy about this. But even happier about getting you."

"You don't have me," I said, raising my fists as if I might win in a fight against the burly man.

"I think you'll come willingly," said Wreckage. "I can't go back empty-handed. Either you're coming with me or they are." He tugged on his end of the jump rope, tightening the wraps around them.

"Where will you take me?" I asked.

"Somewhere safe," he said. "No harm will come to you. I

cannot make the same promise for your mother and friend."

What was I supposed to do? I looked at Avery for help. She always had good ideas. The girl's eyes were big as she looked at me and then to the top of the refrigerator. I glanced over to see where she was drawing my attention.

There, on top of the fridge, was a black top hat. It was resting with the brim up, and as I watched, a white rabbit popped out of the opening like a good old-fashioned magic trick.

"Catch, kid!" Fluffball's deep voice boomed across the kitchen as he pulled something from the hat and tossed it to me. It was an ordinary-looking clothes hanger, but I remembered from Fluffball's list what it could do.

I dropped the atlas I'd been toting under my arm and caught the hanger, throwing it end over end at Wreckage's face. The masked supervillain was too fast, ducking as it whizzed over his head. But he must not have known what the hanger could really do. It came back like a boomerang, the hook catching the length of jump rope he was holding and slicing right through it.

Wreckage grunted in anger as the ropes around his prisoners began to dissolve. I caught the boomerang hanger with one hand, pulling the baseball from my pocket.

Wreckage's short length of jump rope was growing again, and he whipped it toward me as I tossed the baseball over the kitchen counter. It landed next to the dishwasher, and I was suddenly standing over there as his jump rope wrapped around thin air.

I dropped to my knees to take shelter behind the counter. I needed to reach the magic hat on top of the fridge. Pulling the newspaper from my back pocket, I held it up, rising slowly.

"You can't hide from me, boy!" Wreckage shouted. The end of his jump rope whipped out, shredding the newspaper in half and causing me to drop behind the counter again.

So his welding mask would identify any boon I tried to use. And his reflective immunity vest would protect him from magical attacks. It was time to think of a new strategy.

I opened the fridge and popped the top of an egg carton, grabbing three eggs in each hand. Then I sprang up from behind the counter, hurling them like little white bombs.

A couple of them splattered across Wreckage's chest, and he hesitated in confusion. Then I hit him in the welding mask, blurring his vision with drippy yolks.

"Ha-ha!" Fluffball cackled from atop the fridge. "That'll scramble his detector for a while!"

My mom and Avery were almost free of the severed jump rope when I saw Wreckage reach into his vest once again. His gloved hand reappeared, the dreaded drumstick clutched tightly. Before I could shout a warning, he brought it down, sending a shockwave through my entire house.

All of the windows in the house shattered immediately. In the cupboard, I heard plates and cups breaking, while a frying pan and a pot tumbled from the stovetop, cracking against the kitchen floor.

I flew backward, slamming into the dishwasher and whacking my head so hard I saw stars.

"Mason Mortimer Morrison!" shouted Wreckage.

My head throbbing, I pulled myself up to see that Wreckage had taken a new position in the house. He had moved around the kitchen counter, opening the door into the garage and standing in front of the doorway. My mom had retreated behind the dining table, but Avery hadn't been so lucky. She was lashed up in the jump rope again, pinned under one of Wreckage's muscular arms.

"This is your last chance to surrender yourself," he said. "It's you or the girl. Choose!"

"Wait!" I said, standing up slowly. "Leave Avery here. I'll go with you."

"Mason!" she cried. "You can't!"

"Smart boy," Wreckage said.

"We're so close to finding out the truth," Avery continued. "If you go with him now, there's no telling what he'll do to you."

"He said he wouldn't hurt me," I said, moving cautiously toward the enemy.

"Uh-huh," said Fluffball. "I'm guessing he'll buy you an ice-cream cone, too. NOT! He's a bounty hunter, kid! You leave with him and we'll never see you again."

I looked at Avery. "I'm sorry about what I said before. I should have listened to you. You're a good detective, no matter what."

She shook her head. "That doesn't matter anymore. You can't go with him."

"I have to," I said. "It's the only way to keep the rest of you safe."

"That's right," coaxed Wreckage. "Just a few more steps and we—"

There was a loud cracking sound, and Wreckage's body jerked. Then he lost his balance, letting go of Avery, who staggered away. Wreckage fell forward, landing flat on his masked face, motionless.

Hamid was standing in the doorway to the garage, still clutching the frying pan he'd used to knock out Wreckage.

He looked at us with wide eyes. "That dude was a bad guy, right?"

CHAPTER 26

FRIDAY, MAY 15
11:46 A.M.
MASON'S KITCHEN, INDIANA

"Hamid?" I cried. "What are you . . . How did you . . . ?"

"I just clonked that guy on the back of the head!" he said. "That was like a video game! I came in all stealthy . . . The garage door was open. I heard signs of a struggle. Found this weapon on the floor." He hefted the frying pan. "My heart was beating so fast, it was like my strength just leveled up. I went *bam* and smashed that supervillain. Critical hit. He's out cold." Hamid stretched out a toe and nudged Wreckage. "Are you guys okay?"

I stood up and grabbed the top hat off the fridge, pulling Fluffball down with it. "Get me Avery's credit card," I said.

Surprisingly, the rabbit didn't argue. He ducked straight

out of sight, returning a moment later with the card pinched between his two front paws.

I stepped over to Avery, using the sharp boon card to slice away the coils of jump rope that held her. The severed parts began to dissolve while the rest shortened to the size of a normal jump rope, the end still lying across Wreckage's limp hand.

"Oh, Mason!" Mom said, coming around the dining table and pulling me into a hug. "I thought that piano lesson would never end!"

"You know I don't take piano lessons, right?" I asked, stepping away from her and glancing at her wrist. To my surprise, the bracelet was not there.

"I cut it off when I first got here," Avery explained. "Before Wreckage showed up."

"Thanks," I said.

"We're storing the bracelet in the top hat for the moment," said Fluffball.

"It talks . . . ," Hamid stammered, pointing a shaking finger at Fluffball. "The bunny talks!"

"That's *rabbit* to you, kid," grumbled Fluffball.

"I'm still getting used to it," Mom said.

Fluffball turned to me. "I was going to say that stinkiness runs in the family, but she actually smells quite nice."

"You're not freaking out, Mom?" I asked.

"Oh, I'm freaking out, all right," she answered. "I'm just trying to keep it inside right now. Avery told me everything."

"And you believe it?" I said, not able to believe it myself.

She sighed, shrugging her shoulders. "What choice do I have? I was completely convinced that you were at piano lessons for two days straight, had a conversation with a talking rabbit, reached into a bottomless top hat, got tied up by a magic jump rope, saw you teleport across the kitchen with a baseball, and had my house destroyed by a drumstick. I'd say I'm convinced that magic is real."

"Mason." Avery's voice caused me to turn. She was kneeling on the floor beside Wreckage. She and Hamid had rolled the big man onto his side, and I found myself staring at his black, egg-smeared welding mask. There was a face under that mask. If we learned the bounty hunter's true identity, it might help lead us to the Mastermind.

Avery reached out and pushed up the black face shield.

"That's . . . ," I muttered, unable to finish.

"Wreckage is Special Agent John Clarkston," Avery whispered. She rocked back, sighing heavily. "I think we found the mole."

"You should call your dad," I said. "Warn Magix."

Avery shook her head. "Not yet. Even if he believes me, the others won't without proof."

"You could wear the truth shoe," I said.

"The truth shoe?" Mom questioned.

Avery dug the shoe out of her top hat and held it up. "This old thing."

"How does it work?" Hamid asked.

"Whoever is wearing it can only speak the truth," I said.

"No way!" the boy shouted. "Magic is soooo cool!"

Avery turned on him, her eyes narrowing suspiciously. "What are you doing here, exactly?"

"Knocking out bad guys," he said proudly.

Avery didn't look convinced. "Unless you did that just to gain our trust." She threw the shoe at his feet. "Put this on."

"What?" Hamid backed away from the shoe. "It doesn't look like my size."

"It'll still work," I said. "Just do it, Hamid."

"So you can learn all my secrets?" He folded his arms defiantly. "No way."

"We won't ask you anything embarrassing," I promised. "It's just to prove that you're not working with him." I gestured at the unconscious Wreckage.

"How do I know I can trust *you*?" Hamid snapped.

I sighed, slipping out of my own sneaker. We didn't have time for this. The kid could be so stubborn sometimes. I jammed my foot into the truth shoe. "Ask me anything."

Hamid rubbed his hands together excitedly, but my mom beat him to it.

"Did you get into my chocolate stash last week?" she asked.

Mom had already asked me this question when she thought her supply looked lower than expected. I had denied it then, but with the truth shoe on . . .

"Yes," I said, swallowing hard at the admission. "I ate two mint truffles."

"Oh, you little . . ." Mom trailed off, preparing another incriminating question. "Do you ever drink straight out of the milk jug?"

I flinched. She'd caught me doing it a few months ago, and I'd promised never to do it again. "At least once a day," I admitted. "Usually with my snack when I get home from school, but sometimes at breakfast if you're not looking."

"What about the collection of dried boogers that I found on the wall in the TV room?" Mom asked. "Did those really belong to Hamid?"

"Hey! What?" Hamid shrieked.

"No," I answered, my cheeks turning bright red. "They were my boogers."

"One more question," Mom said, her tone the most serious yet. "Do you really think your dad is innocent?"

I took a deep breath. Of all the lies I'd told my mom, this

one was the longest running. I think she'd given up on Dad when the therapist had told us to accept the truth. I didn't like to talk about it, but whenever it came up, I just told my mom what she wanted to hear. *Guilty. Guilty. Guilty.* But inside, I'd never given up on him. And with the truth shoe on my right foot, I couldn't lie now.

"Yes," I said firmly. "I *know* Dad is innocent. They framed him for the bank robbery to stop him from giving me that present . . ."

I trailed off, suddenly remembering the little green box Wreckage had taken. I dropped to one knee beside him, pulling open his reflective vest and seeing the present sticking out of his shirt pocket.

I grabbed it, hands trembling. "Do you know what it is?" I asked my mom.

"Yeah," she said, giving me one of her sad smiles. The kind that seemed to say *I love you, and I wish things were different.*

"I didn't want him to give it to you," Mom said. "That must have been why he asked Carson to hold on to it. So I wouldn't find it and take it away before your big day. But I was wrong. You should have it."

Taking a deep breath, I peeled up the edge of the wrapping paper.

Someone grabbed me from behind.

I dropped the small box, shouting in surprise. Wreckage—Agent Clarkston—was awake. His dirty welding mask covered his face once more, and he'd taken advantage of my distraction to spring up and get me. Mom and Hamid screamed, and I saw Avery's hand plunge into her top hat. But it was too late.

With one arm clamped tightly around my middle, Wreckage used his free hand to hold up a *Get Well Soon* card. It had a cartoon drawing of a walrus with a box of tissues, and a thermometer dangling from his mouth.

"That's a boon!" I heard Fluffball warning. "If he opens the card—"

Wreckage opened the card.

CHAPTER 27

Wreckage and I were alone in a dim building. It looked like an empty warehouse, with only a row of small windows far overhead where the sunlight shone in, lighting up every particle of dust hanging in the air.

The *Get Well Soon* card in the bounty hunter's hand had obviously been some kind of transportation boon, immediately whisking the two of us out of my kitchen and depositing us here. Wreckage shifted slightly, tucking the card away. I took advantage of the moment to squirm against his grasp. I broke free, sprinting for the nearest door in the side of the warehouse. I'd only made it a few feet when something struck me in the back. I stumbled as a red-white-and-blue jump rope began to wrap itself around me. In a moment, my legs were lashed together and I fell, not able to catch myself, with the rope also pinning my arms to my sides.

Wreckage sighed, striding slowly toward me, smoothing his free hand across the Velcro closure on the front of his reflective vest. I traced the other end of the jump rope to his left hand. Tied up like this, there was truly nothing I could do. I was lying on the dusty floor with only my head poking out of a red-white-and-blue cocoon.

Standing at my feet, Wreckage lifted his right hand and pushed up the black shield of his welding mask. "I'll admit, you gave us a lot more trouble than we expected." He wasn't bothering to use his scratchy Wreckage voice now that his secret identity had been blown.

"What are you going to do to me?" I whispered.

"What am *I* going to do?" he said. "Nothing. I'm going to leave you here. A nice little present for the Magix agents."

"What?" I cried. "That doesn't make any sense! *You're* an agent. Why bother with all this disguise? Why not just arrest me as Clarkston?"

"I was working that angle, too," he answered. "But Wreckage isn't restricted by all the laws that Magix puts on their agents. *Don't use this in public. Don't use that.* Wreckage was a more effective way to hunt you. Plus, the Mastermind is paying me very nicely."

"Traitor," I muttered. "Magix will find out about this. They'll know you're a spy."

"See, I don't think so," replied Clarkston, tying the excess length of jump rope high up around a support post in the middle of the large empty room. "I've been the Mastermind's inside man for years."

I drew a surprised breath. "You're the Cleaner, too?"

Clarkston chuckled. "No, no. I did put the Cleaner's note in Avery Lawden's locker, but he's just a pawn in all of this."

"Sounds like more than a pawn," I said. "Talbot told us that the Cleaner is the Mastermind's right-hand man."

"Me, Talbot, West, the Cleaner . . . The Mastermind doesn't play favorites." Clarkston shrugged. "I guess we're all in this for our own reasons."

"What's yours?" I asked bluntly.

He sniffed. "You think I like my job?"

"Which job?" I asked. "The one where you're an agent for Magix? Or the one where you're paid to kidnap children?"

"Either," he said. "I've been involved with Magix for nearly my entire life. But soon I'll be free of my responsibilities. And I'm not the only one who feels this way. The Mastermind has helped many of us to see the truth."

"Whatever you're planning, it'll never happen," I said. "Magix will figure out what you're doing and stop you."

"That's cute," said Clarkston. "But once the Mastermind's

plan goes through, there will be no more Magix."

I swallowed hard. What was he talking about? A plan to bring down the Magix organization? And how was I tied into all of this?

"Why me?" I asked. "I know the Mastermind has been targeting me for years. Why did it have to be me?"

"You'll see soon enough," Wreckage said. "I've got to go now. But once I change my clothes, Clarkston will be back to arrest you. He has a strange hunch that it might be worthwhile to check out this old warehouse." He dusted his hands together and withdrew his *Get Well Soon* card. "Then all that will be left is a celebration while we watch Magix burn."

"Your vest," I called. "How can you use that card if your vest makes you immune to magic?"

"Every boon has its secret," answered Clarkston, tugging apart the Velcro that closed the front. Then he opened the card with the sick walrus and disappeared.

I had no idea how long it would take Clarkston to change out of his Wreckage clothes and come back to arrest me. I wiggled and I wriggled against the jump rope that held me, but Clarkston had tied me to that post so I'd have no chance of reaching one of the outside doors.

I managed to rise to my feet, but the jump rope was tied off too high to reach, and I couldn't exactly climb while wrapped up like a burrito. I tried a few times before finally falling on my side, defeat and hopelessness claiming me.

I wondered about the birthday present I'd been so close to opening. I didn't wonder about its power as a reversal boon. That didn't matter to me. But I was dying to know what the actual item was. What had my dad bought that my mom didn't want me to have? A new video game? A razor?

Now I'd probably never know.

The door to the warehouse squeaked open, and I twisted to see who it was. My heart sank. Two agents in gray suits and top hats. That was fast.

Clarkston and Nguyen.

CHAPTER 28

Agent Clarkston reached me first while his partner swept around the interior of the warehouse, making sure everything was secure.

"Hello again," he whispered quietly so Nguyen couldn't hear. Then he raised his voice and shouted to his partner. "It's him! It's really him!"

Agent Nguyen was at Clarkston's side in a flash. "Unbelievable," she muttered. "What is this?"

"Jump rope boon," Clarkston answered. "It's a trap I set up in this warehouse. Looks like it actually paid off!"

"Liar!" I shouted. "Listen to me, Nguyen. Your partner is a mole. He worked his way into Magix so he could spy for someone called the Mastermind. Clarkston is Wreckage. He's

266

the bounty hunter whose mess you had to clean up at the High Line. He's trying to stop me from finding out the truth—that I was framed for stealing the boons out of the church. That the Mastermind also framed my dad for the bank robbery."

"That's enough," Nguyen said, silencing me. "I've been working with Clarkston for a long time."

"The kid's obviously unstable," Clarkston said. "Not sure what he has against me."

"No!" I yelled. "He's been using you, Nguyen. He staged this whole thing to bring me in. How did he know to search this particular warehouse?"

"Oh, please," said Clarkston. "I've got traps like this all over the country—"

"He's working with the Mastermind to take down Magix," I interrupted.

"Let's pack him up and get back to HQ," Clarkston said to his partner. "He's cost the organization a lot of time and resources. I'm tired of listening to his lies."

"I'm not lying," I said. "In fact, I *can't* lie."

"What do you mean?" Nguyen asked.

In response, I wiggled my right foot.

It took a second for either of them to recognize the truth shoe sticking out through the coils of jump rope around my ankles. They looked at each other for a stunned moment. Then Agent Clarkston pounced on Nguyen.

The two went tumbling across the warehouse floor, Clarkston pinning her in an expert wrestling move. Like an inchworm, I maneuvered onto my side and drew up my legs, planting a solid kick with both feet to the side of Clarkston's head. He rolled off Nguyen and she leaped up in one swift motion, reaching into her fallen top hat.

Nguyen withdrew something that looked like a strap, coming to my side before Clarkston could get up.

"Go," she whispered, reaching around me with the strap. "This seat belt is a transportation boon that will take you back to your last location."

"What about you?" I asked.

"I'll deal with Clarkston—make sure he doesn't follow," she said. "You just get the proof you need to make this right."

Behind her, Agent Clarkston rose. His nose was bleeding, and I saw a familiar drumstick clutched in one hand.

"Hold on!" Nguyen cried as he brought up the stick.

She jammed the metal end of the seat belt into the buckle, and it cinched tight around my middle.

At once, I was in my kitchen again, gasping for breath and shaking from fear. I must have made a crash when I reappeared, because Avery, my mom, and Hamid came running in from the living room.

"Mason!" Mom cried.

Avery used her magic credit card to cut away the jump rope while I told them what had happened. At last, I rose to my feet, sliding out of the truth shoe and into my old sneaker that was still waiting for me on the floor.

I looked around, shocked and grateful that I was back safe. And so soon! For a minute there, I wasn't sure I'd ever see my mom and friends again.

"Here." Mom's voice cut through my thoughts. She was holding the half-unwrapped present. "Hopefully this time you won't get interrupted."

Swallowing against a lump of emotion, I peeled back the rest of the wrapping paper. Opening the little box, I finally saw the present my dad had wanted to give me.

It was a throwing star.

It wasn't bat-shaped, like the ones Batman uses, but I didn't care. This thing looked so cool. It was about the size of my palm, with six sharp silver points. I lifted it reverently, letting the box and wrapping paper fall to the floor. Then I pulled back my arm to throw it against the wall.

"Na, na, na!" Fluffball and my mom both yapped at me in unison.

"No throwing it in the house!" she said.

"And," explained Fluffball, "if you stick that star into anything, it'll send out a blast of magic that'll reverse the power of every boon within range."

"What's in range?" I asked, lowering my arm. "The dishwasher?"

"Actually," Avery said, "there was no boon in the dishwasher. Looks like Ms. Vanderbeek really did know how to repair appliances."

"I'm talking about Avery's top hat," continued Fluffball. "It could basically implode. That's the trouble with reversal boons. Hard to say exactly how they'll reverse each magical effect."

I nodded. It was sort of bittersweet for my mom and dad to finally trust me with a throwing star, only to be told by a bunny that I couldn't throw it.

"I don't think we should stay here," I said, slipping the metal star into my pocket. "Clarkston's going to assume I came back to the house, and I'm not sure how long Agent Nguyen can hold him off."

"I can't believe Clarkston's the mole," muttered Avery. "He's been a top agent for years."

"He admitted to delivering the Cleaner's note to your locker," I said. "But Clarkston doesn't think very highly of him."

"Probably because he knows the Cleaner could expose everything," said Avery. "Clarkston's probably not happy that the Cleaner still has evidence that could prove you and your dad innocent."

"How unhappy would you say he was?" asked Hamid. I could tell the kid was hatching a plan.

"What do you have in mind?" I asked.

"Well, if Agent Clarkston knows we're trying to find the Cleaner, then he might try to get rid of him first," said Hamid.

"Not a bad idea," seconded Avery. "Maybe we could use Clarkston's paranoia and follow him to find the Cleaner."

Mom was shaking her head. "We can't risk going up against Wreckage again. Especially if there's a possibility that the Cleaner could be there to back him up."

"What else can we do?" I cried. "We don't have any other leads!"

"Leads?" scoffed Fluffball. "My nose is always a reliable lead!"

"To find salad, maybe," I snapped.

"I don't like salad," Hamid jumped in. "Unless it's at least seventy-five percent croutons."

"That's just like eating a loaf of dried-up bread," the rabbit argued.

"What does that have to do with finding the Mastermind?" I asked.

Fluffball twitched his ears. "You're the one who brought up the salad, and I think—"

"SHUT UP!" Avery suddenly bellowed. The kitchen fell

silent and we all turned to the girl, who was gripping her forehead as if to keep all her thoughts from spilling out. "Everybody just shut up for a second and let me think." When she spoke again, her voice was much softer. "Let's talk about what we know in order of events."

"Okay," I agreed. "The first thing that happened was almost three years ago. Someone put a magical vent cover in my bedroom."

"A dampener boon," said Avery, "to prevent anything magical from getting to you."

"And the Mastermind had people watching my family all that time," I said, "because two years later, my dad came home with a present for me that turned out to be a reversal boon. They didn't want him to give it to me, so they framed him for robbing a bank and got him arrested."

"One year later," said Avery, "Ms. Vanderbeek and Steve Talbot meet at Gran's Kitchen, where they find a note from the Cleaner written on a napkin. The next day, the boon storage church was robbed."

"And the day after that," I said, "Vanderbeek came to our house to give our dishwasher a free 'tune-up,' which caused it to give us trouble off and on for a month. About that same time, my mom goes to a work party where the raffle drawing was rigged for her to win the music-box boon."

"Only, Tom Pedherson threw a wrench in the Mastermind's plan when he cheated and took your mom's raffle ticket," Avery said.

"He did *what*?" Mom muttered. "We all thought it was too good to be true that the music box collector won the music box in a raffle drawing."

"Because your mom didn't get the music box," continued Avery, "Ms. Vanderbeek had to go to your school as a substitute librarian to encourage you to do a book report using a music box."

"Then, last Tuesday, the same Ms. Vanderbeek came into our house to fix our dishwasher," I continued, "giving her an opportunity to go upstairs and steal the vent cover out of my bedroom floor."

"Now that the dampener vent was no longer in place," Avery said, "you'd be able to use the music-box boon and show up on Magix's radar so they would arrest you."

"But none of this explains *how* I used the music box," I said. "I was just a random Ig with no knowledge of magical boons."

"Not random," said Avery. "Not if the Mastermind has been watching you for years. There has to be an explanation. Let's think about how all the boons involved could work together. A transportation music box, a dampener vent cover, and a reversal boon throwing star."

"The music box is obvious," I said. "It had been used in the robbery of the church, so Magix was just waiting for me to activate it again so they'd have a reason to arrest me."

"Fluffball," Avery said, "what effect would a reversal boon have on a dampener?"

The rabbit twitched his ears. "It's hard to say without examining them. And technically, you can never use a detector to analyze a dampener because it shuts down the detector."

"Then how can anyone get the knowledge of what it does?" I asked.

"If you'd taken a picture of the vent cover, I could have inspected it," he answered. "Boon detection works fine through photographs as long as the magical item is clearly visible."

"But if you had to guess," said Avery, "what could a reversal boon do to a dampener?"

"Well, it would reverse the dampener's power," he said. "Maybe turn it into some sort of amplifier."

Avery snapped her fingers. "That's it!" she said.

"That's what?" I asked, not following her advanced line of thinking.

"If a dampener causes boons *not* to work for Eds," she explained, "then isn't it reasonable to assume that a reversal item *would* cause boons to work for Igs?"

Fluffball nodded his head. "I guess it's possible . . ."

"That's why the Mastermind didn't want my dad to bring home the reversal boon," I said. "Because reversing the power of the vent cover could have caused me to activate a boon without knowledge."

"And the Mastermind wasn't ready for that . . . yet," said Avery. "Once all the pieces were in place to frame you, they wanted you to activate the music box and get arrested."

"But wait," I said. "In order for that to work, the reversal boon would have to be in my house. But the throwing star was at the Kilpacks' all this time."

"Maybe they found another reversal boon that would work," said Avery.

"Those are incredibly rare," said Fluffball, "but it's possible."

"That would mean that the Mastermind's people brought the reversal boon into my house when the time was right," I said.

"Ms. Vanderbeek could have had plenty of opportunities when she was working on the dishwasher," said Avery.

"But why would she take the dampener vent cover if they wanted to use its power in reverse?" I asked.

"The dampener has a lasting effect, remember?" Avery said. "It soaks into the boons around it. Maybe that same lingering power would exist if it were an amplifier. Maybe Vanderbeek exposed the music box to the reversed dampener, letting it soak up some power so you could accidentally activate it in your book report the next day."

"But the music box wasn't even at my house yet," I pointed out. "Tom Pedherson didn't bring it by until after ten o'clock that night."

"And even if that were true," my mom chimed in, "why didn't *I* activate the music box when I opened it to show Mason at breakfast?"

"We're still missing something," I said.

"Let's go back to our suspect list." Avery dug out her pad of paper. "So far we've spoken to your mom, Mrs. Damakis, Hamid, Tom Pedherson, and the pizza guy, who turned out to be Steve Talbot. We also know that the repairwoman, Ms. Vanderbeek, a.k.a. Janet West, was involved. While you were gone, I had Fluffball sniff out the package your mom took inside during her lunch break."

"And?" I asked.

"My nose is a gift to all humankind," said the rabbit. "But I smelled nothing magical."

"We need to find out more about that cleaning salesman my mom talked to," I said.

Avery turned to her. "Did he leave a business card? Or any way to contact him?"

My mom shook her head. "I didn't give him the time of day."

"Wait!" I cried, digging in my pocket for the piece of paper we'd taken from Talbot. "We have this!" I unfolded the receipt and held it out so the others could see the Cleaner's phone number written on the back.

"You think we should just call the guy on the phone?" Fluffball asked.

"What're we supposed to say?" added Hamid.

But I wasn't really listening to them. For the first time, I was studying the other side of the receipt.

"April second," I whispered.

"What?" they all asked in unison.

I turned the receipt over so they could see what I was reading. "This receipt was from Gran's Kitchen on April second, the day before the Cleaner robbed the church."

"Yeah?" said Fluffball. "What's your point?"

"Talbot said that the Cleaner beat them to the diner and left them the note on the napkin," I continued. "But he also mentioned that the Cleaner ate at Gran's Kitchen and left Talbot to pay for his meal."

"That's low," muttered Hamid.

"Look at what they ordered," I said. "A meal for Talbot, and a meal for Vanderbeek. And then this"—I pointed at the item on the receipt—"ordered forty-five minutes earlier."

"A pineapple Oreo milkshake," read Hamid. He shuddered. "I've never heard of that flavor combination."

Avery had gone rigid. I could almost hear her heart beating. "I have," she whispered, locking eyes with me. "Pineapple Oreo. It's the only flavor, in his opinion."

"Who?" Mom asked.

"Lionel Albrecht," said Avery. "The custodian at Magix Headquarters."

Why didn't we see that sooner? "The Cleaner."

CHAPTER 29

"I know exactly where he lives," said Avery, reaching into her top hat and pulling out the atlas.

"How?" I asked. Lionel Albrecht was the custodian at Magix Headquarters. I didn't exactly expect him to be good friends with Avery's family.

"He moved into our apartment building about two and a half years ago," she said.

"He *what*?" I cried.

"I know, I know," she muttered. "It seems suspicious *now*. But we had no reason to suspect him before. I guess it makes sense. The Mastermind needed someone close, to keep an eye on my dad."

279

"Where do you live?" Mom asked her.

"New York City," answered Avery. "Upper East Side."

"Awesome!" Hamid said, pumping his fist in the air. "I've always wanted to go there."

"You're not," Mom snapped. "You need to go home, right now."

"Why?" Hamid asked. "My parents went out for the night. That's why I came over here."

"Besides," I said. "I think we can trust him now. After all, he was the one who knocked out Wreckage."

"I interrogated your friend while you were gone," Avery said to me. "We didn't even need the truth shoe. He spilled everything."

Hamid held up his hands. "I'm sorry I took your *Battlefield 900* poster. I was going to bring it back soon."

"That was *you*?" I shook my head.

"It looks really cool in my room," said Hamid.

I groaned. "Maybe my mom's right. Maybe you should go home."

"Actually, I think Hamid should stay with us," said Avery. "Agent Clarkston knows he's involved, so he might be a target."

Mom glanced around the ruined kitchen like she might find another option. "Fine," she finally said.

Avery spread out the atlas on the countertop. "I guess it's time to go investigate Lionel Albrecht's apartment."

"Hold on," said Mom. "Didn't you tell me that Magix was tracking that atlas?"

"Yeah," Avery replied. "But we don't really have another way to get there. We'll just have to act fast."

"Maybe I can buy you some time," Mom suggested. "Draw the danger away so you'll have an opportunity to check out the apartment."

"What are you talking about?" I asked.

"Maybe I could take the atlas out for a spin once we get to New York," said Mom. "I could keep transporting myself around the city, or even from state to state, making sure the agents come after me, instead of you."

"Ah," said Hamid. "Like a mother bird."

"Did you just call her a bird?" Fluffball asked.

"It's a tactic that some mother birds use to protect their babies," explained Hamid. "Sometimes, if a predator comes near, the mother will pretend to be hurt. She'll flop her wings around like she can't fly and draw the predator away from the babies in the nest."

"Yes," Mom said. "Do you think it could work?"

I smiled at her. "That's very brave, Mom."

"Well, you know I've always wanted to travel," she replied, taking the atlas from Avery, who pointed to the right neighborhood on the map.

"Everybody hold on to each other," I said, grabbing my

mom's arm with one hand and Hamid's shoulder with the other. Avery scooped up Fluffball and touched Hamid. We all held our breath as Mom touched the tip of the pen to the road map.

We appeared in New York City in the blink of an eye. Mom stepped away, hovering the pen over a different neighborhood on the map.

"You kids be careful," she said. "Go find that proof."

"Thanks, Mama Bird," Hamid said.

"Hamid?" Mom said. "Don't ever call me that again." Then she touched the pen to the atlas and disappeared.

"We're close to my building," Avery said, pointing down the street. "Let's go."

The Lawdens' apartment building was pretty nice. We skipped right past Avery's place on the first floor and made our way up the stairs to the third. Fluffball was sniffing and checking every step along the way, but aside from a couple of jabs about my smell, the bunny didn't notice anything. All too soon, our little group was gathered outside apartment 309.

I looked at Avery. "What are we supposed to do?" I whispered.

"We break in and have a look around," she answered. "Just like we did at Vanderbeek's house."

"What if the Cleaner is here?" I asked.

"He won't be," Avery assured me. "It's a Friday afternoon. He'll be at Magix Headquarters, cleaning up for the weekend. Fluffball," she said, taking off her hat and lowering it to the rabbit on the floor, "I need you to get the deodorant."

"Deodorant?" I said. "I don't remember that from Fluffball's list."

"That's 'cuz I didn't tell you about it," he said. "I was afraid you'd try to use it." The rabbit dove into the hat.

"Do you think he could get me a secret weapon while he's in there?" Hamid asked. "I saw she's got that slicing credit card." He turned to me. "What's your secret weapon?"

I scratched my head. "The baseball, maybe? I don't really have one."

"Okay," said Hamid. "Maybe I could get something that deals double damage. And it's invisible, so the bad guys don't see it until it's too late."

"They're not weapons," Avery scolded him. "The whole reason these magical boons exist is to *benefit* regular people, not hurt them."

"Voilà!" Fluffball's head emerged from the top hat on the floor. "This, my friends, is a very special stick of deodorant." Avery helped him out, taking the item from between his paws and sticking the hat on her head once more.

"Is that the kind that gives you a rash?" Hamid asked.

"Because I used some deodorant once, and it gave me a rash."

"This'll do worse than that," replied the bunny. "Wipe it on any surface and that object will disintegrate. But it'll only last a couple of seconds before it rematerializes."

Avery popped off the cap and began swiping it across Lionel Albrecht's front door.

"Oooh," said Hamid. I thought he was commenting on the fact that the wooden door was dissolving. Then he added, "That smells niiiiiice."

"Come on." Avery capped the deodorant and slipped it back under her top hat as she moved through the open doorway and into the apartment.

Finally being here—in the home of the one person who supposedly had all the evidence to free my dad and me—was almost too much to bear. My hands were cold and soaked with sweat. It seemed hard to swallow as I surveyed the place.

Lionel Albrecht wasn't much for interior decorating, which told me that he lived alone. It was a studio apartment—the whole place was basically one huge room. The kitchen was to our left. On the right was a small sitting area with a puny TV and a lumpy couch with a blanket and square pillow with fringe around the edge.

Against the far wall was his bed, a single twin-size mattress on a low frame. But it was tidily made. There wasn't a single wrinkle in the covers, which were folded neatly over his pillow. In the corner of the room was a door cracked open a few inches. Squinting, I could see that it led into a bathroom.

"I don't even see where he *could* be hiding evidence," I whispered.

"Fluffball," Avery said, "do you see anything suspicious?"

"Not yet," he said, hopping across the floor. "But if there's a boon in here, I'll sniff it out."

"Okay," Avery said to me. "You and Hamid check the bathroom. I'll go through the closets."

My ten-year-old neighbor and I moved to the back of the apartment with cautious steps.

"So, this dude's bad," Hamid whispered. "Like, superbad? How would you rank him compared to Wreckage?"

I didn't know how to answer for a moment. "Albrecht *seemed* nice when I met him," I answered, slowly pushing the bathroom door inward. "But it was just an act."

It was very dark in the bathroom. Hamid grabbed my arm. "Where's the light switch?"

"I don't know," I said, palming across the wall for it. "I've never been here before."

"There's a ninety percent chance he's hiding in the shower." Hamid pulled his phone from his pocket and flicked on the flashlight app. As the bright light flashed across the bathroom,

Hamid screamed. That caused me to scream, and we both leaped backward.

"What happened?" Avery called from across the room.

"Nothing," I said. "I didn't see anything."

"Me neither," replied Hamid, shining his flashlight into the bathroom again.

"Then why'd you scream?" asked Fluffball.

"I like to be prepared," said Hamid. "Just in case there *was* something scary."

"Give me that light," I said, pulling the phone from Hamid's hands.

"I've only got thirty percent battery left," he said, "so use it wisely."

I spotted the bathroom light switch and flicked it on, handing the phone back to Hamid.

"Guys!" Avery called from the other room. "I think I've found something!"

That was quick! Hamid and I left the bathroom. I was almost to the bed, where Avery and Fluffball were waiting, when I tripped, my right leg going stiff and causing me to fall flat on my face.

Fluffball laughed, but Hamid reached down to help me up. "Are you okay?" he asked.

"Just a cramp," I said, swatting away his hand. "I'm fine."

But I really wasn't. My leg had cramped so badly that I couldn't bend it. Awkwardly, I scooted the remaining distance to Avery's side.

"Did anyone else think this bed looked a little too nice?" she asked. "I'd say it's never been slept in."

"But Albrecht *lives* here," I pointed out, massaging my leg.

"The couch pulls out into a bed," she explained. "It didn't take much of an investigation to realize that he's been sleeping there instead."

"Yeah," Fluffball said, sniffing at the bed. "But I'm not picking up any magic."

Avery reached down and grabbed the bedspread. Whipping it back revealed only a crisp, clean sheet. A little more carefully, Avery peeled back the sheet, too.

"Still nothing," said Fluffball.

From my position on the floor, I could now see under the bed, since Avery had pulled back the covers. "There's a box," I said, reaching under to grab it. But I couldn't get it to budge. "It's wedged," I said. "Can you lift up the end of the bed a little?"

Avery set Fluffball on the mattress, while she and Hamid grabbed the footboard and hoisted it up a few inches.

The cardboard box slid out easily, and I felt my breath catch in my throat. There was something written in marker across the box's lid. I instantly recognized the handwriting as a match for the note Avery had found in her locker and the message left for Vanderbeek and Talbot on the napkin from Gran's Kitchen.

Personal belongings of Lionel Albrecht

a.k.a. the Cleaner

TOP SECRET

"No way," Hamid whispered, letting go of the bed. "It actually says *top secret*. This is so cool."

Unable to hold it alone, Avery dropped the bed and it struck the floor with a loud clunk.

The cardboard box in front of me exploded.

CHAPTER 30

The entire box didn't explode, but the lid blasted off, smacking me in the face and knocking me backward. Music started playing—a rock song from the 1990s.

Something silver whizzed past my head, missing my ear by less than an inch and sticking into the wall beside the bed's headboard.

It was a CD. But it was glowing red-hot. As I watched, it exploded like a miniature bomb, blasting a fist-size crater in the wall.

"Boon!" I heard Fluffball shout over the music. But he wasn't pointing at the deadly CD. His long white ears were pointing at the box.

289

It looked like there were several items inside, but the only one I had time to notice was a CD player. No sooner did I lay my eyes on it than the small machine spit out another red-hot CD. This one went over my head, narrowly missing Hamid as he leaped face-first onto the bed.

And the CD player didn't stop there. It shot another and another, launching the dangerous disks in every direction across the room.

Luckily, my leg was feeling much better, so I scrambled backward, taking shelter next to Avery and Hamid. Hamid had tumbled off the mattress, and they were hiding behind the bed's footboard.

The deadly CDs weren't slowing down. They stuck into the walls and ceiling like saw blades, each one detonating with a fiery explosion.

Fluffball was still on the bed, mostly burrowed under the single pillow, but he poked his head out to risk a glance at the CD player.

"There's a stop button on the player," he said. "It should shut down the boon's power if we push it."

"How did this happen?" Avery cried. "A boon isn't supposed to hurt us unless we know what it does. We couldn't even see that thing!"

"That's not completely true," Fluffball said. "A boon has to be *activated* by someone who knows what it does. But it can

290

still hurt others. Think about how Wreckage knocked down those Igs at the High Line with his drumstick shockwave."

Two CDs crashed into each other in midair, exploding with a burst of sparks.

"So, someone activated this CD player from a distance?" I said.

"No," said Fluffball. "It was already running when we got here. Someone pushed the play button a long time ago."

"Then how come it didn't start spitting CD blades until I pulled it out from under the bed?" I asked.

"I think we should worry more about turning it off than who started it," said Hamid.

"Right," Avery said. "If that box holds our evidence, the last thing we want is for those CDs to light it on fire."

"How do we get close to it?" I asked.

"Like this," Hamid said bravely, leaping to his feet. He snatched the pillow off the bed, causing Fluffball to let out a panicked scream and dive down next to Avery and me. Hamid moved around the end of the bed, holding the pillow out like a shield.

A CD struck the pillow and exploded, little downy feathers bursting out like a cloud. The fabric pillowcase caught fire and Hamid shrieked, yelling, "Abort! Abort!" He threw the ruined pillow to the floor and sprinted over to take cover behind the couch, two CDs missing him by mere inches.

"I'm going to crawl under the bed and see if I can reach the stop button," said Avery.

"I don't think you're going to fit," I said. "It's pretty low."

She tried to duck underneath, but her shoulder got stuck. "Fluffball," said Avery, pulling herself out. "Go under and shut off the CD player."

"What?" cried the rabbit. "Why me?"

"You're the only one small enough," I said.

"You think I'm expendable," he said, sitting up on his back legs and folding his arms. "I won't go." He closed his eyes and turned up his nose.

Avery grunted in frustration. "I can't think of anything in the hat that would help."

"What about those elbow pads?" Fluffball said.

"Elbow pads?" I asked. "You never mentioned those before."

"They're not in the hat, Stinky. They're over there." He pointed back toward the couch with his ears. "Looks like one of Albrecht's personal boons."

"You mean these?" Hamid asked. His hands appeared above the couch and he pulled a pair of protective elbow pads from an end table.

"Yeah. Those," Fluffball said. "They must have been important to a really bad roller skater who did something good with their life."

"What do they do?" I cried.

"Immunity boons," the rabbit explained. "Once you strap them around your elbows, they will protect your arms from other magical boons."

"Just the arms?" Avery asked.

"Picky, picky," he said. "One of you has to put those on and go out there before this bed gets ripped apart and we lose all our cover. You'll have to use your arms to block all the incoming CDs."

"It should be Mason!" Hamid called, flinging the elbow pads toward us. "He's trained his entire life for this moment!"

"You have?" Avery asked.

I shrugged, strapping one of the pads onto my elbow. "Hamid and I used to play a video game like this."

"Blocking exploding CDs while wearing elbow pads?" she questioned.

"Well, it's not *exactly* like this," I admitted as she helped me put on the other one. In the video game we were blocking laser bolts with force fields around our arms. And if we died, we just started over at the last checkpoint.

"Good luck out there," Avery said, tugging the elbow pads to make sure they were secure.

I took a deep breath and silently counted to three. Then I leaped up with a battle cry, holding out my arms in front of me.

There was a burning CD headed straight for my face. Instinctively, I lifted my arm to block. The disc glanced off my forearm without any pain, shooting upward and lodging into the ceiling.

"Yeah!" I shouted, bringing my other arm around to block the next searing CD.

I advanced slowly, step by step, punching and knocking aside every dangerous CD that came near me. In no time, I was standing above the cardboard box with a clear view of the CD player. But there was a problem. I was working so hard to block the discs—I couldn't possibly bend down and push the stop button.

"Avery! I need help!" I cried, swinging my arms together to block a pair of CDs from hitting my chest. "I'll block for you, but I need someone else to turn it off!"

"Okay!" I heard her reply. "I'm coming out."

I took a sideways step to provide better coverage for her. The number of burning discs seemed to double, and my arms were getting really tired. The video game was way easier than this!

"I'm right behind you," Avery said. Risking a glance back, I saw that she was on her hands and knees. "I'm going to reach around your leg and shut it off."

"Do it quick!" I said, seeing her hand creep past my ankle, feeling for the dangerous CD player inside the cardboard box.

"Got it!" she cried. I looked down just in time to see her press a button. But it wasn't the right one. The music picked up in speed, the voices sounding like chipmunks.

"That was the fast-forward button!" I bellowed. Suddenly, the CDs started flying twice as fast as before. My arms felt like a blur as I followed my instincts and relied on my years of video game training to bat away the hailstorm of dangerous discs.

"Oops!" Avery said, her hand fumbling across the front of the CD player again.

The discs struck faster, and one of them clipped my thigh, ripping my pants and buzzing over Avery's head behind me. I punched away another, my arms feeling like they were turning to lead.

Then Avery's hand finally slammed onto the stop button. The music died, and the CD player made a soft whirring sound as it powered down.

"Is everyone okay?" I asked, dropping my weary arms to my sides. Hamid emerged from behind the couch, and Fluffball tentatively crept around the bed's footboard.

"You were almost out of cover," said Hamid, pointing at the side of the bed that had taken the brunt of the attack. The bottom sheet had burned away, and the mattress was ripped open, exposing smoldering stuffing and springs.

"Yowzer," said Fluffball. "That explains a lot."

"Like what?" I asked, stripping off the elbow pads and handing them back to Avery, who dropped them into her top hat.

"That bedspring." Fluffball pointed with his ears. "It's a boon."

"Why didn't you notice it before?" I asked, annoyed.

"It was inside the mattress, under a sheet," he defended.

"You couldn't see through a sheet?" I cried.

"I'm an Angora rabbit," he stated. "I don't have X-ray vision. Believe it or not, a boon detector like myself has to *see* a boon in order to detect it!"

"I thought you sniffed them out," I said.

"It's a blend, okay?" Fluffball snapped. "You ever smelled something that seems familiar, but you can't quite place it until you see it? That's how it works for me. Yes, technically, I have to *see* the boon to identify it, but my sniffer points me in the right direction."

"What does the spring do?" asked Avery.

"It activates when it's stretched out," said Fluffball. "It freezes other boons that are in close proximity anywhere below it."

"That's why the CD player started shooting," Avery said. "The play button was already down, but the boon was frozen because the spring was stretched out. When we moved the bed, the spring must have contracted."

I nodded, finally understanding. "And without the spring to freeze the CD player, it started launching deadly discs."

"Just another reason to download digital music," muttered Hamid.

"Wait," I said. "Maybe that was how the music box activated during my book report. Maybe someone had planted a boon in my classroom that would freeze the music box until the perfect moment."

"How is this different than the vent cover dampener?" asked Avery.

"The dampener stopped boons from activating," explained Fluffball. "The bedspring froze boons that were *already* activated."

"This was obviously some kind of security system," said Avery. "The only way to get the cardboard box was to move the bed, which would release the spring and wake up the CD player."

I looked over to see that Avery was holding the lid to the cardboard box. It appeared to be slightly charred, but all the handwritten words were still clearly legible.

Avery and I moved over to inspect the box.

"I think it's time to see what the evidence tells us."

CHAPTER 31

I carefully lifted out the CD player and peered into the cardboard box.

"It's mostly clothes," I said, trying not to feel too disappointed. It was sort of like opening a present that you thought was going to be a new video game controller but turned out to be a sweater.

"We need to study everything," said Avery, reaching into the box to pull out a pair of men's black pants—the nice kind of pants, like what my dad used to wear to work. She set them on the bed as I pulled out a blue button-down dress shirt. It was very wrinkly, all tangled up with a long black-and-white striped necktie.

"Hey," I said. "My dad has this same tie." As I said the words, I realized what it meant. "These are my dad's clothes!"

"Really?" said Hamid. "How did they end up in a top secret box in New York?"

"No," I said. "They're not *actually* his clothes. At least, I don't think so. He was wearing this tie when he was arrested. It's probably still locked up in evidence."

"And this?" asked Avery, lifting up a blue-and-orange hooded sweatshirt.

"That's *mine*!" I cried, snatching it from her hand.

"That was the same sweatshirt you were wearing in the security video when you robbed the boon church," Avery said.

"But mine is still at home," I said. "Or at least it was on the floor when we were up there yesterday."

"And I'm guessing these pants are just like yours, too," Avery said, holding up another pair from the box.

"So, the Cleaner has a pair of clothes identical to what you and your dad wore on the days of your crimes," said Fluffball. "Think this is the proof we were looking for?"

"I'm hoping there's more," I said, turning back to the box.

"A picture of you," said Avery, holding it up. It was my school picture from last year. Pretty creepy that an old man had that in a box under his bed. "And a picture of your dad."

That was one of Dad's profile pictures on social media.

The Cleaner must have printed it off. "And an Indiana vehicle license plate," said Avery, holding up the next item.

"That's the same number on our car," I said.

"I'm guessing it was the car your dad was driving when he got arrested," said Avery.

"Whoa!" said Hamid, reaching past us to get into the box. "Why wasn't this the first thing you guys noticed?"

He was holding a couple of huge stacks of cash.

"We're rich!" Hamid cried, lifting the money above his head.

"It's not ours," Avery said.

"Why not?" he asked. "We're already wanted criminals. Might as well be rich." He looked at the money closer. "Dude," he whispered in awe. "They're all hundred-dollar bills! I've got to count this . . ."

"You don't have to," I said. "It's a hundred thousand dollars."

"How do you know?" he asked.

"That's got to be the missing cash from the bank robbery," I said. "When they arrested my dad, they found four hundred thousand dollars in the trunk of his car. But that wasn't all of it. There was a hundred thousand that they never recovered."

Avery nodded. "Albrecht must have kept some as his payment for robbing the bank."

"Why hasn't he spent it all?" Hamid asked. "Wasn't that robbery like, a year ago? I would have bought so much stuff . . ."

"The cash is marked," I explained, sharing what I'd learned from my dad's case. "Albrecht probably realized he couldn't spend it without raising flags that could get him caught."

"Ah, man," Hamid said, dumping the bills onto the bed. "What good is money if you can't spend it?"

"There are ways to clean up stolen money so it can be used," I said. "Albrecht was probably just waiting for the right opportunity."

"Is that enough proof for you?" Fluffball asked.

I shrugged. It was the most we'd found, but it didn't explain *how* the Cleaner had done it. "Is there anything else in the box?"

"Nope," said Avery, tipping it sideways. "Wait!" She reached in and plucked something out. It was a large safety pin, pinched between her fingers as she held it out for our inspection.

"Yep, that's a boon," said Fluffball.

My heart started racing. "What does it do?"

"It's a disguise boon," he explained. "It's been manipulated to fit a very specific purpose."

"Which is?" I pressed impatiently.

"You can pin a photograph to your shirt, and it alters your face and your size to look exactly like the person in the picture."

I snatched the photographs of Dad and me. "Pinholes," I said, holding them out so the others could see the two tiny holes. "This is it!"

"So, last year, Lionel Albrecht put on your dad's clothes, got a matching car with a matching license plate, and pinned Mr. Morrison's picture to the inside of his shirt," Avery said. "Looking exactly like your dad, he robbed the First Central Bank. Maybe he used a transportation boon to move most of the cash into your dad's trunk, and he timed it just right so that your dad would be driving past the bank on his way home from work."

"Then, last month, the Cleaner does it again," I said. "This time wearing my clothes and pinning my picture to the inside of his shirt so he could make it look like I'd stolen all those boons from the church."

"That doesn't work," said Fluffball. "You and your dad were both captured on regular cameras committing the crimes. This pin creates a magical effect. If it were the Cleaner in disguise, the cameras wouldn't have been able to record him."

"Why not?" Hamid asked. "I totally took a video of two flying CDs crashing into each other."

"You *what*?" I said.

"Well, it wasn't actually on purpose," explained Hamid. "I dropped my phone on the bed when the CD player started

302

shooting. I must have accidentally pressed record."

Avery was shaking her head slowly. "That's not possible."

"Look," said Hamid, already holding his phone. "I'll show you." He turned the screen toward us and pressed play.

The video began with a scream as the phone jostled, falling to the bed, landing propped at an angle against the bedcovers. The screen was half-covered, but I could still see the far side of the room—an open closet door with a long mirror hanging on the back.

I heard the music and our conversation on the video, but I couldn't actually see any of the magical CDs. And I noticed that every time Fluffball had said something, the video's audio bleeped out.

"It's just a blank room," I said.

"Shh," said Hamid. "Wait for it . . ." He peeked around at the screen. "There!"

Looking at the reflection in the closet mirror, I saw two glowing CDs collide in a shower of magical sparks.

"That's the only one I got," said Hamid. "For some reason it didn't pick up the others."

Avery turned to me. "The mirror," she whispered.

"Is it some kind of boon?" I asked.

"Nope," said Fluffball, sniffing toward the open closet door. "That's a regular old mirror."

"It doesn't need to be a boon," Avery said. "It's the reflection!" She jumped to her feet. "Hamid! Can you take another video?"

"I don't know," he said. "My battery's already down to twenty-two percent . . ."

Avery grabbed his arm and dragged him over to the closet mirror. "I'm going to pull something out of my hat. I want you to stand where you can see me *and* my reflection in the mirror. You ready?"

"Rolling," he said, holding up his phone.

Avery took a deep breath and reached into her hat, the brim going all the way to her shoulder. A second later, she pulled out the electrifying light bulb we had used at the High Line. She held it up for Hamid to see, then lowered it back into the hat.

"Let's watch it," I said, crowding next to Hamid.

When he pressed play, half of the screen was blacked out, completely covering the spot where Avery had stood. "Whoops," said Hamid. "I must have had my finger over part of the camera."

"But look!" Avery pointed to the other side of the screen. "You can see the magic in the mirror."

It was a view of her back, but Avery was right. The magic top hat could clearly be seen.

"I don't understand what this means," Hamid admitted.

"It's the answer to everything!" I exclaimed. "How many cameras saw me leaving the boon church?"

"Just one," answered Avery.

"And only one camera captured my dad coming out of the bank," I said. "And what do those two cameras have in common? Both of them had bits of broken mirror underneath."

"They did?" Fluffball said.

"Yes," I replied. "When the Cleaner was speeding away from the bank, he hit a truck carrying custom windows and mirrors. And we thought there had been a car accident under the camera outside the church because there were bits of crunched-up mirror."

"But you don't think it was a wreck?" Hamid asked.

"What if somebody installed mirrors around both of those cameras?" I said. "So instead of recording actual footage, it was recording a *reflection*!"

"But wouldn't the image be reversed?" Fluffball asked.

"Not if they used *two* mirrors," Avery said.

"Don't you think someone would have noticed a couple of mirrors strung up around the cameras?" said Hamid.

"Not if people's attention was on a more important crime," I said. "The mirrors only needed to be in place for a couple of minutes. Then they could have been rigged to fall to the street and break. That's why the custom windows truck slammed into the pole holding the camera," I guessed. "And the debris would have hidden the fact that there were already pieces of broken mirror under the camera."

There was a loud bang on the apartment door. All of us jumped, and Hamid let out a little squeak of fear.

"Lionel Albrecht!" called a familiar voice from the hallway. "This is Special Agent Clarkston with Magix Investigation. Open up!"

Avery started grabbing all the evidence—the clothes, pictures, cash, license plate, and safety pin—and stuffing it back into the *top secret* box. Hamid and Fluffball quietly crossed the room and took shelter behind the couch.

"We know you're in there!" Clarkston called. "Open this door, or we'll break it down!"

"Why is *he* here?" I hissed at Avery. Wreckage and the Cleaner were supposed to be on the same evil team.

"If Magix suspects they have a mole," she whispered, "then maybe Clarkston's trying to make himself look innocent by turning in the Cleaner."

It was actually a good strategy, for a bad guy. But where was Agent Nguyen? Why hadn't she stopped him in the warehouse? Avery picked up the cardboard box and moved across the room, following Hamid's example and taking cover behind the small table in the kitchen. I kept up with her, but the two rickety chairs didn't seem like they'd do much good in sheltering us against someone as powerful as Wreckage.

"Agent Clarkston," said another man's voice from the hallway. It was so quiet that I found myself leaning forward to hear what they were saying. "I just got word from HQ. They've found the music box!"

"What?" Clarkston replied. "After all this time?"

"The recovery team pulled it out of the Amazon, fifteen miles downstream," answered the voice.

Clarkston grunted. "Let's get back to headquarters immediately."

"But what about Albrecht?" asked the man.

"Securing the music box takes top priority," Clarkston replied.

"Lawden's going to have questions about that," the man said. "Especially after what happened to Nguyen."

"Agent Nguyen was a traitor," snapped Clarkston. "Lawden did the right thing by sending her to the black site for questioning." I heard them shuffle away from the apartment door, Clarkston's voice fading as they moved down the hallway. "All units be advised: Operation Music Box has just entered the final phase . . ."

I didn't move for a long time, drawing my breath in through my nose and out through my mouth, trying to steady myself.

"We have to warn your dad," I whispered to Avery. "We have enough evidence. He'll be able to help us."

"We still don't know who the Mastermind is," she said.

"But we know his right-hand man," I said. "It'll have to be enough."

Avery sighed. "I guess it's time to turn ourselves in."

"Top three criminals in Magix history . . . ," said Hamid. "This is going to be big."

"No offense," I said. "But technically, you're not wanted, Hamid."

"Still, it's probably not a good idea for you to come with us into Magix Headquarters," Avery said.

"Is it because I'm just too powerful?" he asked. "My very presence could cause the whole place to explode?"

"Umm . . . no," said Avery. "But it will be dangerous to take you in. They'll try to wipe your memory. Besides, we could use someone on the outside."

"Really?" he said. "For what?"

Avery grinned. "I've got a job for you."

CHAPTER 32

"This is a doorbell," Avery said, holding up the little button. It was strange to see it not attached to the wall.

Avery, Fluffball, and I were in the Lawdens' apartment on the first floor now. Hamid was no longer with us, having used the seat belt transportation boon from Agent Nguyen to transport himself back to my kitchen. I hoped he would be safer there. Plus, I wanted him to meet up with my mom and fill her in on what happened when she got back from traveling.

Nobody had been home at the Lawdens' apartment, but Avery had used her key to let us in. It was much nicer and more decorated than the Cleaner's place upstairs. Avery had led us into her dad's home office, entering the director's master code

309

on a small safe and producing the detached doorbell.

"It's an emergency boon that summons the Doorman," Avery explained. "All I have to do is push the button and he'll appear."

I took a deep breath, holding the box of evidence in both hands. "I'm ready."

Avery pressed the doorbell. To my surprise, it still made a little chiming sound. The Doorman appeared immediately, turning left and right with a look of utter shock on his face.

"You!" he shouted, his eyes on Avery. "And *you!*" he yelled louder, his eyes on me.

"We're turning ourselves in," Avery explained, holding up her hands to show that she meant no harm. "Could you please open a door to Magix Headquarters?"

"Don't think you're getting away with this," he said, moving toward the office door.

"Umm . . . we don't," I said. "That's why we're turning ourselves in."

The Doorman reached out, his diamond ring making a soft click as it touched the hard metal doorknob. I looked at Avery as she scooped Fluffball off the office desk.

This was it. Hopefully, the evidence we'd found and the things we'd learned would be enough to convince Frank Lawden of our innocence. He could help us compile the evidence into non-magical proof that would free my dad.

The Doorman yanked open the office door, and we found ourselves staring into the carpeted hallway of Magix Headquarters. The two guards on duty leaped to their feet as Avery and I stepped in, the door slamming shut behind us.

It was strange to think that, technically, I was still inside Frank Lawden's home office, shrunk to a microscopic size and housed inside the Doorman's diamond ring. This thought didn't last long, as the guards all but pounced on us. They knocked my evidence box to the floor and pinned my arms to my sides with a long chain that was definitely a boon, judging by the way it sparkled and wrapped around me on its own.

"We come in peace," Avery said. She was chained up, too, but I couldn't see Fluffball anywhere. "You can tell my father that we're willing to answer all of his questions."

"I'm afraid your father won't be hearing anything you have to say," said a voice from the hallway to the left.

I whirled, gasping aloud when I saw who was striding toward us. It was Wreckage. Not Agent Clarkston in his gray suit and top hat—he was dressed as *Wreckage*. The welding mask was covering his face, and the reflective immunity vest glimmered in the fluorescent lights of the hallway.

And our enemy wasn't alone. Wreckage was flanked by half a dozen Magix workers in gray, though I didn't recognize any of them.

"Do something!" I shouted to the guards. "That man is

Special Agent Clarkston. He's a hired bounty hunter working to take down Magix."

But instead of setting us free, the guards offered the dangling ends of the chains to Wreckage. "They're all yours, sir," one of them said.

"The Mastermind will be sure to reward your loyalty," Wreckage said.

"Stiiiiiinky!" came a battle cry from a familiar deep voice. I saw Fluffball pounce, a blur of white against the dark carpet. He landed on Wreckage's leg, sinking in his huge buckteeth.

Wreckage howled in pain, his gloved hand coming down and slapping the rabbit to the floor. Fluffball leaped up, but before he could strike again, Wreckage had him by the ears.

"You wanna piece of me?" Fluffball goaded him, red eyes wincing in pain as he dangled by his ears. "I've eaten carrots that were tougher than you! It's going to take a lot more than—"

Fluffball was instantly silenced as Wreckage ripped off the red boon collar.

"No!" I cried, trying to lunge at him, but the guard held me back.

Wreckage tossed the collar and the bunny to the floor like they were garbage. "Put them in that box and let's go," he instructed one of his workers. "We don't want to keep the Mastermind waiting."

It took a second for the workers to corner Fluffball. He looked scared, eyes darting around the hallway without a trace of his usual intelligence. Wreckage took the chains from the guard and dragged us down the hallway.

"I don't understand," Avery said. "Why isn't anyone stopping you?"

"Those who would try are currently 'stuck' in a meeting," he said. "Welcome to the new Magix. Some of us have been waiting years for this day."

"It was always more than you and the Cleaner," I said. "How many Magix agents were crooked?"

"Enough to do what needed to be done," said Wreckage. "Finally."

We reached the end of the hallway, and one of the workers scanned her security card, opening the elevator doors. With a jangle of chains, we filed in, the elevator quite full with the nine of us. I could hear Fluffball thumping around inside the evidence box, helpless and afraid.

"Where's my father?" Avery demanded.

Wreckage chuckled. "You want to cry to Daddy? Tell him to make everything better? Frank Lawden is in no position to help you now."

"What did you do to him?" she muttered.

"He's fine," said Wreckage. "You'll see him soon enough. I

thought he'd like to watch everything he has worked for come to an end."

"He'll stop you," whispered Avery. But I didn't think she sounded too convincing.

"Take us down," Wreckage said. The worker scanned her card again, and the elevator began to descend.

"Down?" I said. Weren't we leaving the ground floor of Magix Headquarters? The only thing down from here was . . .

"Lina Lutzdorf," Avery whispered.

The elevator stopped, and I waited with dread for the doors to open. So much had happened since Magix had arrested me two days ago. Despite everything we'd learned, I felt my hopes for justice come crashing down as the elevator doors opened to reveal Lina Lutzdorf.

"So glad you could join us," the woman said, standing in the middle of the large room. She was wearing a glittery red dress, as though she were headed to the Oscars. Her black hair was tucked up and curled, and her makeup was thicker than ever.

There was a new feature in the middle of the suite that I recognized immediately. It was the large thermometer that measured the level of the magic core, the temperature now showing 37 degrees. It had been ripped from its pedestal in the Hall of Justice and was now propped on Lina's glass coffee table.

There were only two other people in the room—Lionel Albrecht, who was seated at the kitchen table, drinking something from a stout glass, and Frank Lawden, who was sitting perfectly still in an armchair with a loose necktie around his neck.

"I'm afraid your father won't be participating much in this conversation," Lina said to Avery. "That boon around his neck is keeping him totally still and silent for the time being."

Ah. So the tie was just like the one we'd used on Talbot. Except it seemed this one hadn't been manipulated to let Mr. Lawden move his head.

"But I assure you," Lina continued, "he can hear and see everything. Would you like to have a seat before we begin?" She gestured to the couches.

"Begin what?" I spat.

"My final plan, of course," she replied coolly. "I guess I should explain. You see, I'm the one responsible for all of this. The one who makes the plans. I'm the one who calls the shots." Lina Lutzdorf put her hands on her hips. "I am the Mastermind."

I felt frozen inside. Of course she was! How had we not seen this coming?

"It doesn't matter," Avery bravely declared. "We know everything."

Lina clucked her tongue disdainfully. "You know nothing."

"We know about the Cleaner," Avery said, pointing across the room at Lionel Albrecht. "We know that you hired him to rob the First Central Bank, using a disguise boon that made him look just like Mr. Morrison. The Cleaner planted mirrors over the security cameras outside the bank so the magical reflection could be recorded. Then he used the same trick to rob the boon church, framing Mason so that Magix would arrest him when he activated the music box."

"The music box," I whispered. "It was always about the music box, wasn't it? You set me up so I'd get arrested because you thought they'd bring the box here. And you need it to transport yourself out of this basement prison."

Lina Lutzdorf laughed. She clapped her hands a few times in mock applause at our words. Then her face suddenly grew serious.

"Like I said," Lina remarked, "you don't know anything. Sure, you figured out how Mr. Albrecht robbed the bank and the church. I warned him that someone would figure out the mirror trick."

"Hey! It worked!" the custodian said, raising his glass to toast his own efforts. "A double reflection made it so the images on the videos were not reversed. It fooled them long enough."

Lina waved a hand at him. "That was Lionel's doing. But

you're wrong about my plans. I don't have the music box."

"But we heard Agent Clarkston say—"

"Exactly what I asked him to say, knowing that you were listening," said Lina. "Knowing that you were starting to put the pieces together. You see, I don't need the music box. I never did. Why would I, when I could just ask anyone in this room to kindly escort me outside? This was never about some transportation boon." She looked right at me. "It was about *you*."

"Me?" I croaked. "What are you talking about?"

Lina Lutzdorf seated herself on a velvet ottoman. "Shall I start at the beginning?"

CHAPTER 33

"When I was eleven years old," Lina began, "I crashed my bicycle in the street, and a car drove over my left leg. Uncle Lionel saw it happen and rushed me to the hospital."

Uncle Lionel? I glanced at the custodian. The Cleaner was Lina's uncle?

"He stayed by my side until they took me back for surgery," she went on. "It was the most intense pain I have ever felt. Most of you wouldn't know how excruciating it is to have your femur snapped in two. But Mason knows. Don't you, boy?"

I stared at her. What did my broken leg have to do with anything? So what if Lina and I had that in common? It didn't mean I was going to be her friend.

"The surgeon who took care of me was brand-new to the job," she continued. "It was his very first operation, and he did a remarkable job, considering it took three metal rods and seventy-two stitches to piece me back together. His name was Dr. Roger Archibald. Does that ring a bell?"

It did. That was the same surgeon who had taken care of *my* broken leg. Where was she going with all of this?

"*Your* surgery was actually Dr. Archibald's last," Lina said. "Did you know that?"

I shook my head. I hadn't realized it. Why did that matter?

"Three months after your surgery, he was in Utah, celebrating his retirement with a skiing trip," Lina continued. "On his drive up the canyon, he came across a vehicle that had hit a patch of ice and gone off the road. Inside the car were a mother and two small children, upside down, three feet deep in a freezing river. Old Dr. Archibald didn't hesitate. He splashed into the water, rescuing the mother and both children. But his legs were severely frozen, the nerves permanently damaged. He's in a wheelchair now, but his act of pure goodness triggered a release of magic deep within the earth." She pointed to the thermometer on the glass table. "The magic reached the top and it bubbled out, soaking into certain objects the doctor had touched. Objects that had meant something throughout his life. That's how I became a human boon."

"That's impossible," Avery snapped. "You can't be a boon. The detectors don't register anything when they look at you."

"That's because the boon is *inside* me," she said, pointing to her left leg.

"The metal rods," I whispered. "They filled with magic after Dr. Archibald saved that family . . ."

"That's not how it works!" Avery cried. "The magic fades as soon as it enters a person's body."

"Also true," said Lina. "After I received my powers, I was confused about how it had happened. Uncle Lionel stumbled across my old X-rays while using a detector. He realized that one of the rods in my leg had become a boon. We set out to make more human boons like myself, building our criminal network. We injected small known boons under our subjects' skin, but the magic faded, just as Avery pointed out. Nothing worked."

"It's because you're making it up," said Avery.

"No," barked Lina. "It's because the boon cannot be inserted. It must already be inside the person when it turns magical. It was an ordinary rod in my leg for over two decades. Then, three years ago, it became a boon, making me immune to all other boons around me. Once we realized how this had happened, my uncle and I stopped trying to create human boons. Instead, we looked for another like me. We knew Dr. Archibald had caused the magic to boil over, so we started there. It was a daunting search—literally thousands of X-rays from his long career as a surgeon. But we narrowed it down. We knew it had to be a permanent implant that Dr. Archibald had touched. We knew it had to be a surgery that meant something significant to the doctor. And that's how we figured it out. I was his first surgery . . . and *you* were his last."

I shook my head, my hand absently rubbing at my old scar on my right leg. "No," I muttered. "I'm not a boon. I don't have any special powers . . ."

"You never had time to discover your powers," said Lina. "Because my people got to you first."

"The vent cover," Avery whispered. "It was a dampener boon that stopped any magical abilities Mason might have had."

"Now you're catching on," said Lina. "The metal rod in Mason Mortimer Morrison's leg was one of the most dangerous types of boons ever known."

"What does it do?" I asked, dreading the answer but needing to hear it.

"It activates other boons *without* knowledge," she said.

"That's how I used the music box during my book report." I spoke softly.

"Yes," said Lina. "Because Vanderbeek removed the vent from your bedroom the night before. You were in possession of the music box by the time the dampener wore off. We knew you'd activate the little box the moment you opened the lid."

Everything made so much sense now!

Avery was staring at me like she didn't even recognize me anymore. "The banister post that you used to break the window on the ninth floor," she said. "I couldn't figure out how you used it when neither of us knew what it could do."

"And the bedspring," I said, remembering the way my leg had cramped. "It froze my leg because . . . I've been a boon all along."

"Well, just for the last three years or so," said Lina. "And it was a full-time job to keep you from finding out."

"You broke up my family," I whispered. "You tried to ruin my life."

She shook her head. "Your dad became a problem when my sources picked up traces of reversal boon magic on his hands—a gift he was planning to give you. But we couldn't let that happen."

"Because a reversal boon would have changed the vent in my room," I said. "Instead of dampening magic, it would have amplified it."

"Which, in turn would have caused your magical ability to flare up before I was ready," she said. "It's difficult to coordinate everything from the basement of a hidden magical building. My two years locked up here really slowed down my plans for you."

Plans for *me*? That sent a shiver down my spine.

"What are you going to do with him?" Avery asked, her voice threatening.

"Magic isn't fair," spat Lina, her beautiful face twisting. "It benefits those who are Ignorant, and it punishes those who are Educated."

"Hey. If you want to forget about magic," said Avery, "we can arrange a memory wipe. We can easily turn you into a happy little Ig."

"Except you can't," said Lina, patting her leg. "We looked into having the rods surgically removed—they were intended to be permanent, even though my leg has been healed for over twenty years. Unfortunately, surgery isn't an option. The magic has fused itself with my leg. Removing it could be fatal. That's why I've been rotting down here in Magix's basement for the last two years. My immunity boon won't allow any memory wiping to take effect against me."

"And you're mad about that?" I asked.

"Millions of Ignorants are bumping into magical boons every day," said Lina. "The magic is rubbing off on them, giving them a great day. Giving them a little boost. So why don't *we* get to benefit from it? Just because we're Educated? Because we have knowledge? When one of us touches a magical boon, we get no extra boost. All we get is more responsibility."

"It's a responsibility we're willing to accept," said Avery. "And we're not left totally helpless. We get to use the boons for their true magical power."

"Which I can't do," barked Lina. "I'm immune. Whether I know about boons or not, they're useless to me. It's not fair. And frankly, I'm tired of it. If we can't *all* benefit from the boons"—her voice dropped dangerously low—"then *no one* should."

"What are you going to do?" I asked.

"Not me," she said. "You." Lina stood up slowly. "Do you know why I asked my uncle to steal all those boons from the Church of the Faith?"

"To get Magix's attention?" I guessed. "So you could frame me later?"

"That was only a small part of it," she said. "I selected the church because it had every kind of boon that I needed for the device."

"What *device*?" Avery asked.

"The largest manipulated boon in Magix history," said Lina. "After the church was robbed, Uncle Lionel began smuggling the boons down to me one at a time. I had done years of research, and I knew exactly what it would take. One by one, I began assembling the boons, linking them together in unique ways that would allow their powers to flow together unlike any boon before."

As she spoke, she crossed the room until she reached the grand piano in the corner. Reaching down, she pulled back the cover to expose the black-and-white keys. "Uncle?" she said.

Lionel Albrecht crossed to the piano, lowering a finger to play a single note.

At once, something magical began to happen. A huge contraption rose out of the piano, individual pieces clicking and unfolding until it loomed almost to the vaulted ceiling.

"My greatest creation," she said, gesturing grandly to the device. At the center was the black piano bench. Random objects leaned over it, surrounding it on three sides—a filing cabinet, a chandelier, a baby's high chair, a porcelain plate, a vacuum . . . The things went on and on, all of them interconnected, too many to see clearly. Too many to count. Instead of a piano, the whole thing now looked like a mad scientist's command center.

"These are the boons from the Church of the Faith," Lina said, "painstakingly assembled and connected. I had only five left over, and I arranged to have them dumped in your bedroom, Mason. I thought it might help incriminate you."

"What is that thing supposed to do?" Avery asked, a quaver in her voice.

"When activated, this device will shoot a beam of

anti-magic straight to the center of the earth," Lina said. "In a matter of seconds, it will permanently fry the magic core, leaving the world a much fairer place to live."

Avery gasped, her eyes darting to the thermometer on the glass table. "You're trying to *destroy* magic?"

"Won't it be nice?" Lina replied with a smile. "No more favoritism for Ignorant people who brush up against a magical boon. When I'm finished, people will have to make their own good days without relying on unfair magic." She walked slowly around the piano, dragging her fingers along the edge of the device. "The problem is, my device is incomplete. It needs one more component—a pilot, so to speak." Her dark eyes pierced into me like daggers.

"Me?" I shrieked. "You expect me to operate that thing? No way!"

"I didn't want it to be you," she said. "But you're the only one who can. You see, combining boons to create magic devices can be tricky business. Sometimes you need a boon with a specific power, though it doesn't really matter what the object is. Other times you need a specific object, regardless of what it actually does." Lina cast a glance at the piano machine. "In order for the device to work, it must be operated by a human boon. The specific power doesn't matter. That was why my uncle and I tried to create our own. When it didn't work to inject boons into people, you became the only choice."

"Not the only choice," I pointed out. "If you're really a human boon, why haven't you operated the device yourself?"

Lina snarled like an angry animal. "Didn't you hear anything I just said? I can't operate boons. I'm immune! It's up to you, boy."

"No way!" I cried. "Not happening! I just barely learned about magic. I'm definitely not going to be the one to destroy it!"

"You are a difficult child," Lina said. "You were supposed to operate the device two days ago. We took advantage of Avery Lawden's desperate need to prove herself and planted a note in her locker so she would break you out of your room. Uncle Lionel was in position on the ninth floor. He made sure you took the wine cork to operate the elevator. But he had already rigged it to overload, carrying you down to the basement. Everything worked perfectly, except you wouldn't—"

"I wouldn't sit down on the piano bench," I finished, remembering the cactus needles in the seat of my pants.

"Yes, yes. Then you had to be clever and call the agents down here so you could slip into the elevator and escape . . ." Lina frowned. "I had to dispatch Wreckage, and the whole thing became a wild goose chase. We knew you were in my uncle's apartment. You set off a signal when you moved the bed. Agent Clarkston could have apprehended you there, but we thought it better to lie about finding the music box and lure you back here on your own."

Avery and I had uncovered a lot of clues, but there were a lot we had missed. Now things were quickly falling apart, and there was nothing we could do about it.

Lina clapped her hands. "All right, then! Why don't you climb up onto that piano bench and stop wasting my time."

"You can't make me," I said. "Knowledge is power. Power is magic. That device will only work if you explain how each of the boons is connected, what each one does, and how it works. I won't learn. I won't listen. I'll plug my ears and scream and shout until—"

"Your boon," Avery said, her voice weak but intense enough to capture my attention. "You are a human boon that activates other boons *without* knowledge." Her face was crestfallen, and I felt sick when I realized what she was saying.

"The girl is much smarter than you," said Lina. "I don't have to give you any knowledge about the device. Your magical leg will automatically activate it. You will burn up the magic core, and you'll never even know how you did it."

I tried to run. It was the only thing I could think of doing. But I only made it a few feet before Wreckage yanked on the chain around my middle, tugging me to my knees.

"I don't want to hurt anyone," Lina Lutzdorf said. "I just want to end magic forever. But if you don't cooperate, I'll be forced to take more severe actions."

"What can you do?" I shouted, my face red. "You can't kill me!"

"No," said the woman. "But there are other people in this room who are more expendable."

Panicked, I looked at Avery, then at Mr. Lawden. He remained perfectly still on the armchair, but I saw a tear running down his face.

"Don't do it, Mason," Avery whispered. "It doesn't matter what they do to me. You can't help them destroy magic."

"Of course, we also have your mother." Lina's sentence made my blood freeze.

"That's a lie," I said.

Lina shrugged. "My people picked her up in Maine. She was quite the fast traveler with that atlas boon."

I shook my head. "Don't threaten me."

"And then there's your father," she said. "Mr. Morrison might seem safe, locked away in prison. But sometimes inmates meet with accidents. . . ."

My dad. I could picture his face, laughing, always cracking jokes. I thought about how he'd never actually broken the law. How Lina Lutzdorf had stolen a year of our life together by sending him to prison. I knew he'd be proud of me for getting this far. He trusted me. My mom trusted me, too. And that was all I needed. Suddenly, I had a plan.

"Okay," I said. "I'll do it."

"Mason!" Avery shouted, her face crumpling under the betrayal. I couldn't look at her. I had to focus on what needed to be done.

I had to activate the device.

CHAPTER 34

Wreckage untied the chain around me, but I didn't even think about running. Where would I go? With enemies on all sides, the only thing I could do was get into the device and hope that my friends and family would be safe.

On shaky legs, I approached the grand piano. I had to duck under a microwave that was wired into a lampshade in order to reach the bench. Behind me, Lina Lutzdorf was giving Frank Lawden some sort of classic villain monologue, but I wasn't listening. I was thinking of my dad. My hand wandered into my pocket. I scooted past a large grandfather clock that was leaning precariously over the seat. Then at last, I was in position.

With no other option, I seated myself on the padded piano bench.

"Behold!" cried Lina. "The end of magic!"

For a moment, nothing happened. Then the device began to hum. A deep resonant vibration filled the room, accompanied by Lina's victorious cackle. Glowing energy started to swirl around me, churning through the boons as if I were seated at the center of a glowing tornado.

"Magix will always remember you as the boy who destroyed magic!" called Lina.

But I didn't feel like a traitor and a destroyer. In fact, I felt great!

"What?!" Lina shrieked, darting across the room to check the magic meter on the glass table. "Why isn't it working? My calculations were perfect. My manipulation of the boons was flawless." She let go of the thermometer. "What is happening?"

I stood up from the piano bench, but the device didn't shut down. It was like a train on a downhill track now, and I knew it would keep working until it completed its purpose.

"Sit down!" Lina screamed. "Wreckage, make him sit!"

But I had already stepped away from the seat. My leg was aching, and based on the way Lina was limping, I'd say hers was, too. Wreckage took a step toward me, but he paused, head tilted as though he was in pain.

Behind him, Avery suddenly gasped. "The chains . . ." Her voice was barely a wheeze. "They're crushing me . . ."

"Let her go, Wreckage!" I threatened.

"It's not me," the big man rasped. His voice sounded pained, and he dropped the chains. "I'm not doing anything." He grunted, his gloved hands coming up to slap his face shield. "I can't see," he muttered, finally pushing back the welding mask. "I can't see!" he howled, scratching at his eyes.

With a grunt, Avery suddenly tore through the chains. They clattered to the floor, and I saw her magic credit card in her hand. Two other agents moved to stop her, but Avery swung the card through the air. From ten feet away, it split a couch down the middle, causing the agents to draw back and cower.

Avery darted across the room, ripping the necktie from around her dad's neck and hurling it against the wall. Strangely, it stuck there, quivering like a spear.

Wreckage suddenly gasped, falling to his knees as he blindly tried to pull off his reflective vest. His body jerked in pain, and he strained for breath, falling onto his face.

Frank Lawden rose to his feet. "The magic meter," he said, turning all heads back to the thermometer.

The magic level was *rising*.

"No!" Lina screamed. "Why?" She took a step toward me, but her leg gave out and she collapsed to the floor. By this point, mine was really hurting, too, but I knew what was happening. I was probably the only person in the room who did.

The existing boons were growing more powerful as the magic level rose. Wreckage's boons had overcharged, his detector mask blinding him. The chains had tightened on Avery, but her credit card had had a surge of strength, suddenly able to slice from a distance. . . .

"What did you do?" howled Lina Lutzdorf.

I grinned. "I added one more piece to your precious device." I pointed back to the piano.

There was my throwing star, one of the sharp points stuck into the piano keys.

"The birthday present from my dad," I explained, "a powerful boon that can reverse the effect of any other boon it touches. Your magic-destroying device just became a magic *booster*."

"Stop him!" she ordered.

The six workers moved toward me, hands clenched into white-knuckled fists. Lionel Albrecht stepped into my view, holding a toy truck that was quivering with a sudden surge of energy. I didn't know what his boon could do, and luckily, I never had to find out.

The elevator doors flew open, and Agent Nguyen burst in. And she wasn't alone. A dozen Magix agents backed her up, all of them holding regular-looking items that could only be explained as boons.

Lina's workers fell to the floor in immediate surrender, no match for special agents trained to use boons with precision and skill. Even the Cleaner dropped his toy truck, falling to his knees with his hands in the air.

"Uncle!" yelled Lina. "You coward!"

Hamid appeared in the doorway, dusting his hands together. "Good work, team. That's a game-over for these baddies."

I smiled at my video-game-loving friend. "Glad you made it," I said. "And just in time."

"Avery's instructions led me straight to the black site," said Hamid. "Once I convinced Agent Nguyen that I was one of the good guys, she was happy to rally the others and summon the Doorman."

I turned to Lina Lutzdorf, who was still lying on the floor, gripping her leg. "It's over, Mastermind," I said, choking down my own pain.

"I don't understand," she muttered. "The device shouldn't be able to affect my leg. I'm an immunity boon!"

"This power surge isn't coming from the device," Avery said, pointing our attention back to the thermometer. "It's coming from the magic core. Straight from the source."

The hum in the room grew to an almost deafening level. There was a bright flash of light as the giant boon device imploded on top of the piano. I saw the thermometer spike upward, the red level of magic rising so fast that it shattered through the top.

Lina Lutzdorf screamed, and I felt my leg break from the inside. I grunted against the intense pain, but it was too much. My vision started to fade, and I slipped into unconsciousness.

CHAPTER 35

I woke up in the hospital and thought I'd gone three years back in time. My entire leg was in a cast, slightly elevated at the foot of my bed.

"Well, it's about time you woke up," said a voice to my side. I turned, blinking my eyes, not daring to believe it.

"Dad?"

He reached out and ruffled my hair. "Your mother and I have been worried sick!" He looked to the hospital room door and called, "Honey!"

Seconds later, Mom came rushing in, smothering me with hugs and kisses.

"How long have I been out?" I asked when she finally gave me some room to breathe.

"Almost a week," Mom said.

"A week?" I cried. "What happened?"

"Your leg was in bad shape," Mom said. "They had to do surgery to remove one of the metal rods that had exploded."

"The boon," I said. "It's gone?"

Mom and Dad nodded. "Just a regular kid again," Dad said. "Although your friends filled me in on all the details, and it sounds like you used to be a pretty awesome *magical* kid."

I shrugged. "I didn't really know I was a human boon until it was almost too late," I admitted.

"I'm sorry they couldn't leave it in," Mom said. "The folks from Magix said that the broken boon was poisoning you. It's why you were unconscious for so long."

I sighed heavily. "Actually, I'm glad it's gone. Magic was hard enough to figure out when it wasn't inside me." I turned to my dad. "I'm guessing you're free?"

"Thanks to a couple of young detectives," he said, smiling. "Frank Lawden was able to take the evidence that you and Avery found in Lionel Albrecht's apartment and convince a non-magical jury that I was innocent. The missing cash, the clothes, the fake license plate . . ."

"A complete raid of Lionel Albrecht's stuff turned up a cell phone with a lot of incriminating messages recorded on it," said Mom. "He basically confessed to robbing the bank."

"So, what happened to him?" I asked.

"He took my place in prison," said Dad. "He'll be there a loooong time, so we don't have to worry about him anymore. Oh—" Dad pulled something from his pocket. "It's about time I officially gave this to you." He handed me the throwing star. "Happy birthday, Mason. You should probably give it a throw."

"Here?" I said, gripping one of the points between my fingers. "Now?" I glanced at Mom.

She shrugged. "They're not my walls."

With a grin, I hurled the metal star across the room. Instead of sticking, it clattered off the wall, dropping to the floor without leaving a dent.

"I guess I need to practice," I said sheepishly.

There was a knock at the door.

"There are a couple of other visitors anxious to see you," Mom said.

"Come in!" I had a pretty good idea of who it would be.

Avery entered timidly, her dad right behind her, carefully closing the door.

"How are you feeling?" Avery asked.

"Non-magical," I answered. Then I looked up at her dad. "I hope you're not here to arrest me."

Frank Lawden smiled. "Quite the opposite," he said. "The evidence that you and Avery found was more than enough to clear both your names. It doesn't mean I'm happy about what you did." He cast a stern glance at his daughter. "But I'm willing to overlook a few things. I owe you both my thanks. For uncovering the truth. For revealing a network of traitors inside Magix Headquarters. And for saving the magic core."

"Speaking of traitors," I said, "my parents told me about the Cleaner. But what happened to Wreckage and Lina Lutzdorf?"

"Clarkston didn't make it," said Avery. "He was wearing so many boons that when they all supercharged, the force was too much."

"We tried to save him, but he died before we could get to the hospital," finished Mr. Lawden.

I actually felt a little bad about Clarkston. He'd been a smart guy, but he'd been too willing to follow the Mastermind's dangerous plans.

"And Lutzdorf?" I asked.

"When the device reversed and boosted the magic core, the boon in Lina's leg exploded like yours," said Avery. "We got her to the hospital, and she woke up two days ago."

"Of course, by the time she recovered, she didn't know who she was anymore," said Mr. Lawden. "The committee had considered her crimes and sentenced her to a full and total memory wipe. We gave her a new name and a one-way ticket to Argentina. She's just a regular Ignorant now. You don't have to worry about seeing her again."

"So, Lina sort of got what she wanted in the end," I said.

"What do you mean?" asked Dad.

"She didn't want the responsibility of knowing about magic," I said. "She wanted to be Ignorant so she could benefit from touching random magical items to brighten her day. But the boon in her leg made it so Magix couldn't erase her memory. That was why she built the device to destroy the core."

"Well, I hope she has many good days," said Mr. Lawden.

"You aren't mad at her?" I asked.

"Of course I am," he said. "But wishing her a bad life doesn't make anything better. Lina Lutzdorf has the chance to start her life over. Magic exists to give Ignorant people good days. I hope she rubs up against a lot of boons so she never starts thinking like the old Lina Lutzdorf."

The door opened, and Hamid came into the room. "Sorry," he said, "We got distracted by a vending machine. There was a bag of chips dangling on the edge, so I bought a candy bar hoping it would fall and knock the chips down with it."

"It failed miserably," said another familiar voice. That was when I noticed that Hamid was holding something soft and white.

"Fluffball?" I cried.

"Yeah. Good to see you, too, kid," said the bunny.

"I don't understand," I said. "Wreckage tore off your collar. It lost its power."

"True," said Fluffball. "Until you went and used your throwing star to reverse the Mastermind's device. When the magic core surged, it revived my collar. Avery let me out of that evidence box and put it on me again. Good as new! You thought you could get rid of me so easily?"

Hamid released Fluffball, and the rabbit leaped onto the edge of my bed, his pink nose bouncing as he sniffed me. "Much better," he said.

"What do you mean?"

"You don't stink anymore," answered Fluffball. "When Avery put the collar back on me, I noticed something interesting. Lina Lutzdorf had the same kind of foul odor as you."

"Umm . . . thanks?" I said.

"I thought she smelled nice," Hamid admitted. "Like perfume."

"Maybe to a human nose," said Fluffball. "But to a detector nose like mine, she was rotten. That's because she was a boon that I couldn't quite get a reading on. Just like you. The magical rods in your legs threw off my sniffer, but since I couldn't see them, I didn't know why you smelled funny."

"I'm glad you're alive, Fluffball," I said.

"I never actually died, you know," replied the animal. "I just turned back into a regular bunny for a while."

"Hey!" I cried. "You said *bunny*."

"What?" Fluffball looked around, his ears twitching nervously. "No, I didn't. You're clearly having trouble with your hearing, kid."

Mr. Lawden reached out and put a hand on my arm. "The doctors tell us you'll be in that cast for a couple of months." My shoulders slumped with discouragement. "But we might have some healing boons to speed up the process," he finished. "And as soon as you're out of that cast, I'd like you to pay a visit to Magix Headquarters. I've got an offer for you."

"What kind of offer?" I asked.

"Avery?" said Mr. Lawden, stepping back so his daughter could explain.

"Magix has decided to start an official apprentice detective program," she said, beaming. "Students will partner with full-time agents for different kinds of training. They might even have us go out in the field for practical experience."

"Us?" I said.

Avery nodded. "You've been accepted into the program. You'll get to come into Magix Headquarters three times a week."

"If you can find time between your piano lessons," my mom joked.

"I'm doing it, too," said Hamid. "Maybe we could carpool."

"That won't be necessary," said Mr. Lawden. "You'll both

get transportation boons that will take you directly to the Doorman."

"It's going to be so fun, Mason," said Hamid, bouncing up on his toes. "What do you think you'll choose for your secret weapon?"

Avery sighed. "They're not weapons . . ." She trailed off in frustration, turning to me. "Thanks for all your help, Mason Mortimer Morrison."

"Thank *you*, Avery Lobster," I said. "I wouldn't have gotten very far without a real detective on my side."

She smiled. "Not bad for our first case together."

"I'd say we make a pretty good team."

Case closed.

ACKNOWLEDGMENTS

The idea for this book came to me after I wrote a short story for a book titled *Super Puzzletastic Mysteries*. I had so much fun writing a short mystery that I decided to try my hand at writing a longer one! Of course, I had to mix the mystery with magic. Because magic is just plain fun.

I would like to thank my wonderful editor, Elizabeth Lynch. You were so great to work with on this project from day one! Thanks for your patience with me. Your keen eye and thoughtful insights helped make this book better.

Thanks to Simini Blocker for her fun, eye-catching cover art, and the whole team at HarperCollins Children's Books for making this book a reality. And thanks to my stellar agent, Ammi-Joan Paquette.

I dedicated this book to my fifth-grade teacher, Mrs. Foster. She fostered so much creativity in the classroom and motivated me to spell words correctly (a handy lifelong skill for an author).

And thank you for reading! Now let's make the magic level rise with some acts of pure goodness!